JEFF PERILMAN

The Escape Velocity Project

An Exquisite Jeffcore Publication

Learn more at: www.jeffcore.com

First edition

ISBN: 978-1-7373813-0-3

Cover art by ebooklaunch.com

This book was professionally typeset on Reedsy.
Find out more at reedsy.com

This book is dedicated to our dog, Loki, who passed during its creation. You were all heart and snuggles, duder. You never let being a ninety pound labrador deter you from being a lap dog. May you have rabbits to chase and holes to dig for eternity. You left a dog-size hole in all of us.

Backward we traveled to reclaim the day
Before we fell, like Icarus, undone;
All we find are altars in decay
And profane words scrawled black across the sun.
Still, stubbornly we try to crack the nut
In which the riddle of our race is shut.

-Silvia Plath
"Doom of Exiles"

Acknowledgement

There are very specific and important people that I would like to recognize for their part in helping make this story. Each of them deserves more than a few sentences, they deserve volumes and volumes of praise for the impact they had on me. Without them, there is no question that these pages would not exist.

My mother, Pam, and my late father, David: When I began writing stories, poems, and songs as a child, both of you took sincere interest and support in it. Mom, you took me on trips to the library and Books & Co. on a frequent basis, and even took me to signings so I could talk to real live authors. Dad, you bought me my first musical instrument (a Samick bass and amp combo package) and paid for lessons. No matter how loud I played my music or how bad my stories were - and even when my schoolwork was obviously suffering - you both never once wavered in your encouragement of my creativity. I will never repay either of you for the foundation you paved in my soul.

My absolutely *amazing* wife, Erin, and our children, Jacob and Callie: you give me the strength I didn't know I had. Starting a business, publishing a book, and recording an album? I knew how absolutely crazy it sounded when I told you all about it. Regardless, you rallied around me and got me to the finish line. Kiddos, take this book as physical proof: you can do *anything* in your life that you set your sights on. You all are both the reason that I do anything and the reason that I'm able to do anything. I couldn't dream of a better group of bears to be a part of. You truly make being a husband and father both fun and easy.

My senior high school Humanities teacher, Carol Lewellen: by the time I entered your classroom, I'm sure you had already heard about me and how terrible of a student I was. You must have been *thrilled.* But because you were passionate, stubborn, and accepting, I actually thrived. By my senior year, I didn't care about much except cutting class and partying with friends. Yet somehow you also had me completely engrossed in the thirteenth-century Italian art scene. No small feat. You opened up Pandora's box for my education and inflamed an enthusiasm for learning. If not for you, I likely would have never have attended - or completed - college. You set a standard in teaching that cannot be understated.

One of my best friends: Matt Reynolds. My mind was quite a sheltered place when we first crossed paths. You brought me before not just an explosion of musical initiation, but a cultural one as well. Without "Matcore," there would not be a "Jeffcore." Bogart's and The Newport are hallowed grounds because of you - and you alone. We're now worlds apart but we will *always* be Brothers of Metal. Troo and kvlt.

Another one of my best friends, and the best supervisor I have ever had the privilege of working for, Nick Creech: your friendship has only been surpassed by the amount of leadership knowledge you have taught me. Without your guidance, my attitude of "I don't care what the fallout is, I'm doing what I think is *right*" would be a foreign concept. Without that, I don't write this book. Full stop. We got into Hell together, and dammit, we got out together. We've seen each other's lowest, and now we're on the other end living our best lives. I'm your biggest cheerleader, and I know you're mine - no matter the distance between us.

To all the aforementioned, and Elon Musk, the future God-Emperor of Mars: thank you.

1

The Gift

Washington, D.C. April 12th, 2053. 4:51 AM.

Dr. George Sansor was sprinting wildly. He had already dropped his collection of binders, cell phones, and NASA security clearance cards so many times that it would probably be more prudent to walk. But Dr. Sansor was sprinting, sweating, eyes darting around the florescent labyrinth hellscape that was the secure floor of NASA Headquarters.

He wasn't the only one. The entire staff had been activated. He hadn't seen this many people in the building in his entire 34-year career with the Administration. It was a beehive mixed with an anthill strapped into a roller coaster. Sansor smashed into a wide-eyed engineer with a crushing *thud* as he rounded the umpteenth corner on his mad scramble.

"Watch where you're-" the engineer cried out, but George had already recollected himself and was pushing forward. He wasn't used to physical exertion, pain, or anxiety on this level. He hadn't ever played sports, and his idea of working out was completing this route, except at an extremely leisurely pace.

He typically would be exhausted being awake at this hour, but the adrenaline surging through his body was a new drug to him, and it was working.

He finally reached his destination: a nondescript door with a placard to its right identifying it as "Briefing Room U-A." "U" meant that the room was in the confidential section of the building, and "A" meant it was the largest, nicest, and most opulent. There hadn't been many critical incidents in his career that warranted the room. It was typically used when high-level ranking officials wanted a "dog and pony show" of headquarters, and U-A had the fancy NASA logos emblazoned on the tables, chairs, and even the drinking glasses. Most of the briefings or meetings he was invited to were in rooms that were comparable to storage closets, with stained furniture retained from the Obama administration.

The room's significance on this day suddenly hit him. He stood up straight, collected his breath, and wiped what sweat he could away from his forehead. His hair, an unkempt brown mop that he usually kept down around his face, was moved over in a half-effort at combing. The stains that had quickly amassed in his armpits would have to wait. He fished his access card from his bundle of disarray in his arms. As he moved it leftward to the door's card reader, the door abruptly swung open, striking his right arm. Yet again, his grasp abandoned him, and all his materials went tumbling to the ground. He didn't even get a look at who had rocketed out of the room, as he had reflexively started gathering his mess.

"Sansor, quit messing around and get your ass in here, *now!*" bellowed a familiar voice. It belonged to the Associate NASA Administrator, Cullen Boddaring. Cullen was widely renowned for his pettiness, back-stabbing, and temper tantrums. His face was utterly forgettable except when he wore his trademark semi-rimless framed glasses. There was a halfway substantiated rumor that he didn't even need them, and wore them out of pretentiousness.

He was a dedicated micro-manager. However, he always pre-empted any forthcoming complaints about him from his subordinates with discipline or formal counseling. That way, complaints to the acting administrator appeared to be retaliatory from the rank-and-file employees. Therefore, Boddaring always kept his image clean with the rotating cast of people who served as the acting Administrator. He was widely loathed by everyone else.

Boddaring brought in a culture of nepotism and degradation of morale to the entire Administration. Often, highly-qualified employees were passed over for specialty assignments for the less skilled. Even people that consistently sucked up to managers sometimes found their careers turn stagnant. Only the "chosen ones" continually got premier mission responsibilities. George never played into that game, despite his stellar credentials. He watched top-level talent walk out the door for the private sector at a rapid pace, though. Often for less work, and more pay. He only got to his position because he refused to die or quit, he often mused to himself.

George pushed his mass of messy, dark brown hair backward and mumbled a response before he found the first available seat, like a student arriving late for class. As he surveyed the room, his doubts were erased. *This is actually legit,* he realized. Boddaring, acting Administrator Glenn (who had been on the job for less than a month), and every subdivision head were in the room. Flanking the NASA leadership were no less than a dozen military members. He didn't know who they were, but the number of accommodations pinned on each of them might as well have been large neon signs that read "I'M IN CHARGE."

Looking upward, he saw ten large screens with more top brass military members on video calls, with off-screen aides frantically pushing notes to them. One screen caught his gaze, and then also caught his breath. Seated at the end of a large table was the only person outside NASA personnel that he actually recognized: President of the United States of America, Adam Buynak. President Buynak was surrounded by other suits George could only assume were his Cabinet. He never kept up on politics, especially after the legendary failure of the e-ballot apps in the 2036 presidential election. NASA had almost been shuttered completely because of a hashtag in 2033. *This isn't a briefing room anymore,* George realized. *It's a situation room. A command center. It's real.*

"Don't tell me what you *think* you know, Tom," one of the screened soldiers barked at Administrator Glenn. "What *do* you know?" George didn't have any bad opinions of Thomas Glenn. The only bad talk he'd heard from coworkers usually came from the same people like Boddaring. One had to take their criticism with a few thousand grains of salt because they talked badly about everybody. He just knew nothing of the man outside of his title. George realized he was a career NASA guy when he lost count of how many administrators had come and gone during his tenure.

"Well, general..." Glenn began before another screened crew cut interjected, yelling "...goddamn waste of my time here! Did anyone just *happen* to consider that this is an offensive counterintelligence op? This smells like shit, Mr. President. Pure shit!" George rolled his eyes as another wave of fighting began, with everyone yelling, nobody listening, and the testosterone levels so high he wondered whether the fistfights or ass-slapping would start first.

"Everybody shut up."

"Everybody shut up!" The second time worked. Everybody shut up and looked to the screen with President Buynak. He ran a hand through his unkempt mop of hair, obviously having been roused in the middle of his sleep for this. "Tom, which of your guys is most qualified to look at this? To tell us if it's 'pure shit' or not?" Glenn shot a *help me* look to Boddaring that the whole room recognized. Boddaring cleared his throat and responded "Sir, Dr. George Sansor is our... our most *tenured* quantum physicist. But as Associate Administrator, I have personally-"

"-Is Dr. Sansor in the room?" George's face immediately flushed crimson as the entire table of NASA heads turned to look at him. He sheepishly raised his hand, then remembering his armpit perspiration from the mad dash in, quickly dropped it. *The one day you throw on a blue shirt, George...*" he thought as the President continued. "Dr. Sansor, are you up to speed on what this meeting is about?"

"Only rumors and gossip, sir," George responded. Other NASA employees had been asleep, or out socializing. But he had kept up on every detail in every group chat he was included in. He had no wife, pets, or friends to keep him busy after he left work. So when this scandal had begun circulating among his colleagues, he had been following it in real-time, from speculation to speculation.

The President leaned forward as if he needed to assert more weight to the situation. "This morning at about midnight, a package arrived at the White House. After it was deemed safe, it was opened. There is what we think to be a construction manual inside. Now, no one here can make heads or tails of it, not one page. So I called up Administrator Glenn here, and he said that you guys would be able to read it and tell us if it's real or not."

"Who sent it, sir?"

"Also a complete mystery. I've had the Secret Service, CIA, NSA, hell, every letter agency we have trying to figure that out. We even called the Postmaster General. So far, no one has one shred of an idea how this thing got past security and onto my doorstep."

"The doorstep?"

"Right by the welcome mat."

"Sir?" George began, more fear in his blood than ever in his life. He felt dizzy and like he weighed a thousand pounds all at once. He was about to ask the question that had been on his mind since he'd been called in the middle of the night to report to headquarters. An absurd question.

"Yes, Dr. Sansor?"

"You said it was a construction manual?

"Yes, Dr. Sansor." Boddaring stared at him with his signature stick-up-the-ass glare.

"So is the gossip true?"

The President paused and glanced at one of the Cabinet members.

"Yes, Dr. Sansor..."

"...we think it builds a teleportation device."

2

Pilot One

Sixty-one. Sixty-two. He glanced at the clock. *Three seconds behind. Dammit. Sixty-three sixty-four sixty-five sixty-six. One second behind. Sixty-seven. Sixty-eight. Sixty-nine (heh). Seventy.*

Seventy sit ups in sixty seconds. Christopher Wendell patted his abdomen, muscles still aflame and waxed chest still thumping. He would never get fat simply because he chose not to. He was constantly surrounded by feeble, mouth-breathing bags of cellulitic waste. Even when they weren't spewing out of their binge-holes about how they *just couldn't lose the extra weight,* or nearly having a heart attack climbing a set of stairs, he knew they were still thinking about Ore-No's (literally: Oreos began selling bags of just the creme filling years ago. You could buy up to a five-pound bag of the stuff). It was like a radio turning on in his head every time he was unfortunate enough to be around the fleshy bastards. *Oh God, you're pushing the button for the elevator, but I know you're just dying to push an extra-large pizza down your vacuum trap right now, huh Bub? You'd like that, wouldn't you?*

Christopher finished his daily workout routine with stretches - had to retain his limberness - and turned on the news as he warmed up his shower. He didn't care about the talking head that was currently being broadcast on EverNews all but copulating President Buynak. He didn't necessarily care what was going on in the world, but he did like to keep up with current events. Being left out of a conversation because he wasn't versed on the topic felt like having his skin slowly removed piece by piece. He missed out on a great piece of ass in a tight pink dress at Club Particle because he wasn't even aware that Korea had re-unified. In other cities he'd partied in, he could get laid on his good looks alone. But in the D.C. District, you had to be able to hold your own in a conversation about politics if you wanted to seal the deal. It was so annoying.

"Next up, should the country consider going to a Parliamentary-style government if President Buynak can't stave off this latest scandal? Stay tuned." Christopher rolled his eyes and stepped into his waterfall shower. He forced his medium-length, jet-black hair to the back, spiking it up as he did, and admired his chiseled, naked body in the mirror just before he did - no tattoos, scars, or piercings to be found. His parents both had full-sleeve tattoos, and it was an act of rebellion against them to keep his body bare of any modification. Most people his age had neck tattoos by the time they were twenty. He would sleep with a girl with tattoos or piercings, but too many were certainly a deal-breaker. His head was buzzed on the sides, and the top was pushed back to avoid falling outside military regulations, with the right amount of hair product. His jaw was firm and square, even when he was flashing his signature smile.

For his shower, he used a combination of a hair volumizer

shampoo, tea mint conditioner, exfoliating and detoxifying face scrub, skin repair body wash, dead skin body plane tool, and premium subscription aloe shave gel. He had six different mirrors mounted to make sure no square inch of his body was neglected. The entire routine had been honed down to fifteen minutes.

As he exited the shower, he put on a cool face mask. It would chill his face so that he wouldn't sweat from the hot steam, thereby reducing the chances of pimples. Next was his diet and vitamin pills: twenty-four of them. The oldest living person in the world was 132. Medical experts believed people of his generation could likely live to be 200. He fully intended to, and dedicated time every day to extend his stay on Earth.

Christopher checked his messages on his mirror's built-in computer interface: social media likes and comments were the most prominent. He'd check and respond to those throughout the day instead of right now to avoid appearing needy. Dozens of emails through his .mil.gov address, which were all likely garbage. DatrApp notifications. That would definitely occupy his morning commute. A drunk text message from his high school friend Blitz who was hilariously named after Santa's reindeer.

And six texts from his ex-wife Grace. *Why don't you just block her?* his friends always asked. The diplomatic answer was that he still needed to be in contact with her because of their two kids together: Luna and Mark. However, if he was ever honest with himself, he'd admit that it was because he liked the attention she still gave him. He enjoyed toying and teasing her with mind games. She had never remarried after the divorce or even taken back her maiden name, which Christopher found deeply satisfying.

* * *

The two had met while he was at the Naval Officer Candidate School in Rhode Island, and she was attending college at Stonehill College in Massachusetts. Christopher had a knack for slacking off but still managing great grades, which drove his classmates mad. So while most of them were busy studying, Christopher was busy sneaking off the base to drink with the local rich college girls. He was having the time of his life with a never-ending supply of vapid, but beautiful girls when his gaze met Grace's one night.

He had been perusing the party, chatting with one pretty face to the next, and noticed someone noticing him from the rear of an apartment. Grace was shorter than him, with her forehead just reaching his chin. All the other girls were wearing their designer clothes, heels, and makeup, which Christopher recognized very early on as simply "my parents overpaid for this getup just for you to look at my tits." Grace, however, was wearing plain shorts, a purple Stonehill t-shirt, and tennis shoes. He looked her up and down, trying to evaluate her body's features first, but her clothing left more to the imagination than any other girl had dressed that night. However, he could ascertain that she was slender, with long, straight auburn hair in a braid that was resting on her shoulders and chest. He decided she was surely a B-cup. Finally making his way up to her face, he saw it was cute but plain. A slight, almost unnoticeable smattering of freckles dotted her cheeks below her eyes on her cheeks. Her pharmacy store-bought lip gloss was the only sign of makeup on it. Her green eyes and small mouth pursed into a slight grin, sipping beer out of a plastic cup.

"Something funny?" he said, sliding over to her and return-ing the smile.

"Just wondering if any of these girls here are going to fall for your bullshit," she responded, smugly taking another sip. Her eyes never left his. *Now* he was interested, B-cups or not.

"What do you think my odds are?" he smirked, as his hand crept onto her waist.

"Probably good. They're all pretty fucking dumb and stoned," she cracked back as she rejected his hand with a flippant push. "I'm neither."

"Neither? That a family name, or did your parents just hate you that much?" Now he was invested. Most times all he had to do was ask a girl what her major was, mention he was in the Navy, then nod the rest of the night until the clothes came off. She was making this interesting, even though there were plenty of other sexier females within spitting distance from them.

"Har har. I'm Grace," she said with another smile and a slight roll of her eyes. And damn, he was starting to really adore the hell out of those emerald stunners.

"Well hello, Grace. I'm Christopher. It's a pleasure to meet you, ma'am."

"Ma'am?" she looked at him, puzzled.

"Sorry. Force of habit. The Navy forced a bullshitter like me to start having manners," he added with a grin. Now that he was in, he'd still try his tried-and-true methods.

"Oh? Navy? I just figured you were a UMass fratboy," she shot back. It was a bigger rebuff than smacking his hand away. He couldn't tell if he wanted to dump his beer on her and call her a bitch in front of the whole party, or grab her up and kiss her. *Man. This girl...* He had to recollect himself before she could tell that the verbal punch had landed.

"No, UMass was too hard to get into for me. Hence, the Navy." The smile returned to her face as she enjoyed his self-deprecation. They stood in silence for a few awkward seconds, both of their heads racing to try to get the next witty one-liner in on the other. Taking a shot at himself interrupted the flow.

"So... the Navy? You gonna go sail a boat, Captain Cassanova?"

"I wish. No, they've got me lined up to fly planes." This turned her smile to genuine intrigue, he could tell. "But tell me," he continued, "what does a beautiful girl go to Stonehill to do?"

"To major in general eds, right now..." she offered, obviously a bit deflated that she didn't have more to go on than that. He opened his mouth to offer up some sort of reassuring note, but another party-goer moved in between them to attempt access to the apartment's back deck. Failing at opening the latch, the inebriated girl began spraying vomit all over the door, her shoes, and her hand, as she tried in vain to cover her mouth.

The two moved out of the way in disgust, as the stench from the mixtures of the regurgitated alcohol began circling the area. "And, on that note... I think the night is complete," Grace said with a grimace as she dumped out the remaining of her beer in a nearby trashcan.

"Hey. Let me see your phone," Christopher said, taking one last shot.

"Oh? What for?"

"So I can put my number in it."

"What if I don't want your number?"

"Then delete it. But I'd prefer if you didn't," he said as he held his hand out. She hesitated for a moment, now sizing *him* up. He was definitely in chiseled military shape, which she liked. And his smile could stop a room. But he also had the military bravado, swagger, and machismo that she loathed. Still, she thought there was something behind that thin veil of chauvinism. Something that maybe she liked a little. She unlocked her phone and handed it to him. His smile turned mischievous for just a fraction of a second as he entered his digits into her contacts.

Dating, followed by a full military wedding, followed very smoothly. Their children, Mark and Luna, were born in what seemed like the blink of an eye after. Luna had her mother's long, copper hair, and Mark was a carbon copy of Christopher in every single way. Christopher graduated from OCS, and she finished at Stonehill. He was constantly traveling to different flight schools the Navy put him through on his pipeline to being a pilot. Grace eventually became an assistant development director at a large environmental philanthropy group, Giving to Earth Foundation. They spent money to raise awareness against multi-national efforts to begin terraforming the planet, commonly referred to as "eco-improvement" by politicians and corporate lobbyists.

Christopher nodded along when Grace spoke of her work, but he was typically thumbing through his phone to read the news on his social media apps. One night in a heated argument, she challenged him to name three of her colleagues. He responded, "they only hired you because they're a bunch of old stuffy men that are trying to fuck you."

Marriage began to suit Christopher less and less. Dating, even being engaged, was *exciting.* He remembered the first time he slept with Grace, realizing that he'd never actually *made love* before then. He'd bedded much more "classically attractive" women before, but that skinny, quivering naked body under him he was *connecting with*, and more than at their genitals. It was all about the future, about the take-off. Marriage was already having landed, and just aimlessly gliding through a random spit of water on an aircraft carrier. It was nothing but addressing one problem after the next, and being expected to do so with the elegance and dignity of a saint in the process. Kids only exacerbated the issue. He wondered sometimes if they were actually his. Not because he suspected Grace was unfaithful, but because it would somehow justify his misery.

And Christopher was most certainly miserable. Grace began spending more time at "doctor's appointments," which he used to directly accuse her of having an affair. Even when he trailed her one day to some of her supposed appointments, and she actually did enter buildings full of doctor's offices, he just assumed the affairs were with doctors. He began secretly building new profiles on DatrApp to start preparing to leave her.

Christopher arrived home one day and found the house eerily quiet. Usually, Mark and Luna, both toddlers, were busy destroying the house he'd worked so hard to get. He hung his duty bag on a hook in the mudroom and opened the door leading into the kitchenette area. Grace was sitting there with a large envelope and other documents in front of her on the table. She'd obviously been crying, her once-astonishing green eyes were red and puffy. She was staring down at the table, chewing on her thumbnail. He was relieved, angered, and betrayed.

Divorce.

"So go ahead. Go ahead with it," he said as he collapsed into a chair across the table from her. He was disappointed he didn't do it with more authority, but instead just slumped down, showing his true emotions. He felt like he gave up some kind of phony dominance in the situation, even though she obviously had the upper hand in serving him the papers.

She breathed deeply and looked at him before starting to cry again. He remained quiet, unflinching. If she were going to do this, he was *not* going to guide her through it. She stifled a tear, wiped her face and snot, and began talking. But the words coming out of her mouth didn't sound like a conversation about divorce. She started saying words like "cluster," "oncologist," and "chemo." He started getting increasingly confused, and the more confused he got, the less he listened. Because *here it was again*, yet another problem he had to address: cancer.

That was marriage for him. A cancer.

"Grace, stop." She had been rambling about the kids and her mother, but he couldn't take another second. This wasn't something he could just go to the basement and drink away like her normal bullshit.

"I want a divorce. Keep the house and kids. I don't care. But I can't do this anymore."

He remembered her face the most as he immediately left to go pack his necessities. If cancer hadn't taken everything from her resolve, he certainly just had. *Well now she understands how I feel,* he thought as he left the room.

3

The Master Project

"Sir? Dr. Sansor? G...George?"

George was in between dream and waking, and he couldn't quite figure out which one he was being beckoned from. But his brain craved sleep and he succumbed to it for a few more moments. He lost track of time and sank back into the depths.

"Sleeping at work is against policy, Sansor! *Get up!*"

He let out a sigh as he opened and adjusted his eyes to the low-lit misery he'd lived in for the past six months. It used to smell like office furniture and fresh coffee down in U-118, which was a common work area. Now it smelled like body odor, vending food snacks, and the coffee was days old. The team NASA haphazardly assembled to work with him had set two small fires from leaving coffee pots on too long in their scatter-brained work.

George glumly looked up to see his assistant, Kevin Yim, looking at him with concern. He whispered "sorry," with his pudgy mouth to George, due to the other presence in the room. Kevin was an aspiring physicist at MIT and had been awarded a very prestigious internship from NASA. To George's disdain, Kevin was assigned to work directly under him in what George had gruffly told him was a "government-funded babysitting gig." He spent his first month getting George's coffee and had never complained once, so he started getting actual assignments within the unit. Kevin was a medium build but held fat in odd places like his neck and cheeks. His round glasses didn't complement those features, but George had quickly grown fond of his eagerness to learn and amazing work ethic.

The other presence, of course, was Boddaring. His cold, displeasing stare had gotten half amusing, half psychotic lately. "I've contacted the Swiss. They think they can take this over and give better insight," he said matter-of-factly.

George's forehead and ears became ruby red. Boddaring had been trying to proclaim from the get-go that he was "front line" on the build design. He'd even named it the Master Project without any input, assuming that no one would discover his full name was Cullen Master Boddaring. However, from the second it began, "the Master Project" was rife with errors, communication breakdowns, and infighting. Once thought to be potentially the greatest technological advancement of the human species since the wheel, the assignment was now largely regarded as career suicide for whoever touched it. Boddaring spent a great deal of every day unsuccessfully trying to pass the buck and get it out of NASA headquarters for good.

"Pretty funny that the Swiss even know about this," muttered George, eyes falling back to the hundreds of papers strewn about on the table in front of him.

"That's above your pay grade. I decide who or who *isn't*

involved in this project," Boddaring shot back, peeling his glasses off his face, crazy eyes still glued on George. *Mother-fucker*, he thought, *does this asshole want a salute or something?* He had never been much for cursing in his entire adult life, but lately, he thought and spoke like a Pantera album. His own mother spoke to him at a declining rate because she hated how flippantly he colored his expressions with expletives. He was wearing the first goatee he'd ever grown, and the twenty gray hairs he had before that fateful day in Room U-A had spread like wildfire throughout his head. He had begun to avoid mirrors because he didn't recognize how he looked anymore.

"Anyway, you and your lackey are to organize these... notes, deliver them to the Swiss, brief them on your findings, and return. Your plane leaves in four hours. I expect a full report on this unit's failure on my desk - and no one else's - tomorrow." Boddaring wanted to make sure he could cherry-pick details from the project to give to the new NASA Administrator, so that he came out looking good and everyone else dirty, as usual.

"You're putting us on a flight across the Atlantic with no notice and no rest?" George's voice was exposing him, becoming higher in pitch and rhythm.

"It looked like you were plenty rested when I walked in here. Consider this verbal counseling for sleeping while at work. Get a move on," Boddaring said behind him as he was already walking out of the room.

"That guy is such an asshole," Kevin said in both disgust and awe.

"Yeah. Rumor is that his mother abandoned him while he was still in the womb," cracked George. "But it is what it is. Another signature punch in the dick from U.S.S. Boddaring. Help me get all this shit together. I guess 'the Master Project' is officially DOA."

The two began collecting the ruins of the lost project, gathering large heaps of notes, sketches, and diagrams. Some were hastily scribbled on napkins with stale bagel crumbs still stuck to them. George's gaze caught an early design of the entryway to the device, which was surrounded by crossed-out equations. Underneath, the author had obviously given up on the design aspect and had angrily scratched in large letters "*WHERE DOES IT GO???*"

George's tepid nostalgia suddenly turned to a wrinkled frown, as that question brought him to a set of notes on a steel workbench behind him. The papers were mostly still readable, despite all the blood. The heated arguments at that point in the project were a daily norm, but that day the stress had hit a boiling point. He forgot the names of the men involved, but no one in the room was a fighter.

That didn't mean a thing in the melee that broke out. It was messy, savage, and nothing like anyone in the room had experienced before. Noses were broken, pocket-protector sporting men were wearing blood on their faces like full red masks, and NASA careers were ended. More than one bystander was vomiting in nearby trash cans when the mayhem stopped. Others received medical retirements from PTSD (a NASA scientist first). At the end of the week, when George had to go to Boddaring's office to get chewed out, he didn't have anything to offer up in his defense. After witnessing such carnage, he was completely drained of any fight.

That no one could agree on where the theoretical teleporter would theoretically transport something was about the only thing they *could* agree on. Someone offered up that NASA should build it, send a satellite through, then connect with it to see where it had gone. Homeland Security denied that plan, lest some alien civilization catch a foreign machine materializing in front of them and deem it a declaration of war. Rumor among the disgruntled masses throughout the halls was that the Pentagon hadn't been able to strike a deal that was amenable enough for EverCorp's profit margins, which had a full monopoly on satellite deployment. NASA had to clear its own missions with the conglomerate for years, even for shuttle launches. That corporate entitlement stifled an undertaking *this* important kept George's blood pressure impressively high. It wasn't enough that he had to fight incompetent NASA bureaucrats, he also had to contest with nameless CEOs making decisions for him from their turboyachts.

"Dr. Sansor?" Kevin's decorum broke George from his jaded stream of consciousness. "Should I bring my thesis draft, too? It's not like they'll look at it. And I wasn't allowed to store it anywhere but on this local hard drive." Kevin had been hoping to use the Master Project as his educational magnum opus, which would have likely launched a promising career for him. Now, he'd probably be better served to be a group psychologist with the same paper.

"I'd love for you to be able to take that home with you, Kevin. You've earned as much. Transfer it with the rest of the files to the argentibyte drive. Wouldn't want to get strung up by our toes for treason," George said with a grin and eye roll. He kept shuffling papers into boxes, mostly treating them like discarded litter. He took more time to study the reports labeled "Mars," however.

George had a special place in his heart for the Mars Theory. The blueprints had been coded in a language that was not - and had never been - used on Earth. Every time they made progress in translating one part of the code, it affected other parts they presumed they had already cracked. It was almost like a living, breathing, volatile thing; constantly changing and toying with the beleaguered minds of NASA. However, one part of the plans, depending on who you asked, spoke of Mars quite a bit. George was firmly in the camp that it *did* read Mars. But just like every other disagreement within the project, nothing was officially resolved.

Why would we *need* to teleport to Mars? To that, he hadn't a clue. Manned missions to the planet had discovered next to nothing in the last decade that robotic missions hadn't already revealed. A variety of companies, all under the EverCorp umbrella, had been shuttling VIP "space tourists" there for the past ten years. If you had twenty million dollars to spare, you could fly all the way to the red planet, look out the window, then fly right back to Earth. It was just a giant middle finger for rich pricks to give other rich pricks: *"Look at this selfie I took by MARS. Do YOU have a selfie by MARS? Naa-naa-nah-boo-boo."*

Mars never passed the NASA administration, either. Eco activism was at a white-hot temperament. Most demonstrations against eco-improvement had turned violent, and a lot of times, deadly. One of the most challenging aspects of the Master Project was the "why?" Why would an extraterrestrial existence just drop us these plans? Was there a trade-off? The answer to that, from project workers in the Mars camp, was that Earth was beyond repair (which was true), eco-improvement efforts were futile (which was up for debate), and the project was to build something to transport a massive amount of mankind for a permanent relocation on Mars. He wasn't sure about a lot of things, but this theory was at least one slimmer of logic in his newfound nonsensical work.

However, if this *was* a device to "move to Mars," NASA never supported it. George assumed they wouldn't want to set off a worldwide Doomsday-esque panic; telling the world that it was ending, and also that most of them wouldn't be invited to the after-party. The project, he very quickly found out, wasn't about what the designs built. It was what they could sell to the public that they built.

Kevin stood up from a computer terminal, giving a thumbs up across the room. His transfers to the secure argentibyte drive were secure. George finished collecting what scattered notes he could until the cardboard box he was using was filled. They both paused and gathered a look at U–118 before crossing the threshold of the door. It looked like an apocalypse had ripped through, skewered an otherwise orderly office space, then come back again for good measure. *All for nothing*, George lamented to himself. *All for goddamn nothing.* George flipped the lights off as the door shut behind Kevin, him, and the Master Project.

* * *

George and Kevin landed at Dübendorf Air Base the way they had left NASA Headquarters: in a fog, exhausted, and badly needing showers. They were corralled like sheep from the tarmac to hallways, rooms, and walkways by quiet and polite Swiss Air Force officers. The two followed pointed fingers and half-interested shrugs without question, mostly because they were too defeated to ask any.

A tall, bald man wearing glasses in small, modest frames met the two when they were led out of a side exit. He was thin, and his pursed lips had wrinkles around them that showed little signs of ever smiling.

"Dr. Sansor and Mr. Yim?" He said it with more of a declaration than a question. The two nodded glumly in response. "Please get in. I am Jan Bachmann." He opened the door of a black, nondescript Volkswagen and motioned for the men to enter.

"Are you the butler?" Kevin said. It sounded like a wisecrack, but his expression told George that he might actually be serious. In the day's sudden haste, he hadn't appreciated the fact that Kevin had probably never been outside of a hundred-mile radius of either Boston or Washington, D.C., and spent the majority of that time immersed in studies. He was probably still a virgin. Shipping him halfway across the planet in a shoddy EverLift 5500 without notice? To call it culture shock was probably putting it mildly.

"I am Bachmann. Get in," scoffed Jan.

George began to fall asleep soon after as the vehicle began zigzagging the pristine views of the Alps. He felt like a baby being gently rocked to sleep. Before drifting off, he smiled as he saw Kevin's breath fogging up the rear passenger window, his face pressed up against it to take in the view. *He probably doesn't know there used to be snow on these mountains. And the grass was a luscious green carpet*, he thought. Now, the fields and hills were scratched with barren streaks of dirt and rot. Switzerland was the birthplace of eco-improvement, and its scarred face wasn't a good look for its PR image. Eco-activists and talking heads on television loved to throw that out as an opening salvo in an argument, and people for eco-improvement always maintained the "break a few eggs to make an omelet" defense. It was enough to make one's head spin - or lose one's lunch.

"Sir? Dr. Sansor? G...George?"

He opened his eyes to see Kevin sitting up, staring at him. Bachmann was turned around in his seat, also staring at him. "We've arrived. Please exit," he ordered them.

"Where *are* we?" Kevin exclaimed.

"CERN. The Future Collision Collider," George said, eyes upward through the window at the large, bulbous building. He knew it well. He knew that Kevin did, too, but only in the context of research studies and theoretical reviews. Now they were sitting at its doorstep. Kevin's jaw dropped in reverence.

"It's... amazing. It... it looks like..." Kevin trailed off.

"A big boob," George replied. Kevin's face burned with embarrassment from the juvenile joke, but George was only half kidding. From the moment he first saw the building, it was a boob, and nothing else. And the large tube, buried hundreds of feet beneath them? The boob tube. He chuckled to himself at his own brilliance as he popped open the door of the car. No sooner had George and Kevin stepped out with their belongings, Jan put the car into gear and sped off. George curiously peered at the car, turning wide at the edge of the empty parking lot, Kevin's door still ajar and swaying in the mid-morning sun.

The two looked at each other. Kevin's look of bafflement screamed out to George to say something. "C'mon, Yim. Let's go turn this crap in and be done with it," he mused, "and maybe afterward they'll give us the Boy Scout tour."

4

Hounds of Hell

"Commander Wendell? This is Lieutenant Kreisch. SOCOM's been up my ass about your ETA to Andrews." Christopher took his attention from the rearview mirror of his Mercedes E15. He'd been inspecting both his hair – which was perfect – and the cute Latino woman standing on the sidewalk looking at her phone in horror. C-cup.

"Tell SOCOM I'm five minutes out."

"Are you?"

"In *this* traffic?" He laughed as he hung up. He didn't see what the big fuss was over. *So terrorists blew up half of Philadelphia? Had they seen Philly? Talk about kicking a dead horse...*

Another warning alert interrupted his music, blaring in every car stuck in the traffic jam with him. *Okay, this is getting a little excessive. Time to actually get to the base where the alarms are a bit more subdued,* he decided. Looking around, he found backed-up cars as far as he could see. None of them moving, a lot of them honking, and more than the norm of fender benders. The only way was around, and the cops probably had other things to worry about.

Christopher flashed his big smile and laughed as he took his car off of E-Go Mode and pulled up onto the sidewalk. Alarms in the car started going off again, this time warning him that he had driven off of the roadway. "Hey sorry, can't keep SOCOM waiting!" he squawked with puckish delight.

When he finally turned the corner to pull into the main gate of the base, he groaned with disappointment. Hedgehog barriers were littered across the front. The bulky, orange, spiky things were called "lawn ornaments" by his unit and were meant to stop vehicular threats in their tracks. All he ever saw them do was cause slower entry time to the base. Also, he knew what was next. He motioned his car forward, only steering with his thumbs, and his issued Common Access Card wedged between his left pinky and ring finger. As he neared the front guard shack, he was met by four perimeter guards with their rifles pointed at his car. They bellowed orders at him, which he couldn't hear because they all yelled at the same time. *Probably all these pups' first time above DEFCON 4*, he joked to himself. One of the guards snatched his card out of his hand and scanned it. "State your business and rank," he commanded him.

"Oh me? I'm here to ask you one question: does your vacuum really satisfy your home cleaning needs? Because have I got a *deal for you!*" Christopher looked to see if he had properly agitated the young man. The glowering stare he received told him that he had.

"Rank."

"Commander."

The guard looked at his identification, then at Christopher, then let out an exasperated sigh and handed it back to him. "Come on in, Commander Wendell," he said through gritted teeth as he performed the mandatory salute to a ranking officer.

Christopher saluted back and coasted forward, quipping back "you're doing a *great* job. Thank you for your serviiiiiiiiiice..." in a sing-song retort. His phone rang again, with the caller ID completely blank. He answered, letting the irritations of the morning show in his voice.

"I'm *literally on the damn base!*"

"Dude, you were supposed to be here a half-hour ago. You're holding up the briefing. We're in Hangar 18. *Hurry.*" Christopher's best friend, and also a Navy pilot, Erik Stormer, was on the other end, trying to keep him out of trouble. The two usually got into trouble as a tandem, but would pull one another back if the other was going on the plank by himself. They had courted girls together, saved each others' lives in combat, and saved each other from being arrested more times than he could count.

"Hangar 18. Got it. Save me a seat." Christopher kicked the gas pedal down and his urgency up. He shot past rows of cars, breaking every traffic law he could without having his own squadron scrambled to apprehend him. Finally, after what seemed like eons, he saw the sign marked "HGRS 12-18." He pulled up and parked next to Erik's Honda E-RX and bolted towards the entrance door.

As the door slammed shut behind him, the entire hangar turned to look at him. In his haste, the occupancy took him for pause. Usually, briefings were with his unit - the Cerberus Squadron - and a captain. A dozen or so squids. Today, there were at least seventy-five people present. *Shit*, he thought, *not the best day to be thrown in the barracks.*

Rear Admiral Garland stopped his speech midway and breathed heavily through his nose. He was a large man in stature, and his demeanor was always either joking or over-stressed. He never physically imposed on anyone, but at the same time commanded the respect of the room when he talked. He was obviously put off by Christopher's tardiness. Erik supplied a much-needed tiny fist bump to Christopher as he slunk into his plastic-molded seat at the back of the ensemble.

"Now that everyone's actually *arrived*," Garland paused as he stared down Christopher, "let's review the mission for anyone that isn't up to speed. We have been attacked on an unprecedented scale, ladies and gentlemen. Make no mistake about it: we are now officially at war with an unknown enemy. You are the front lines here. There will be reinforcements available, but to what I have no fuckin' clue and I doubt I will know anytime soon. We don't know if this is just the first in many attacks, we don't know if it's a dirty bomb, nothing. SOCOM and the DoD are telling me they don't know anything, either..."

The entire room grumbled in irritation. They were all used to being told what the actionable intelligence was before the mission, only to find out afterward it was horribly wrong, misinterpreted, or worse: held from them on a "need to know" basis. Christopher and Erik had personally wiped out a Ukrainian village on intelligence that it was a Novi-Bolshevik hotspot. Hundreds of innocent civilians died. The two got commendations in their service records. Needless to say, the bonds forged between pilots were largely due to the failures of the entities that were supposed to be their guiding lights.

"I know, I know," Garland reassured the masses. "But trust me, there's nothing I know that you don't. If you're in the dark on something, rest assured that I am, too. As per usual. Survey and report, and watch your asses. Dismissed."

Chair bottoms scraped against concrete as the mass separated into their respective assignments. Christopher and Erik gave each other the "well here we go again" eye roll as they stood up. "Stormer, Wendell. A word," Garland ordered from his post. Looks were flashed yet again between the pair. They couldn't even sit in silence without being whisked aside into secret scoldings, it seemed. The idlers that hadn't yet fled took heeding to the imminent scene and hurried their exit from the area like a grenade had just been tossed to the middle of the assembly.

The two slunk towards their supervisor. As if by reflex, when they neared, they both stood up straight and feigned confidence. Erik gave a serious, attentive gaze while Christopher flashed a big smile to bluff normality in the situation. Both were internally prepared and readied in defense, despite their bravado.

"Get your shit together, commanders," he growled through gritted teeth, "I've got more brass than I knew existed up my ass about getting your squad in the air. We don't even know who's behind the attack, or whether there's more coming. Today's *not* the day for your bullshit. *Do I make myself clear?*" The two nodded in humble obedience. "Good. Report for pre-flight. You're in the air an hour ago. Wendell, I need to speak with you. Privately."

Christopher and Erik glanced at each other uneasily. A reprimand in front of others was always safer in the military. The *terrible* shit happened by oneself. They both knew and feared what was about to become of Christopher. He followed Garland to a far corner of the hangar, slinking his head in defeat like a dog being led to a kennel.

Garland spun around suddenly and tucked his head down,

taking a step towards Christopher. "Why the *fuck* are you such a colossal waste of command, *Commander?*" he barked, sticking a rigid finger into Christopher's chest. "You think that flight talent *alone* can justify those bars and stars? I've got W-1's that have more dedication to this unit than you! If you can't even be bothered to make it here during World War Four, why the hell should I bother putting you in the air? Please inform me, because I don't have a clue what the hell you're worth to this country, force, or unit anymore."

The condemnation hit him harshly. His mouth was agape and he knew it. Garland had ripped his ass before, but nothing near what he'd just spat out. He knew it was time for capitulation, and not his usual bluster, if he wanted to professionally survive. Christopher took a deep breath and chose his next words very carefully.

"Sir, there is no excuse for my tardiness." Garland rolled his eyes at the trite response, but he continued. "You say we're on the brink of World War Four? Well, I'm who you want in the skies for that fight. We can talk about commitment and task after the mission, but I urge you: today, right *now*, who is best behind the controls for this purpose?"

Garland huffed and shifted on his feet. He gazed over Christopher's shoulder and took in the scampering of personnel for the flight preparation. He returned his watch to Christopher's dubious eyes. Garland's face hardened ever-so-slightly, his slight frown turning more powerful.

"Get your head on straight, for once in your career, Commander."

Christopher tightened his body and saluted as Garland shuffled his binder, returned the salute, and immediately was on a phone call. He briskly walked away, barking at the other end of the line. After he departed from view, Christopher relaxed from his pose and walked back towards the briefing area, searching for Erik. He caught his tall, lanky frame inspecting a flight helmet. Christopher grabbed his elbow and pulled him mid-stride, making his way to the locker rooms. As they walked by, people took notice. They caught the view of most as they strutted by, like peacocks in full parade.

The military, and especially elite units like theirs, tended to be like sorority houses with camo and guns. There was endless petty gossiping, rumor mills, and cliques. Christopher and Erik tended to be the topic of conversation more than most, due to their antics. Christopher attributed it to pure jealousy, so it didn't terribly bother him. He took it more as a badge of honor. Erik would be far more discontent, however, and would attempt to track down every salacious claim about them, which was a fool's errand in that culture. He'd once spent a week trying to fight the nameless person that had begun the rumor that Christopher had gotten cosmetic surgery, without avail.

Folding tables were lined up alongside the Cerberus Squadron's pewter E-2 fighter jets. Large aeronautical charts, laptops, binders, and EverCorp portable coffee makers were strewn about on them, with flight crews scrambling around, marking notes, and yelling into their radios. Pre-flight was usually controlled chaos, and this was no exception. Christopher paused for a second to take it all in. He loved it. All of it. The pandemonium was amusing to watch, like watching an anthill after being knocked over. He took great pride in being the calm within a storm.

"Commander Wendell? We're as ready as we can be, given the orders. As soon as you guys are suited and booted, we are go for take-off," one of the crew members informed him. Christopher and Erik hurried off to an adjoining locker room, where there were flight suits and toiletries stocked. Most of the squadron was already there and beginning to change. Someone was banging loud, annoying rap music as a pre-flight motivation ritual. As the group suited up and sauntered out towards their jets, they began banging on lockers, walls, and windows with growing excitement. "*Who's ready to fly to Hell?!?!*" Erik whooped to the group. They responded with exuberant barks and woofs, reaching a fevered pitch by the time they were handed their flight helmets. Christopher admired his own before climbing into his jet: silver flaked, polished, and *ROVER* adorned across the rear. He looked over and made eye contact with Erik, who was holding his own helmet displaying *THUNDER*. They shared a grin before climbing into their respective planes.

Because of the emergent circumstances with the mission, the runway authorizations, which usually meant sitting, taxiing, and sitting some more were skipped. Airspace in the entire city had been completely shut down, except for them. *Garland wasn't fucking around on this one*, Christopher thought as his aircraft roared into the skies and his group raced off to Philadelphia.

* * *

Christopher usually would have used his compass and way-points to navigate toward the destruction in Philadelphia from Washington, D.C. But the plumes of smoke were visible the minute his squadron reached maximum altitude. "Jesus..." someone muttered into the group communications. "Did we get nuked? That's a nuke, right?" someone else exclaimed.

"Mission Control to Cerberus, active your FLIR cameras. We need eyes," they heard over the radio. Twelve buttons were instantly mashed and screens lit up at Andrews. Those screens elicited gasps and curses. Three people collapsed into their seats. Thus far, the only images anyone had seen were from the ground level. EverCorp built into their phones the function to immediately activate cell phone cameras when a terror alert was pushed out. It turned the populace into walking surveillance during an attack (whether the customer wanted to or not). This was the first "wide view" anyone had observed.

The smoke from the blast reached up to the heavens. Even higher than the Cerberus Squadron was flying, there were parts of the pillar that were on fire in midair. As the jets grew nearer, the blast looked almost to be vibrating. "Zoom in," Garland said in the Mission Control room, eyes never wavering from the screen. He was still on the phone, but the conversation between both him and whoever was on the other end had fallen silent. Heeding his orders, the camera operators enhanced the view. The "vibrating" was just an optical illusion: automobiles, semi-trucks, and even large chunks of entire buildings were raining down from miles high within the blast.

As the squadron neared closer, still miles out, the thunder from the maw of the inferno grew louder than their own supersonic jets. Medical sensors attached to the inside of the pilots' flight suits began spiking back at Mission Control in ways the medical staff had never seen. Combat pilots were notorious for being able to keep a resting pulse even in the middle of the most frantic dogfights.

"Does POTUS have this view?" Garland gasped into his phone. "Good," he said from the phone's affirmation and hung up. "Ladies and gentlemen, we have begun Exercise Cocked Pistol. We are now at DEFCON 1. No one leaves this base unless the President of the United States has personally granted it. No outgoing phone calls from anyone ranked below me. Turn in your cell phones to your line leaders immediately."

Christopher stared at the windshield of his aircraft. It was supposed to be able to withstand anti-aircraft rounds, yet it was beginning to chip and spiderweb. White-hot pieces of cement were beginning to strike and compromise it. "Cerberus, jink three o'clock on me!" he exclaimed as he banked his E-2 hard to the right. "Mission Control, you have your views, do you need it in a sepia filter or do we return?" he spewed with frustration.

"Negative, Rover. Establish a flight perimeter and continue with mission objective," someone responded through the comm line, which had become electrostatic.

"Hooyah. Cerberus, on me. We're taking a trip to Atlantic City," Christopher ordered. "Hooyah" reverberated back to him eleven times as the group shot towards the ocean to circumnavigate the blast. As he altered course and took in his new surroundings, his throat fell into his intestines: Atlantic City had been reclaimed by the ocean. Literally broken off from the small sliver of New Jersey that hadn't been directly hit by the nuke and just swallowed up to a watery burial.

Christopher's eyes began to dart around wildly and his mask began to fog up. His windshield shattered and a miasma of Hell enveloped him. He couldn't breathe. The smoke cloud refused to stop climbing and he couldn't breathe. The whole world was on fire and he couldn't breathe. "Rover? Rover check your horizon. *Rover come in!*" his radio screeched at him. He only caught parts of it because the leviathan clawing out from the ground in Philadelphia was deafening and he couldn't breathe. All he could see was black and red and white and his ears were splitting and he couldn't breathe.

"...remote eject on Rover, Control..."

"Clear."

"I'm ejecting as well, Mission Control. I'll go get him."

"*Negative*, you are not authorized. *Repeat, you are not authorized. Thunder!*"

"Have search and rescue deployed. Cerberus, return to Andrews. Comin' for ya, Chris."

Christopher and Erik plunged into the scalding-hot waters of the Atlantic Ocean by parachute - as always - together.

5

Colliding with the Future

George and Kevin entered CERN headquarters with trepidation. George hadn't been to the facility in nearly two decades, so some changes were bound to be in store. He remembered large banners, magnificent displays proudly boasting CERN's latest business, reception clerks, music, and tourists. His nostalgia died the second he took his first step inside. The historic monument to science - now a vapid, barren, corporate graveyard - gave him pause.

He took in the cold, austere, lifeless lobby. The walls had been stripped of their marble vibrancy and replaced with white drywall, holding generic modern art prints. The chairs and tables were all cheap office furniture, the kind that they were used to seeing at NASA. It reminded him of a large-scale adaptation of his tax attorney's office. Or any attorney's office. The Washington County DMV had more charm. As they progressed through the lobby, George took a glimpse into the gift shop. A large green sign with white lettering at the entrance gaudily proclaimed it the "Gift Shoppe at CERN in partnership with EverCorp." But Kevin raised the most prominent issue.

36

"Where *is* everyone?" he asked. They were the only two people there at all. George's nerves began to rapidly surge, his chest rising and falling in vigorous succession. *Is this some sort of high-level, government assassination setup? Why would anyone want to take peons like us out? I'm not some secret spy, I'm a goddamn physicist!*

A door suddenly swung open from ahead of their route, partially obscured by an old, battered filing cabinet. George reached his hand out across Kevin's chest to stop him, the way his mother used to in her car. Kevin, conversely, had never even sat in a vehicle that wasn't self-automated.

"Dr. Sansor said Mr. Yim, yes?" a thick Scandinavian man's accent called from behind the filing cabinet. They both glanced at each other with apprehension and remained frozen.

"Yes?" the voice called again, with a slight tinge of confusion. George composed himself, somehow trying to suppress the paralysis he was experiencing from his waist to his feet.

"Yes," he fluttered out.

"Oh good, we've been expecting you. If you would follow me, I will take you to the meeting room." George and Kevin didn't budge.

"Please, sirs. If I hold the door much longer, the alarm will sound and we will be fined. This way, yes?"

George let out a sigh of defeat. "C'mon," he mumbled to Kevin and began shuffling his feet. Kevin hesitated, still uncertain of his surroundings. As George reached beyond arm's reach, however, he quickly launched himself forward to keep up with his mentor.

As they crossed the veil of the filing cabinet, they found not a government hit man, but a short, bald man with prominent ears, round spectacles, and an olive green dress shirt. George felt instant humiliation for being afraid of such a docile-looking, harmless person. The man smiled fondly and held his hand out, motioning for them to enter. They stepped in, and he quickly scooted past them to lead them. A short distance in, the door closed behind the three, snapping closed with an unexpectedly loud *bang*, followed by a buzzing of the magnetic locking mechanism reactivating. George and Kevin slightly perked to the jolt, but not as much as the bewildered men typically would have, as the entire afternoon had been loaded with over stimuli.

The two followed the bald dome in front of them as the man glided down the hallway. "My name is Dr. Järvinen," he said over his shoulder. "When we heard of your Master Project, we couldn't believe it. It sounded of typical American boasting," he said with a slight chuckle.

"Then why do you want it?" George responded as the trio approached a T-intersection in the hallway.

"Because it should've been here in the first place, Dr. Sansor," Järvinen responded as he came to a halt at the crossroad.

"I don't understand," George said, summarizing the day.

"End of the hall," Järvinen said, motioning to the rightward corridor. "Last door on the left. Thank you, sirs," he said as he pointed. "This way."

The three continued down to where Järvinen led them. Two double doors opened into a massive room, engulfed by a circular desk with lamps illuminating the darkness around it. Mindless chit-chatter among those in the room came to a brisk halt as they entered. Everyone stared and gawked as they entered the room.

"I thought we were just dropping these off," Kevin whispered to George. "*What* is going on?"

George wished he knew. The Master Project never had such gravitas. In the NASA cafeteria, those associated with it were viewed as social pariahs. He got used to eating lunch alone, or at best with Kevin. Janitors got better experiences with career staff. These men seemed awestruck by their appearance.

They climbed down the amphitheater stairs, following Järvinen. He led them to the front of a taller stage as everyone took a seat, patiently waiting for something. Järvinen went to a wooden podium at the front of the stage, adorned with a CERN logo at its center.

"Ladies and gents, it has arrived," he marveled with delight. The room erupted into cheers and applause. Coworkers high-fived and hugged each other. One computer was toppled in the madness. Järvinen turned and tried to shake both George's and Kevin's hands, but the gesture fell apart with the baggage they were carrying.

George had been through enough. He shifted his cardboard box into his armpit and pulled Järvinen aside. "Okay man, enough," he growled into his ear. "Take this shit and get us out of here."

Järvinen looked at him with genuine surprise. "Dr. Sansor? Yes? Are you really going to leave us without telling us about what you've discovered about Mars?" George stepped backward like he'd been punched. *Mars? What does this whole fucking thing have to do with Mars?*

Järvinen knew the shot had landed. He leaned into the podium's microphone and informed the crowd. "You all, you've done great things. Now we leave greatness behind, and the *extraordinary* begins. Please continue your work and thank you." As he concluded his address, he grinned at George and Kevin. He scurried off the stage and towards the large circular desk, and they followed out of involuntary complicity. George had never been one for the spotlight, despite his academic prowess. He found out early in his formative years that making a name for oneself in science was one part genius, ten parts theatrics. The number of people less qualified for his position, yet more considered for it, was vast. When he started his career at NASA, science was a broad complex of people just trying to make the world better. Over time, it had simply become another device to make money.

They sat in two empty seats to Dr. Järvinen's right. George let the box he was lugging fall to the desk with an emphatic *thud.* He glowered at Järvinen. The scowl was returned with a bemused smile from the old man. He reclined backward in his chair slightly and put his hands behind his head.

"Gentlemen, what can you tell me about your Master Project?" he asked.

"Everything's here in these files," George returned with a matter-of-fact snipe and a motion of his head.

"I'm sure it is. But I find the character of research gets lost in words. Words are lies written by men. I want to know what *you* can tell me about it," Järvinen explained.

"It was delivered to us. We can't decipher it, but it's a blueprint for something." George was being coy on purpose. *Because screw this guy, that's why,* he thought.

"For teleportation!" Kevin suddenly blurted out. George grimaced at his outburst. Järvinen's demeanor changed to earnest as he leaned forward towards them. Other workers in the proximate area stopped working to eavesdrop on the conversation.

"And to what ends have you developed this technology?" he asked.

"Not a damn thing. Like I said, we couldn't translate it," George pushed back.

"Ah. A pity. Would it help if you had the key to such a code?" Järvinen said with a sardonic grin. George's eyebrows raised. He was at a loss for words.

"D...Do you *have* the key?" he stammered out. Järvinen let out a hearty laugh.

"My dear Dr. Sansor, do you really believe I needed Mr. Yim and you to hand-deliver these notes? No, I could've easily had them sent by e-mail. I need you to *work*. We have much to do, and time is of the essence."

"Then why did my boss tell me that we were just dropping them off?" George challenged.

"Ah, you refer to Mr. Boddaring?"

"Yes, him."

"I did not care for him in our conversations. He was less than pleasing. I told him what I did to get you and Mr. Yim here without revealing the truth because I don't believe him to be trustworthy," Järvinen said. George and Kevin exchanged knowing grins.

"You don't know the half of it, Järvinen," George cracked.

"So you'll help us, yes?" he implored. George glanced at Kevin again. He made a face and shrugged his shoulders. George sighed.

"Sure. We'll help. But you need to show us what it is we're working on. Seems you've made an awful lot of progress on a project that was *supposed* to be top-secret."

"Dr. Sansor, it's hard to keep a secret like that when your country was not the first to be given such plans," he said with a boast. Järvinen slid his chair out from the desk and stood up. He motioned for George and Kevin to follow him. The trio walked to the far side of the room, where a bank of elevator doors lay in front of them.

"Let me show you what our mutual friends supplied to *us*," he said to them with a sly grin.

6

Down the Rabbit Hole

Järvinen retrieved an access card from inside his coat and waved it in front of a black panel next to the only single-door elevator in the row. As he waited for entry, he turned around to see George fuming with anger. His brow was furrowed deep into his eyes and his face was slightly twitching.

"A problem, Dr. Sansor?"

A problem? Yeah, you could say there's a fucking problem!

"Yeah, you could say there's a fucking problem!" he echoed himself.

Järvinen chuckled. "Yes, Boddaring said you could be… difficult… to work with. I don't mind working with brash arrogance, sir, but I need my employees to keep a propensity of composure."

George checked himself. He was fatigued, temperamental, and at the end of his rope. He took a long, deep breath. "Given the circumstances, Dr. Järvinen, you'll have to understand my irritation. We've been deprived of sleep, we've been given bad information, and we've been undermined by our superiors every step of the way. We *just* found out that we should've been

43

collaborating here from the start. One guy quit NASA and shot himself. Another one drank himself to death. Kevin and I have given this project every ounce of our careers, of our health, of our *souls*, only to find out we were rats running on a wheel."

Järvinen's eyes widened with empathy. "I assumed as much, my dear Dr. Sansor. Americans have money, but the disorganization is... startling. I wanted you here because I have read your works. You are thorough. When Boddaring said you were on the project from its inception, and that you were the only one who could claim so, I knew you were dedicated. And that's what I need here: thoroughness and dedication."

George was baffled. His reputation at NASA, and within the American scientific community, had been in shambles for so long, he wasn't mentally prepared to accept compliments. He glared at Kevin, daring him to react to the acclaim, and found him rolling his eyes.

"That *all* Boddaring said?" George demanded. Because he knew *damn well* it wasn't.

"No, Dr. Sansor. It was not. He was careful to tell me about your... episodes," Järvinen shot back. "In fact, he felt necessary to tell me about your *two* failed marriages. How many years difference in age was your second wife from you, sir?"

George gritted his teeth and flared his eyes. "Twenty-two," he buzzed like a chainsaw.

"Ah yes, sweet Kinsley. Mr. Boddaring sent me screenshots of her social media pictures. Quite the looker, Dr. Sansor. Quite indeed," Järvinen toyed.

* * *

Kinsley had started as an intern at NASA four months after

Erika, George's wife of ten years, had packed exactly three suitcases and left him. There was no discussion. No attempts at fixing their problems, which were mostly centered around George's career ambitions. One unusually warm November night he returned home from a fifteen-hour workday, completely exhausted. Erika was packed and ready to go: an EverRide car was idling on the curb waiting to jettison her away from their marriage.

He was blindsided. He felt cut down at the knees. He was both furious and perplexed.

But Erika didn't care. Any rationale he felt she owed him, she felt he should know. He still didn't know why she felt entitled to such disrespect: He couldn't even remember that conversation any more than he could remember a conversation with a toll booth worker. It was so paltry, and he was so indignantly seething, that he developed tunnel vision for the first time in his life. He remembered seeing a packet of divorce decree papers with red arrow stickers indicating his signature was required. A marching band could have waltzed through their kitchen and he'd have been oblivious to it.

Maybe she told him why their marriage was dead. Maybe she told him off. Every scenario of the exchange reverberated in his head for months, turning him into an automated shadow at work. His career trajectory began to remarkably tumble.

And then, like the first warm, sunny day of spring after a brutal D.C. winter, Kinsley walked into the employee entrance of NASA headquarters. Erika was a slender, blonde, olive-skinned woman who was stern, serious, and compassionate. George couldn't tell if Kinsley was Hispanic, Asian, black, or a mix of them all. But she was curvaceous, vivacious, and bubbling with cheerful energy. She reminded him of old pictures his father showed him of Jessica Alba or Danica McKellar. His world ignited from a gray, fatigued blur of weariness to an explosion of color and feverishness.

Obviously, George never approached or made a move on her. She was entirely out of his league. It was never a position that left him resentful: he was otherwise thankful that she'd unwittingly managed to awaken his zeal for the world around him. Admiring her from afar was just fine to him.

Until the day she sat down with him at lunch.

George was very busy that day with his daily lunch ritual of dejectedly unwrapping a sealed, air-tight, egg salad sandwich that he procured from a vending machine. Inspecting the dusty, uninteresting bread labeled as "artisan" by EverCorp. Playing with the sour gunk in between excused as mayonnaise. Itemizing every appalling aspect of the feast, if only to corroborate the foundation for his misery. Months prior, he'd have brought his work on his laptop with him to work on quantum fissure equations while he stuffed a caloric necessity into his mouth. But since Erika had deserted him, something about centering his focus on his lunch felt necessary. He *wanted* to see her face in his thoughts. He *wanted* to feel the pain.

A soft *clank* interrupted the self-examination of his torment. He peered upwards at his disturbance, only to feel his stomach cave into his ass. Kinsley stood over him, one hand perched on her left voluptuous hip. She was obviously used to posing, and she casually accomplished it with remarkable talent.

"Is this seat taken, sir?" she hummed. George opened his mouth to stammer a foolish response but surprised himself with his indifference.

"Not yet. Better hurry before the crowds form," he jeered back at her. *Holy shit, where did you get that finesse, you bastard?*

he remembered thinking to himself.

Kinsley snickered a burst of high-pitched laughter and sat down in a graceful, exquisite move. A week and a half later, they had sex for the first time. George felt like he was getting a virtual EverHub video for free - without pesky advertisements. He'd never been romantically involved with anyone nearly as tantalizing as her. He studied every inch of her perfect naked body as they made love, to the point that it made her uncomfortable, she'd later reveal to him.

Male co-workers attempted to give him juvenile accolades for "hitting that." Female co-workers sneered at him in discontent for being yet another boorish chauvinist. Kinsley's reputation grew from beautiful darling to office slut almost overnight. Such was life in a government office workspace.

Foolishly, the two married approximately three months later. If they were both being honest, they'd admit: George did it for the thrill of being with a younger, more attractive woman than he could have ever imagined; Kinsley did it to prove to an office she never had a desire to work in that she wasn't a harlot. It was a union damned before it started.

Still, George never saw the betrayal coming. Kinsley seemed entirely devoted, no matter why. She never seemed to crave any of the urges that other younger women like her had: going out on the D.C. nightlife, social media, or wild drinking nights. Rather, she seemed more comfortable bundling up on their old sofa on her laptop, researching deep space with George while watching old episodes of Supernatural. *She's truly a unicorn*, he used to admiringly tell himself. That blind faithfulness to their vows further made George trust her even more. If she were to double-cross him, wouldn't she have done it by now? Even his strongest corners of paranoia couldn't find a trace of infidelity in her, no matter how hard he may have tried.

He didn't need to go find it. George and Kinsley held an annual Capital Cup party, celebrating the bitter college football rivalry between Georgetown University and Columbia University. Twice since its inception, the Ivy League schools had participated in bench-clearing brawls. It was a giant spectacle, especially in the District. One didn't need to care about football (George and Kinsley certainly didn't) to delve into the experience.

While entertaining their guests, George noticed that Kinsley was noticeably absent for an extended period of time. He casually looked for her, figuring that the three-meat chili he was famous for had upset her stomach. Nothing.

Back yard. Nothing.

Garage, perhaps for a drunken e-cigarette? Nothing.

Genuine worry set in. *Where could she be? Is she hurt?* he remembered wondering. He made his way to the street for answers. He found them in a white Ford E150. Parked two doors down from theirs, it was rocking with fervor and the windows were steamed in passionate iniquity. He crept further and saw Kinsley getting violently screwed in the missionary position in the back seat of the truck. Just as his brain registered what was happening, she reached up and placed her hand around her suitor's head and pulled him in closer to her.

Numbness. Pain. Rage. Humiliation. Powerlessness. Betrayal. Assault. Inadequacy.

George felt all these emotions ripping through his veins, pounding through his temples, and piercing his stomach like a treacherous disease burning him from the inside out. The worst part, he'd remember later, was that goddamn pull of the head towards her. That was an act of pure affection. Something she had never done or shown to him. That wasn't her being drunk and horny: that was infatuation. She'd forever deny it. He'd never forget it.

He crept up on the truck, trying to be covert and failing. He tripped, stumbled, and dropped his beer. No mind, as the two lovers in the truck were so enthralled in their tryst that a supervolcano wouldn't separate them. He yanked the door open with resolve.

"Whatchya guys doing?" he facetiously asked.

"Uhhhh....talking...." the man who had literally just exited his wife's vagina answered. Both he and Kinsley looked down to the ground in shame.

"I think you should leave," he growled back at the absconder. The man considered his options for a second, gazing at Kinsley.

"No, I'm not gonna," he submissively mumbled as he covered his genitals with a piece of discarded clothing. George's eyes blazed with a fever that made the man recoil with even more alarm than he already had. He wasn't used to anyone - let alone another man - writhing in fear from him. In retrospect, he enjoyed the fleeting experience of command.

"That's going to be the best offer you're going to get tonight. *Get the fuck out of here*, and *now*," he said, surprising even himself. He barely cursed before, not even if he stubbed his toe. He wasn't feigning anything he was feeling. There was no filter between his heart and his mouth.

The man glanced at Kinsley, who was huddled on the opposite side of the truck, also trying to guard her private parts. He climbed into the driver seat, and Kinsley got out, wrapping herself in the garments she'd retrieved on the way out.

George walked into their townhouse and furiously ejected every guest they had, including Kinsley's father. Initially, he tried to refuse. When Kinsley walked in, half nude, and George began bellowing at her, he also left. In the mad scramble, their Goldenschnieser dog, Orion, also fled.

Everyone left him.

He walked around in a numb haze for a period of time. It could have been days or weeks. He didn't know. He *did* know that he felt punched in the stomach in a way Erika had never made him feel. He'd always felt in control of his emotions, and yet here was another woman forcing him into another avenue of agony against his will. Kinsley kept trying to explain away her impieties: it was the only time, George was emotionally unavailable to her, she was too drunk to know what she was doing. Every excuse was just another lie. Every subsequent lie was promptly revealed until she had no choice but to admit everything.

Instead, she chose to run, while George was at work.

Almost one year to the day, George found himself divorced a second time over. Technically, the marriage to Kinsley was annulled, since he wasn't even able to track down her whereabouts. The last location he could place her was in Las Vegas. After a documented account of her infidelity, that locale alone was enough for him to abandon the mirage of their love. He turned in the notarized copies of the annulment on a Friday.

Monday afternoon, at lunch, he ate a crusty egg salad sandwich by himself.

* * *

Järvinen relaxed and gave a dismissive wave. "As I said, Boddaring is less than pleasing. I needed him to authorize your and Mr. Kim's transport here. Nothing more." The black panel beside the elevator suddenly illuminated with a green LED horizontal line as a bell chimed. The door quietly slid open and Järvinen stepped inside. "Please, sirs. Let me show you what you were *actually* working on." The two joined him and checked the floor display. There was none. Järvinen waved his access card in front of a similar black panel inside the elevator, then pressed his right thumb on it. A numerical display lit up, and he punched in a ten-digit code. A bell chimed again as the door glided shut.

The elevator began a swift hum downwards. All three men looked upwards, looking at the floor indicator that wasn't there. The elevator kept moving for minutes upon minutes. There was no elevator music to save them from the awkward silence that became torturous.

Kevin coughed. George began impatiently looking at his watch, then looking at Järvinen. He had twice been to the Zhansu Tower - the tallest building in the world - and couldn't remember it taking nearly this long to reach the observation deck. "Just a few more minutes, gentlemen, I assure you," Järvinen said, noticing the discomfort in his guests.

Finally, the elevator crept to a halt. The door emerged and the three stepped into a small room with panoramic windows. George and Kevin were both stunned. They were in the center of a giant mechanical beast. Perhaps a mile up from the bottom of it, which they couldn't see, and another to the top. A large, metal tube sat in the middle of the room. It was entirely metallic, set with accented white lights to illuminate it. George felt as tiny as an ant compared to the sheer size of the place. Järvinen began to operate levers near the window and the entire room began to descend at a forty-five-degree angle towards the mammoth tube "What... what *is* this place?"

George wondered aloud. Järvinen gave a smug grin.

As the transport room finally reached its destination inside the massive tube, two doors to their left yawned open to meet it. The room rotated halfway around, and the three exited the room the same way they'd entered it. Turbocomputers lined the inside, and plasma lines snaked their way across the inner skin of the monstrosity. Catwalks reached up to the top and intertwined in a metal embrace all throughout.

Järvinen led George and Kevin down metal steps at the end of the beast, where they'd entered it, at one lone computer terminal stand. An empty, lined-off space sat in front of it, approximately one hundred feet wide and long. It stood out as obvious to George that something was missing from there, that should be right where the three were standing. Awkward silence turned into grave sincerity. Järvinen stood between the two and the belly of the tube and gestured at it.

"Dr. Sansor, Mr. Yim: welcome to the Escape Velocity Project."

7

Recovery

Christopher Wendell woke up annoyed and confused. He knew exactly where he was.

Andrews Hospital. The dated wallpaper and stench of slow death were ones he'd experienced before. *Beep. Beep. Beep.* He checked his surroundings. IV machine. Naked, except for the standard assless hospital gown and footies. A half dozen or so leads hooked up to his chest. Bandages haphazardly coated his body from his waist to his neck.

Beep.

Beep.

Beep.

His head was throbbing. Nurses loudly gossiped in a nearby workstation. He rolled his eyes at their lounging.

Beep.

Beep.

Beep.

"A little help?" he called out. Nothing. He let out an exasperated, excessive sigh. Still nothing.

Beep.

Beep.

Beep.

"Aight, to hell with it." He lowered his legs over the side of the bed and thrust himself up. Searing pain shot up from his butt to the top of his head, making the end of every hair on his body tingle. He sucked in a deep breath between his teeth in agony. The monitor beside his bed wobbled, then crashed to the ground, yanking most of the leads from his body.

Beep.

Beep.

Booooooooooooooooooop.

One sole nurse finally meandered in, clearly in no rush. He glared at her in disbelief.

"Commander Wendell, you're in no shape for these games. Get back in bed," she bossed.

"Doing just fine," he retorted while gauging her bra cup size. "Just get me my discharge papers and I'll be on my way. And some ibuprofen." *Probably a C-cup, but her scrubs are too loose to know for sure*, he decided.

"Not a chance. You're staying here until Rear Admiral Garland approves it. I'll go call his office. In the meantime, get back in bed. Don't *make* me get the restraints again."

Again? You hardass, Christopher. Fighting people in a blackout, he mused to himself. He slid back onto the bed, not breaking eye contact with the nurse. He'd been to enough VAs to know that to get anything done, you had to be half cooperative, half homicidal. But it was a very delicate balance of the two.

Overwhelming depression suddenly sank in as he realized his phone wasn't with him, and he was cut off from information from the outside world. Throbbing panic hindered his thought processes. "Nurse?" he called out. She turned, as she almost had passed the doorway. "Is my unit okay?" She nodded in confirmation.

"The only other patient we took from your squad is three doors down from here. A Commander Stormer." Christopher catapulted off the bed in a reflex and pushed past her. Ignoring the pain, he drug his monitor and leads into the hallway. Nurses from the workstation looked up in bafflement.

"Erik! Erik, you hear me? Where you at, buddy?" he hollered. His room was situated in the corner of the hallway, so three rooms down from his was a fifty-fifty shot. His nurse followed him and began to scold him.

"*Erik!*"

"Yo! Calm your ass down, dude!" Erik's voice rang out to Christopher's right. He shimmied as best he could, tracking his friend. He entered a room and found Erik, lounging on his bed, fully clothed, scrolling through his phone. He rushed over and gave him a hug, ignoring the pulsation of agony that touching anything did to him.

"Anyone else hurt?" he questioned.

"Not a one. We ejected and they were ordered to boogey home. S & R picked our sorry asses up floating in the Atlantic Ocean. I looked pretty heroic. You were crying, though. Like, a *lot*." he cracked with a sarcastic grin.

"You know I cry when I get too aroused," Christopher joked back. "So did they figure out who it was? Russians? Chinese? When do we start kicking some teeth in?" Erik's face grew long and solemn.

"It wasn't anyone," he answered. Christopher blinked rapidly.

"I..uh...huh?"

"It wasn't a nuke, man. It was Mother-fucking-Earth

herself," Erik said. "Apparently some kind of 'supervolcano.' Right under Philly and we never even knew it."

"A supervolcano. Under *Philly*. Come on, man. Quit your bull-shitting," Christopher said with growing agitation. And fear. Erik picked up a remote and turned on the television. He clicked through the channels, but they were all the same. Scrolling bars of information lined the bottom of every channel:

"DEVASTATION IN PHILADELPHIA"

"MILLIONS FEARED DEAD"

"SCIENTISTS BAFFLED AT UNDISCOVERED VOLCANO"

"ECO-IMPROVEMENT TO BLAME?"

"QUESTIONS MOUNT AS BODY COUNT RISES"

"ECO ACTIVISTS PLAN MARCH ACROSS WORLD"

"PRESIDENT BUYNAK TO DELIVER ADDRESS FROM SECURE LOCATION"

Christopher sunk to the bed and sat next to Erik. His nurse charged in and started yelling at him, but he couldn't be bothered to take his eyes away from the screen. He held up his hand to cut her off, but his shoulder wouldn't allow his arm to raise high enough. The images kept flashing on the screen. Destruction like nothing he could ever fathom. Entire miles of Philadelphia sunken underground and on fire. People, chalk-white from dust and ash except for the blood pouring out of them, hobbling down remnants of streets like zombies. Video from ash falling like a blizzard in Cincinnati. Boats capsized on the Outer Banks in North Carolina.

He started itching feverishly under his bandages and realized he was sweating profusely. Erik looked at him with concern. "We're getting extended leave from this, man. By all accounts, that blast should've killed you ten times over." Christopher looked down and remembered his cockpit, melting and bright orange. He felt himself reaching for the controls to try to maneuver his plane, losing his grasp on his surroundings.

"Dude, you alright?" Erik's question snapped Christopher from his confusion.

"Yeah, I'm good. Garland's gonna be *so pissed* that we're not dead, though," Christopher murmured.

"Well, we are the number one and number two worst pilots in the Navy, need I remind you," Erik bantered back. Garland had infamously given the two that title during a heated spat, but never specified *who* was deserving of the 'number one' or 'number two.'" The pair constantly used it as a badge of honor in rebellion against the upper ranks of the Navy. Christopher smiled with fondness at the joke.

"I hear you're doing your best to go AWOL, Commander Wendell," Garland said as he entered the room. His face was sagging from stress and fatigue. His uniform, usually clean and pressed, was probably the same one he was wearing when they had spoken to him last in Hangar 18. He normally stood to address people unless he was at his desk, but he quickly slumped into a chair next to the two in quiet resignation. "By the way, Wendell, the damage done to your E-2 is getting docked from your paycheck," he dryly joked. Garland always rode the two especially hard, but he cared above all about the safety of the people assigned to him.

"Put it on my tab," Wendell bantered back. "Sir, they said I can't leave without your sign-off. Could I possibly get that? I'm gonna catch a staph infection in this hellhole."

"You look like shit, Wendell. No chance. Plus I've seen the women you bring home. I'm confident in your ability to fight off diseases," Garland answered. The three refused to let their eyes betray the television. Cell phone video showed

Christopher's jet tumbling into the water like a wounded bird. Erik's was shown exploding midair a short time later. It was a feature EverCorp had built into the eject function, so reverse-engineering by enemies would be next to impossible. Christopher felt surging humiliation and defeat. He had rarely experienced a mission go so badly, and at his expense, no less. He punched the bed between his and Erik's legs in aggravation.

"What's our next move, Rear Admiral?" Christopher demanded.

"*Your* next move is getting healthy. The Pentagon has gone radio silent since we found out this wasn't terrorism. I can't even get a damn aide to return my calls. From what I've heard, this is a FEMA issue now. We're to standby and be ready, should they come calling," he responded.

"So handing out water bottles and photo ops," Erik groaned.

"Consider it a blessing, gentlemen. This could've been the biggest SNAFU in military history, and I personally don't want to be on this end of it. You're both on medical leave until my office authorizes your return to duty. Rest up, relax. Don't get arrested or anyone pregnant. I have a feeling this isn't the end of this headache."

8

Short Notice

Järvinen let the silence fall between the three for dramatic effect.   George's eyes darted to and fro, trying to understand the maze they'd just been led into. He couldn't.

"I thought this project was the Future Collision Collider? Experiments with accelerated particles and black holes?" he wondered aloud, not necessarily to anyone. Järvinen nodded.

"All true. The name and *reason* for that project are essentially the only things known to the world. And..." he added, "...what they think is the FCC is a mile above our heads. *This* is the principal work we have been doing."

"Let me guess," George replied, "space teleportation?"

"Indeed, Dr. Sansor. When you Americans received your instructions, you believed in some proud way that you had the entire puzzle. You never even thought to question that you only had one piece. As it happens, we believe you have the *final* piece."

"And you think this will teleport to Mars? Why? What could be so important on Mars that aliens would want us to go there?" George implored.

"Life sustainability," Järvinen said matter-of-factly. It hit George like a ton of bricks. Kevin was holding his breath without realizing it, and let out a loud inhaling gasp. George and Järvinen broke eye contact to simultaneously glare at him.

"Earth is fucked, huh?" George said. Järvinen grimaced at his vulgarity but nodded in affirmation.

"Our planet isn't just dying, sirs. It is, for lack of a better term, deceased. What we are living on now is just a planet that hasn't completely broken apart. Planets die all the time, across the galaxies. Ours has run its course. Not without some help from mankind, unfortunately. We tried to stop it, and the best minds in the world brought us terraforming."

"Eco-improvement," Kevin corrected him.

"So it was named. Public relations isn't our expertise. It was actually quite a novel idea when it was devised. However, we quickly became horrified when we saw the damage it reaped on the planet. We tried to put a stop to it..." Järvinen trailed off in regretful memories.

"But by that time you realized you weren't in charge of your own monster anymore, were you, Frankenstein?" George said, with a rather accusatory inflection in his voice. Järvinen took the shot with another dose of guilt. He swallowed and cleared his throat, attempting to redirect the conversation.

"Dr. Sansor, Mr. Yim. Our mutual friends have supplied us with a fascinating alternative to extinction: relocation. Escape. A lifeboat. We can begin again, with new technologies, and the knowledge of our past. *Will you help us?*" his voice reverberated high into the metal behemoth.

"We're in," George said. He looked at Kevin as if to ask "right?" Kevin nodded.

"Yeah, I mean... I don't want to *die*," Kevin said with a shrug.

"Fantast-" Järvinen began to say but was cut off by loud, blaring sirens. All the cool white lights turned red. George tried to ask Kevin, and then Järvinen what the alarm was for, but had experienced better luck at conversations in the front row of rocket propulsion demonstrations. The three hunched down, the sound was so deafening. Järvinen motioned to the lift they had arrived in, and the three ran back up the network of steel entanglement to it.

As they entered, Järvinen worked the controls and began the ascension back to the elevator. When the doors closed, the sirens became much more tolerable. George collapsed on the floor.

"What the hell's going on? Are we under attack or something?" he screeched as he gasped for air. Järvinen looked at the control monitor and swiped between notifications eyes widening with each word he read.

"Yes, Dr. Sansor. We are. Äiti Maa"

"*English?*"

"Earth. Earth is attacking."

* * *

The elevator reached the main chamber after what felt like an eternity. George swore that it was twice the time that it took to descend. They had left the main chamber room in a positive, celebratory atmosphere. When the door crept open, they found that cheer was replaced with absolute chaos and pandemonium. The room was also outfitted in a red hue, and the scientists were running from one computer terminal to the next, shouting and pointing at notes and the screen. George felt like he was reliving the Master Project at NASA.

61

The three moved quickly to the closest computer. "Järvinen," George shouted over the turmoil, "what the hell is going on?" Järvinen's eyes were wide with dread as the computer monitor reflected in his glasses.

"I don't believe it. It actually *erupted.* We didn't anticipate this for decades," he said. George wasn't sure if he was responding to his question or talking to himself.

"*What* erupted?" he pressed, his patience already worn down with stress.

"The supervolcano. In your Philadelphia," Järvinen revealed. As if on cue, large monitors that were perched high on the walls of the walls began to switch from data readouts to news channels. George and Kevin started rotating around, taking in the savagery they unveiled. A large, gaping hole - easily a mile wide - was spitting magma and ash up into the skies in the large metropolitan area of Philly. Images of the water banks of the Atlantic Ocean churning out thousands of dead fish onto the shores. Corpses piled up in the streets like fortress walls. People were being turned away at hospitals that were missing limbs. A video of a little girl, caked in dirt and blood, missing her left arm, crying and desperately trying to find her mother. Video from Greenland, where the smoke cloud was visible.

George looked over at Kevin, who was frantically trying to use his phone, to no avail. He was crying and breathing so rapidly that he was near hyperventilating. George's mouth went dry and he realized his mouth had been hanging open in shock for several minutes. He knew he should try to give Kevin comfort, but his brain wasn't processing words. He put a hand on Kevin's shoulder and slunk his head in defeat. A speaker monitor hummed to life behind them.

"Excuse me? Excuse me. Mind the interruption. Please,

if I could have your attention. Please take your seats and quiet down. Thank you," Järvinen's voice came through the workplace's speaker. Everyone obediently filed to their respective chairs. An uneasy hush fell over the room. Järvinen cleared his throat and scanned the room from the podium, where he had slipped to during the commotion. He took a deep breath.

"Today, it appears our greatest fears have been realized. We have both been proven correct in our planet's future, and proven incorrect in our expectation of time to plan accordingly. This, ladies and gents, is catastrophic. If any of you have loved ones you wish to go be with, please turn in your credentials and you will be permitted to go." He paused as he surveyed the room. "But I must appeal to you: our work here has become ever so much more crucial, given the events that have just transpired. CERN doesn't need you, *mankind* needs you, now more than ever." He paused again, gauging for any dissent. "We must begin work immediately. Sleep only when necessary. I'll phone for more provisions."

Järvinen stepped away from the podium and wiped a line of sweat from his brow. He strode over to George and Kevin. "Do I still have America's support in this project, sirs?" George's brain began to swim as he tried to find words to use.

"Yeah. Yeah, you do," Kevin quietly responded, his eyes trained on the floor. George nodded in agreement.

"Good. I'll build you into our CAD on my computer. I can walk you through the decryption algorithm we wrote. We need your piece ready for assembly with the utmost haste. And Dr. Sansor?" Järvinen asked. George's eyes had wandered back to the large screens, captivated by the scenes of ruin. He turned his attention back to Järvinen.

"Call NASA, if you please. We'll need a brave wanderer to be a test pilot. Immediately."

9

Aftershock

Christopher let the warm water from his shower drip down onto the back of his head. He focused on the water droplets reverberating off the glass enclosure around him, pinging tiny echos into his aching head. The water stung his burns on his upper body, not unlike anything else that touched it. He hadn't even worn a shirt in a week since returning home. Erik had been diagnosed with shingles on his sides years ago and described the pain of even a breeze like Christopher was experiencing. His own competitiveness assured him that his suffering was worse, though.

He hung his head lower as he tried to shake away tears that were threatening to break free. He didn't cry as an adult - not ever. But he had been battling with an overpowering urge to sob every time he showered. It left him annoyed, confused, disoriented, and furious all at once. *Why are you being such a pussy?* he'd argue with himself. He prided himself on being a "man's man," and crying was the farthest thing from that which he could imagine. That he didn't know *why* he was crying was the worst aspect. He couldn't admit it to himself, but his psyche was imploding on itself.

The water started to turn cold, but it didn't help the agony coursing through his midsection. He shut it off in disgust and frustration. Standing still for a moment, he stared at the metallic shower handle he'd just used. His body, morphed from the convex curve of the handle, looked macabre. It was small, so he couldn't identify much, but it looked like a shrunken zombie. He turned his head as he studied it, and the zombie did as well, as if studying him back. He shuddered as his body began to chill from the water still dripping on him.

Christopher tenderly stepped out of the shower and located the mirror. Torrents of dejection again shot through him as he took himself in full view. He was a monster. His skin was a mix of deep maroon, pastel yellow, and black throughout the entire middle of his body. The muscles he so carefully sculpted were hidden under unsightly waves of blisters and sores. He looked like a victim of the Black Plague. Thankfully, it stopped at his lower groin, just short of his penis. *That* was something he was certain he wouldn't be able to handle.

He began to gingerly apply the prescription ointment he'd gotten from the hospital to his ailments. That offered short and minimal relief. He cursed the Andrews medical staff the whole time he did it. When he was properly lubricated, he began the excruciating process of applying adhesive bandages and then wrapping his body in one large elastic bandage. He winced and grunted at the pain, becoming short of breath very quickly.

When he was nearly finished, his mirror notified him of an incoming call: *User Number Blocked.* He rolled his eyes. "Ignore," he said in an irritated tone. The computer beeped in response and sent the notification scurrying away. He continued his wrapping when another call immediately rang:

Erik USN. Christopher sighed. He'd been dodging Erik's calls since being released, only responding by text. That way, he could properly put on a cloak of bravado. He made sure there weren't any straggling tears in his eyes.

"Answer."

Erik displayed on the screen, eyeing Christopher with intrigue. "Oh, sorry, is this your pay site? I thought I called your normal number," he quipped. Christopher rolled his eyes and kept wrapping. Erik read his face and steadied his tone. "Garland was trying to set up a conference call with us. He's got a mission or something for us."

"I'm on leave. So are you."

"Yeah well, you know what they say about leave..."

"It's just been revoked?"

"Yep. So answer the call when it comes in again. If I gotta get yelled at, I at least want you there, too." The words cut Christopher deep, even though Erik didn't mean anything by it. *He jumped into the Atlantic Ocean for you, and you can't even pick up the phone for him. God, you're such a prick.*

"Got it. See you in a minute," he responded. Erik nodded and hung up. The sudden silence of the room left Christopher momentarily alone with his thoughts. He quickly began to scowl in self-loathing. *What did this crash turn you into, Christopher Wendell?* he wondered as he continued to have to look at himself. He never had anything but admiration for himself. He was never short on self-esteem. Now, he felt like a shell of his former self.

His mirror mercifully rang to break him from his mental torment. *User Number Blocked.* "Answer," he said, this time much more defeated. Garland and Erik both appeared, neither one saying anything. Garland peered into his screen on his end.

"Wendell? You mind covering up?" he said. Christopher shook his head and reached for a towel. As he did, he did his best to hide the pain that stabbed him like lightning bolts. He glanced at the mirror to see if the other two noticed. Their faces told him they absolutely did. He carefully wrapped his lower body in the towel, then continued wrapping his midsection with the bandage.

"Sir, how can I help you?" he responded, trying in vain to move past their judgment.

"I wanted to check in on you and see how your recovery is going," he responded.

"Just as I told you in our last text, sir. Feeling great," he lied.

"And just as I told you in our last text: that's bullshit," Garland said. He sighed deeply. "Look, Wendell. I need you and Stormer back in the saddle as soon as you possibly can. Something's coming down the pike and I don't have the faintest clue what. But it's going to involve your squad."

"How is it that you, *Rear Admiral Garland*, are never in the loop?" Erik asked with a smile on his face. But he wasn't joking.

"Shit, Stormer. There are E-1's walking around here that are more in the know than I am. You know this and *what is that sitting next to you?*" Garland turned from disgruntled to enraged mid-sentence. The "what" he was referring to was a giant water bong, prominently displayed on Erik's screen. Erik took it and showed it with pride to his commanding officer. Flashy neon logos adorned it, with small lettering warning of cancer, diabetes, and death, below them.

"Oh, this? It's a new EverCorp energy drink! Bomb Rips! Comes in this fun container, and look, it's got two places you can drink it out of!" Erik demonstrated for the two. Christopher shook his head and grinned for the first time in days. Garland sank his head into his hands and grumbled.

"Gentlemen, just... Just get combat-ready ASAP. They need pilots, and if I'm not sending the both of you, I'm not sending anyone in your unit," he finally groused.

"Sir? Who are 'they?'" Christopher asked.

"The Pentagon. DoD. The White House. I dunno, but someone closer to God than me," Garland answered. "And Stormer? You're dropping piss for me the next time you step foot on base," he said with a glare as his screen went black. It scuttled away and Erik's half enlarged to full-screen.

"Jesus, dude. *Now* what? Another supervolcano?" Christopher said to Erik. He shrugged and smiled.

"Probably another suicide mission," he said as he waved and signed off. As the mirror turned fully translucent to a reflective piece again, Christopher looked at himself intensely. *Do you have what it takes for another suicide mission?* he wondered.

10

Key to Salvation

George's eyes darted rapidly around the tabletop monitors that Järvinen's lackeys had set up in the designated "USA" space of the Escape Velocity Project. He moved documents displayed on the screen, and as he did, hieroglyphics shifted, coded, and decoded. Colors flashed from aqua to red in a dancing fashion. He was still as confused as he was when his team was trying to translate their piece in Washington, but the puzzle was beginning to make sense to him. He had at least translated the title of America's portion: "Mars is the Door to Salvation. This shapes the Key." *Amazing*, he thought as he shifted the document image below him. It trembled with haptic feedback as it changed back to its original title:

𝄋iiiiii⇚⊠ڥ▨ ▩฿▤◉,◂◃n6.TY1vXC ▦TY1vXC ◪◩௰82588◩◩⇶
|kWJ◜ ◕⨦⨦R‘ Ξ∠|uo⊛ᕱ⍡29.209⍋⊛ᕱ⍡29.209⍋฿▤◉,◂◃n6.
◪◩௰82588◩◩⊛ᕱ⍡29.209⍋]₴~,6fc5⊠ڥ▨
▩{ζ~⊳⊠▫₢G,4.⊠ڥ▨ ▩◪◩௰82588◩◩▦⊛ᕱ⍡29.209⍋⌋]]⨧∨⨧⨧Ss
Fd⊠&6.301⇶|kWJ◜ ▦TY1vXC TY1vXC⇶|kWJ◜ ⊠ڥ▨ ▩◘7ri,9.⍭
◕⨦⨦R‘TY1vXC ◪◩௰82588◩◩⇶|kWJ◜ ◕⨦⨦R‘ ₠\₣10⌇01◕⨦⨦R‘⌂

7.912.六

The math involved required quantum turbocomputers, which was something NASA, CERN, or anyone else George knew of didn't have. This machine, however, was probably the closest thing mankind had ever gotten to it. He'd love to have it back at his research lab someday if he survived that long. The learning curve was steep but manageable. Kevin stood across the table from him, jotting down numbers and punching algorithms into a calculator. He'd written a program from scratch in just four hours to shortcut some of the more tedious work. He was really starting to shine under this colossal pressure.

"Kevin," George said, pausing his studies, "I need to apologize to you." Kevin looked up from his notes in confusion.

"Apologize for what, Dr. Sansor?" he responded.

"I've been making all the decisions for both of us ever since we landed. I never once asked if you were okay in going along in all of this bullshit." Kevin shifted his weight on his feet, obviously uncomfortable with the discussion. "Are you?" Kevin put his pen down and took off his glasses.

"I wasn't, no. Not at the start. I didn't trust Dr. Järvinen and this is all a little... *much*," he said.

"But you are now?" George asked.

"I have to be," Kevin said. "You don't really know that much about me, do you, Dr. Sansor?" George's cheeks flushed with shame. He didn't. The workload at NASA could chew you up and spit you out if you let it. Recreational time was non-existent, and George worked through his lunch like most career employees. He realized at that moment that this was the first conversation he could remember between the two that didn't involve a mathematical formula or a scientific theorem. His eyes sank downward and he sighed deeply.

"No, Kevin. That's fair. I never really asked you more than what I knew from your résumé. I'm kind of a dick and I don't really talk to people. I don't have any friends outside of work, so I *should* make friends with the people that I *do* work with. But I don't. And people that have been around the Administration long enough can screw off if they don't like that. But you're a young, inspired, developing mind with his full career ahead of him. You shouldn't be around someone so toxic like me. You don't deserve that," George said, taking a paternal, yet apologetic tone with his protégé.

Kevin snorted through his nose. "That's exactly why I *wanted* to work with you, Dr. Sansor. Heck, that's why *most* people want to work with you. You eat and breathe physics at a level that no one else can even fathom. Sure, you might be a little... rough around the edges... but what great scientist wasn't?" he revealed. George leaned in over the monitors.

"So what does this have to do with the Escape Velocity Project, then?" he questioned. "What changed your mind?"

"Because you don't know where my family lives," Kevin responded quietly. George's blood turned ice cold and he stopped breathing. Because with that one sentence, he knew everything else that would follow.

"Oh, fuck. Oh, no, Kevin," he bumbled. His eyes felt wide enough to allow them to fall out of his head. His brain began racing so fast that he stopped hearing the soft hum of the machinery around them. "Not–"

"–Philadelphia," Kevin answered. The two stood in silence, watching the table monitors blink and flicker. George reached for the right words – for any words – of consolation to a young man that had just lost everything. The videos being shown on the news were harrowing and ominous but still felt like it was happening *out there* and they were *in here*. George, nor anyone else at CERN even knew anyone that lived remotely close to the area of destruction. He couldn't imagine the helplessness that Kevin must have been feeling to see what had transpired. There was no communication with the outside world in the depths of the project, save for Järvinen's food and hygiene requests.

"How many...how big is your family, Kevin?" George finally driveled out.

"My grandma, parents, sister, and brother. My brother, Jian, he's a sophomore in high school. He wanted to go to MIT like his big brother," Kevin said with a grimace as his eyes began to dampen. "So that's why I stayed. That's why I'm here. Because if it's as bad as Dr. Järvinen says it is, I have to *try*." The two stood looking at each other as the silence enveloped them. Minutes passed. "Do *you* think Järvinen's telling the truth?" Kevin finally asked. George considered his question deeply.

"Why would he lie?" George offered.

"I dunno," Kevin sighed, "I don't know what to make of the world anymore. What if this machine is really meant for something *else*? And he's just feeding us a bunch of lies to get us to follow along and do the work that needs to be done?"

"Hot damn, Kevin. You really *have* been around my toxic ass too long. I've already turned you into quite the cynic!" George said with a half-smile.

"No, but I mean-" Kevin protested.

"-I know what you meant," George interjected. "Look, I'd probably be a bit more skeptical myself. But look at it scientifically: doesn't what he said make *sense*? I mean, a *supervolcano?* Under *Philly?* I don't recognize this world anymore, Kevin. I truly don't. When I was your age, I got all up in arms about which politician won what, or what war was true or fake. And all my young friends and I would scream and declare 'the world's gonna end if *this* happens or if *that* happens. We'd be in the fetal position," George added with a chuckle. "After enough time, I realized that shit didn't mean anything. We were always getting upset and emotional over real trivial shit, in the grand scheme of things. The world would keep spinning, short of nuclear war, or..." George trailed off, the lingering wound of Kevin's losses still hanging fresh in his mind. He tried to think of some way to soften the blow.

"Or something equivalent?" Kevin offered in a deadpan tone.

"Yeah. Something 'equivalent,'" George said. More silence cut through them. "So yeah, I don't necessarily *trust* the guy, but I do *believe* what he says about the planet going down the drain. Don't worry about him. Let's just get this thing figured out."

* * *

Dr. Järvinen watched George and Kevin's conversation from his office computer. The monitor reflected off his glasses as he kept his lips firmly pressed against his two extended pointer fingers. As the two submerged back into their work, he breathed deeply. "Iloinen kuulla se, Tohtori Sansor. Mutta kiroat liikaa. (*Glad to hear it, Dr. Sansor. But you do curse too much*)."

11

Back in the Saddle

"Rover, you are clear for takeoff, repeat, clear for takeoff," Christopher's radio buzzed to him. He grasped the controls of his new E-2 jet firmly. It had been six weeks since Garland had cleared him to resume normal duties, but he had gone through a gauntlet of testing to prove he was ready for combat. He had aced the physical agility tests since he had been working out against medical advice virtually the minute he'd been released from Andrews Hospital. The psychological tests and mandatory counseling had been much more challenging. "Appears ready to resume duties but obviously hiding extreme pain" was the consensus from every professional he'd been sent to. No one in his chain of command even mentioned it.

"Rover, do you copy?" Christopher's mind had wandered. He gazed outside the jet to see the ground crew staring at him. Beyond them, additional companies had been brought in solely to drive E-78's around the tarmac, sweeping up the blizzard of falling ash that had been relentlessly falling since the Philadelphia mission. It was a fool's errand: by the time one of those cumbersome, slow machines had finished plowing one line of ash, the beginning of that succession had already risen to the same level it was cut down from. It didn't take a pilot to understand that swirling, pallid sky wrapped in windstorms of embers was not military flight-ready standards. He couldn't even see to his liftoff point. But these were hardly standard times.

"Copy, ready," he responded as he fired the jet's thrusters to their maximum levels. He shot the plane forward and was off into the darkness.

Garland had decided to put him through an augmented reality exercise. It began with basic maneuvers, then progressed to defensive and offensive pivots and banks. If those were cleared, he had AI enemies to dispatch, then more as he had to re-enter the maneuver section of the exam. Finally, he would corkscrew, pitch, twist, and turn while withstanding five G's of gravitational pull, closer to the Earth's stratosphere than the ground. If that was accomplished, his runway to land was a quarter of the size he normally touched down upon. One mistake was a course failure. He had aced this course before. But now, he was doing it blindly. *That man hates me with a passion*, he thought of Garland to himself.

He breezed through the maneuverability section with ease, even with an obsidian backdrop. Most of it was rehashes of previous tests. *Lazy programming*, he chuckled to himself. *Bet you never wrote programs for something this fucked, EverCorp.* He buckled down his concentration for the combat section. A few close misses, and probably a bit of luck later, he had cleared it as well. To his advantage, the AI was being remotely communicated to his aircraft instead of being directly installed into the onboard terminal. He had inquired about that before the flight, passing it off as inspection diligence. Due to the weather, there was noticeable lag and glitches from the onscreen opponents he comfortably terminated.

Christopher rocketed skyward as he began to feel the nauseating tug of extra gravitational pull. "Two G's," his radio crackled at him. "Three. Three-point five. Four. Almost there, Commander." he tried to respond but couldn't. He started relaxing his grip on the controls. *I can't do it*, he told himself. *This is going to kill me. I can't do it.* The roar of the terror he'd encountered in Philadelphia crept into his ears like a surging infection.

"Losing climb ratio, Commander, keep your foot on the gas!" his radio urged him.

"Repeat traffic!" he responded, "I cannot clear, I repeat, I cannot clear your traffic!" No matter. He couldn't hear a thing over the roar of the supervolcano pounding his brain against his skull.

"Increase climb, sir! Increase climb!" his radio mumbled through the thunder. *You get up here and try it then. I can't*, he answered in his head.

"That's five! Come on back Commander, great job sir!" he heard. He exhaled loudly and realized he'd been holding his breath for a while. He nudged his flight controls and moved back to normalcy.

As he landed, the blood in his body was finally returning to the proper places. He taxied the jet inside the hangar as the ground crew started its tear down. One of the crew members patted his helmet and gave him a thumbs up. As he did, his face turned into an awkward stare and he clamored back down the escape ladder. Christopher climbed out after him and felt the warm hangar lights hit his flight suit, punctuating the dampness in his crotch. He froze in fear and embarrassment.

He'd wet himself. His head burst with rage and humiliation, and suddenly he felt like the entire crew was staring at him. Most of them were. He jumped down the ladder from too high, punishing his ankles as he landed. He limped off towards the locker room as fast as he possibly could, his head tucked down to his chest. The crew was all wearing helmets, but he swore he heard them all laughing as he reached the exit.

Christopher heaved his flight suit into the nearest laundry cart but made sure to bury it at the bottom to obscure the evidence. He shuffled into the shower and turned the water on, not even waiting for it to warm up. He knew what was next. His breathing started to increase, and he felt like he was suffocating. In the midst of that, he began sobbing uncontrollably. Large, loud, crying that he tried to stifle to no avail. He leaned against the shower wall to steady his balance as his body gave in to the tears. He despised himself. *Why couldn't you have just botched the crash, you asshole?* he demanded of himself. *No questions and you wouldn't have to live with being such a goddamn disgrace.* Ropes of snot hung down from his nose, twirling and spinning against the water running down his head.

A loud slam broke his self-deprecation short. He sniffled and put his face into the shower stream, now adequately heated. "Mmmm *mmmm*, I could take in this view all day!" Erik's voice echoed off the shower walls. Christopher turned to see him, leaning against the entryway to the shower room, arms crossed in front of his chest and an amused grin plastered upon his face. Christopher feigned a smile back and pretended to wash.

"I hear you passed the training course. People are saying you're number one," Erik continued. Christopher's stomach sank and his neck tightened. *Did he hear?*

"Yeah," was all Christopher mumbled in response.

"Yeah man, they say you're a real *whiz* in that cockpit," Erik said. *Shit,* Christopher thought, *that's definitely-*

"-But I thought you were a loyal United States Navy Pilot? Guess this whole time we shoulda known that you were actually *you're-a-peein!*" Erik's knockout line was accompanied by loud belly laughs and slaps on the shower wall. Christopher slammed the shower handle down in frustration and turned, standing fully nude and pointing his index finger.

"Listen motherfucker, it happens to people all the time at that many G's. I've seen better pilots shit themselves at two G's! When's the last time you went to *five?!*" he exclaimed, voice getting lower and louder as he went on. Erik raised his hands in defense, smiling and pushing off the wall.

"Okay, okay man. Just messing with you. Shit, calm down. I just wanted to come by and tell you Garland wants to see you once you're decent." Christopher kept his finger pointed and glare composed. "But... I'll go tell him that you're going to be a bit." He turned his tall, slender frame away and pulled the shower room door handle open. As he stepped out, he paused and turned back to Christopher. "A *wee* bit." He ducked out of the room as a shampoo bottle rocketed against the wall directly behind where his head had been.

* * *

Christopher walked down the hallway of the administrative offices on the other side of the base. Secretaries and service staff shuffled from door to door, mostly talking on phones or composing emails on tablet devices. He had already checked his DatrApp before leaving the locker room. Twenty new requests and not a single one piqued his interest. He was annoyed and confused by his emotional turmoil. Eight of the online candidates were at least D-cups and scantily clad in their profile pictures. Traditionally, those would be reliable seductions for his appetite. Now, he didn't know what he wanted: from women, from the Navy, or even from life.

He stopped as he reached a set of wooden double doors. Garland's name was posted upon one on a gold placard. The doors were usually open, leading into the reception area of his office. They were closed. Christopher swallowed hard and immediately started recounting everything he had done wrong in the last year. Bar fights. Sexual escapades. Gambling. Drinking and driving. Sometimes all in the same evening. Closed doors in this section of the base were rarely good, especially for people of his rank. He rapped his knuckles on the door and tried to slow down his racing heart.

Garland's secretary, Jennifer Wright, opened the door. She was quiet and homely, with a definite "cat lady" vibe. But Christopher had been "matched" with her on DatrApp before and discovered through her profile that she also had a slightly naughty side to her. They had never spoken about the matches before, which at times left awkward silences between them. "He's waiting for you in his office, Commander," she directed him and strode back to her desk. He tried to read her for a better indication of what he was walking into, but she was a stone wall. He started to mentally prepare for a dishonorable discharge, or worse.

Christopher opened the door to Garland's office. He was furiously typing into his computer, and his desk was a cluttered mess of disorganized papers. He glanced up through his reading glasses and motioned Christopher to approach him. Christopher walked across the large office and saluted Garland. "At ease. Take a seat, Wendell," Garland responded. He eased into one of the chairs across the desk from his boss as if the thing was booby-trapped.

"I hear you passed the test today. Congratulations," Garland continued, eyes never betraying his computer monitor.

"Thank you, sir," Christopher responded.

"Wendell, what are your career aspirations? Where do you want to be in five or ten years?" Garland asked. Christopher was puzzled. *Where is he going with this?* he wondered.

"Well, um... I plan to try to make Captain at my next review, if that's what you're asking, sir..." Christopher bumbled his way through his response.

"Anything else? You know, naval combat experience opens plenty of doors elsewhere. Private sector. Hell, we even get people into NASA," Garland said. Christopher became suddenly defensive. He *liked* the Navy. He'd dedicated his entire life to it, and more. Garland seemed to be pushing him towards an exit. Why would he want to leave? He sat forward in the chair towards his commanding officer.

"Sir, it sounds like you're wanting me to resign my commission or something. What are we talking about here?" Christopher finally demanded. Garland chuckled.

"Come on, Wendell. Every single squid this side of Fort Worth knew your career trajectory the second you enlisted," he demurred. Christopher felt the back of his neck start to boil. "Please tell me you *aren't* planning on following in Daddy's footsteps? Going down 'guns-a-blazing?' Because I've seen you in action. It's almost like you can't help yourself." Christopher felt betrayed. His father, Admiral Patton Wendell

III, was his personal hero.

* * *

Admiral Wendell had enjoyed a lengthy, successful career in the Naval Corps. Christopher, unlike other military brats, never minded picking up and moving at a moment's notice. To his knowledge, he never developed a complex from it and found it refreshing to leave old friends behind for new ones. He felt it an honor, to sacrifice his own personal happiness for what his father was doing for the country.

When Admiral Wendell became stationed on a more permanent basis in the Washington, D.C. area, he deployed less and began taking on more administrative roles. Christopher's mother, Martha, was relieved. Admiral Wendell was less so. "Bullshit paperwork queen is all they've made me," he'd mostly grumble when anyone asked him about his day at work. Not as if he would have been able to give much more than that, with nearly all of his work being top-secret. But Christopher, young as he was, could tell his father was not happy behind a desk.

Then came the presidential election of 2040. William Horn, a third-party outside contender for the throne of political power, won in a hotly-contested race. After the e-ballot fiasco of the previous election, paper affidavits were re-instated. Some claimed that reeked of racism, sexism, and a dozen other "isms". Others screamed government mismanagement. No one could agree on why they hated the outcome, but everyone could agree that they had to take matters into their own hands. Beguiled, extremist factions from every political corner - left, right, up, and down - were marshaled on the National Mall on Friday, January 20th, 2040. It was a powder keg of emotion and entitlement the country, nor the world had ever seen before.

As President Horn began to be inaugurated, the masses gathered for the event began to sway and push against each other. People who were in an elevated position remembered it as a "storming sea of humanity." Fires quickly started in the crowd, which was attributed to the tremendous amount of signs and banners displayed. One spark sent the whole turnout into a pulsating, organic brushwood. People began to scramble in panic. The seas, ablaze and frightened, pushed outward in all directions. The security detail, understaffed and overwhelmed, didn't see people scrambling for their lives. Themselves frightened, they saw what their founder described as "actionable threats." One single shot was fired, followed by uncountable responsive volleys. In between reloads, screams and groans raised up through the smoke and haze that had covered the entire event grounds.

When the dust settled, several thousand corpses both were both lined and submerged in the Lincoln Memorial reflecting pool. The private security team, an upstart outfit called EverCorp, stood with their rifle barrels smoking in the morning sunlight. They were the first private entity to ever be hired for a presidential security detail.

Christopher was witness to the massacre. He remembered the silence more than anything else. Once the screaming of the dying stopped, and somewhere in between the whimpering of the critically wounded, there was a crisp, deafening silence. He remembered gazing upon the bodies, shredded into bits, lying out as if a bomb had just gone off in front of him. Once his hearing returned when he looked down and saw his father.

The Admiral was dragging himself along the stage's deck by his right arm, his service weapon readied in the same hand.

His left arm was severed at the bicep from a high-caliber bullet strike. Christopher leaped into action, trying to pull Admiral Wendell to safety. As he did, his father resisted, causing Christopher to fall backward on his heels. He didn't relent his grip on his father, pulling the wounded man on top of him.

Admiral Wendell's face was missing from the ears forward. A gurgle of muscle and bone spat back at his son, involuntarily flapping the few teeth that had survived the injury. Christopher's eyes widened as his father's viscera splattered onto his face. If his father was trying to tell him anything before he died, he was unable. His head was collapsing into itself with every splatter of brain matter that exited onto his son's dumbfounded face. Blood and bone fragments poured down into his son, nearly drowning him in gore and carnage.

Christopher watched as his hero literally crumbled into mush down onto him. Before he succumbed to his injuries, Admiral Wendell squeezed off one last final round from his service weapon into the air. It would be his last conscious action.

* * *

Garland continued. "No no, you're a fine pilot. The Naval Corp would hate to see you go, even if you are a giant pain in the ass. The reason I'm asking is that I just got a phone call this morning from Admiral Reynolds. Who had just been on the phone with the SECDEF. Apparently, NASA has cooked up something top secret, and it's a real spicy one at that. Only thing is, the nerds there can build it, but they can't fly it. Which is where we, specifically *you*, come in."

Christopher thought for a moment as he took everything in. "So basically, you want me to be an astronaut? Why me? And

84

why not Space Force?" he asked.

"Honestly, Chris, I don't know what I'm asking you to be. Everyone I've talked to either doesn't know shit or is pretending they don't know shit. They asked me for my best pilot, and that's either you or Stormer," he replied. Christopher felt pangs of guilt as he remembered Erik. Military aviation was an extremely competitive field, and it never came between the two because they achieved their successes in very close proximity. There were only a handful of months in their entire careers that they weren't at the same rank.

"Does he know about this?" Christopher asked.

"What part of super, mega secret do you not understand? The only person I've spoken to about this is the Admiral and you. I can't even tell my dog about this. But, if you're feeling noble, you can always pass and I'll move on to Stormer," Garland said with agitation. "Wendell, I need to know, and I need to know *now*: are you in?"

Christopher felt weighted down with his conscience. A mission with no details, yet probably the best career opportunity he's ever had? But without his best friend being considered, he felt like a traitor. The large grandfather clock in the office ticked loudly as the two sat in silence. Garland leaned back in his chair and placed his hands behind his head, watching him intently. Christopher sighed deeply.

"I'd be a fool to turn down something like this, sir. I'm in. Let's put a man on the moon!" Christopher said, forcing a joke. Maybe he was betraying his friend, maybe he wasn't, but this was a chance for him to get his head back in it. He needed a win.

"I never said the mission is going to the moon! I didn't say what planet if *any* is the destination," Garland said as he rolled his eyes, "and we *have* put a man on the moon. *Several* times."

"Wait, there are *other* planets in space besides the moon?" Christopher feigned sincerity as he stood to salute his boss.

"Wendell, get the hell out of my office. Check your email for your orders. For my sake, I hope they're shooting you into the sun," Garland said, shaking his head and planting it into his hands.

12

Curtains Down

George and Kevin looked up as they saw someone climbing down the stairs to their improvised workshop. "Good evening, Dr. Järvinen," George said dryly. He was beginning to tire of the constant interruptions, the lack of sleep, and the terrible coffee that had quickly become his only source of nourishment. Järvinen stepped down the final set of stairs with a smile on his face.

"Dr. Sansor, Mr. Yim: how does our progress go?" he said.

"*Our* progress is fairly steady. We could have this done in a matter of weeks, at this pace," George replied.

"Days," Järvinen flatly announced. George was immediately confused. Conversations with Järvinen were never easy. The little man had a distinct, odd way of communicating with people. It bordered on authoritarian without actually being, and his pleasant yet peculiar manner of talking was difficult to decipher. Also, George couldn't remember being engrossed in a project like this in his entire career. Whenever breaks happened, it was burdensome on his brain to "switch modes." He had developed a routine for his workflow, and it countered his mind's function for dialogue. He and Kevin traded glances.

"Days... days of what?" he blurted.

"The project needs to be fully operational in days," Järvinen said matter-of-factly.

"What's the rush?" Kevin asked.

"It is the necessary time for what we need to properly see our task to completion, Mr. Yim," Järvinen answered with the closest thing to a glare they'd seen from him. George put down his control stylus and compass for the monitor board and rubbed his eyes.

"So basically, if I'm understanding this correctly: you want us to *not* sleep, eat, or shit for the next few days? And you expect this work to be of outstanding quality?" George said gruffly. The agitation was clear in his tone, which Järvinen brushed off with a hand wave.

"Nonsense. We have provided quite amenable facilities and nourishment for you. I've noticed that you have rarely taken use of them. I'm merely keeping you informed on the project's new specified launch date," Järvinen explained.

"Gee, thanks," Kevin sarcastically drawled.

"If something's changed with this project, you need to let us know about it, Järvinen," George demanded. "You're talking about drastically altering the trajectory of this entire thing. What aren't you telling us?" Järvinen small body stiffened up at the insubordination. *Typical Americans*, he thought.

"Fine then. We have your American military sending us a test subject. Our window for securing him here is quite small. We view this minor inconvenience as a rare opportunity to get the project functional so that we can begin further colonization attempts. Every second spared is of the utmost importance," Järvinen said. His phone began buzzing in his pocket, and he silenced it. "Are you now satisfied, sirs? Can our work continue?" George shook his head in frustration and brought his attention back to the tabletop monitors. Kevin looked at him, then at Järvinen, then back at George. He shrugged and dove back into his computing, as well. "Very well then," Järvinen said as he spun around and left the two. He picked up his phone, which was vibrating once more, and began talking as he left.

"This stinks," Kevin said to George.

"Mmm–hmm," George murmured absentmindedly.

"No I mean, what was that about? Colonization? What would CERN have to do with that? Aren't we just *building* the device?" Kevin implored. George looked up from his work and checked where Järvinen was on his exit out of the large structure. His eyes darted around apprehensively.

"Keep your voice down with that shit," George hissed under his breath. Kevin looked bewildered.

"Um, what?" he responded.

"I said, *keep your voice down*. They've got this place bugged up or something," George said in a whisper.

"Dr. Sansor, no offense, but–" Kevin was cut off mid-sentence by George slamming his fist down on the table. The alien scripts shuttered and danced wildly in response to the touchscreen impact.

"You don't believe me?" George said, glaring holes into Kevin.

"I mean, I believe that you *think* there's–"

"Don't patronize me, asshole. *And keep your voice down!*" George whispered. "Here, use my stylus."

"But I–"

"*Use. My. Stylus*," George commanded with a deliberate nod.

Kevin hesitated for a moment, but after a few seconds took the stylus from George in a hand-to-hand that made him feel like he was purchasing black market turbomeds. He looked at the digital pen. Taped to it was a tiny lens, no bigger than the end of the stylus, with frayed wires coming out the back of it like an optic nerve. His confusion climbed higher.

"I don't understand. Where did you get this?" Kevin asked.

"Corner of the room, next to the stairs. It looks like it shorted and fried itself. Who knows how many are in here. Or in our rooms," George answered.

"I mean, it *is* a top-secret facility. I sort of assumed the whole thing was video monitored?" Kevin said with a shrug.

"By who? Have you seen any security, or military, or anyone? As far as I can tell, it's nothing but a bunch of scientists here. If we're on camera, who's on the other end of it? And why are they *hidden* cameras? What the hell is Järvinen not telling us?" George rattled off under his breath.

Kevin searched the tabletop as if the alien cipher would have an answer to any of George's questions. He finally shook his head. "I don't know anymore. I don't know what we're even doing here anymore, but even worse: I don't know if we're allowed to leave or not."

George's stomach turned. He'd never considered that they were possibly there against their will. Normally that would sound far-fetched to him, but "normal" had ceased to be for Kevin and him long ago. He started to place his head in his hands, then stopped, not wanting to look unnatural to his hidden watchers.

"I liked it better when this was a dead-end project," he muttered. As he restarted his work, a portion of the code caught his eye: φj↵P\J⊠ِ▨ ▓Þ▤◉,

◂◃n6.◪◩ゐ82588◩◩⇶|kWJ◜ ▦TY1vXC◪◩ゐ82588◩◩⇶|kWJ
◜ ◕±±R‘ ₪y‰◕±±R‘⊠ڧ▨ ▩₪y‰-◕±±R‘⌋⌉⌉∔∨∔∔Ss₪y‰
⌼7ri,9.∔฿▤◉,◂◃n6.⊛ᕳ⩲29.209⍙NO⟁◍∭∭◕±±R‘
◪◩ゐ82588◩◩,]₴~,6fc5⊠ڧ▨ ▩⌋⌉⌉
∔∨∔∔SsTY1vXC⊛ᕳ⩲29.209⍙฿▤◉,◂◃n6..

He rotated the key to align with the symbols. The characters bounced and danced, then revealed: "*Earth is the dead-end project, Sansor.*" George drew his hands away from the table in terror and gasped. Kevin stopped and looked at George, who was trembling and hadn't taken his eyes off the table.

"What was it, Dr. Sansor?" Kevin asked. George said nothing in response. "Dr. Sansor? Your color doesn't look so good. *Dr. Sansor*?" George finally brought his eyes up to Kevin's to see deep concern troubling his young face.

"It was uh... Just some real shitty static. On the machine. You need some more coffee? I need some more coffee. I'll be right back. With coffee," George stammered.

"You're leaving *now*?" Kevin said, rightly agitated with his mentor's desertion.

"I'll be right back. I need some, uh... coffee," George reiterated as he began his trek, weaving his way across the labyrinth of servers, machinery, and makeshift hallways of turbocomputers. As soon as he was out of eyesight of Kevin, he collapsed to the floor, sitting against a steel wall. He began breathing rapidly and unbuttoned the top of his shirt for cooler air.

It fucking spoke to me. It spoke to me and - did it threaten me? Is it warning me? It can hear me. Of course it can hear you George it spoke to you. Can it hear me right now? Is this from aliens or gods? The Devil? Jesus Christ George, you're having a psychotic breakdown. No. A heart attack. Yes, definitely a heart attack. Is it worse to go from a heart attack or an apocalypse?

George's vision crept inward and dulled in the darkness. The hum and rumbles of the project turned into buzzes and shrieks in his ears before he finally gave way to total loss of consciousness.

13

Curtains Up

Red flashes and roars screamed through George's dreams as he trembled and sweated in his blackout. Bloodthirsty aliens stalking the arid landscape of Mars, howling and grunting, chasing down humans in carnivorous rampages. The planet turned an even deeper shade of crimson with bright teal highlights.

George inhaled loudly as he escaped to consciousness. His eyes danced around as he gathered his surroundings. He was lying on a bed with one thin sheet next to a metal table with basic aid equipment scattered on it. The white fluorescent lights above him hummed softly. Small water bottles and EverCorp antiseptic solutions lined a supply shelf on the far wall. *This must be the infirmary*, George realized.

Voices outside the room gave him pause. He didn't hear Kevin's. *Do they know about the message? Are we in trouble?* His confusion overwhelmed him and he felt his heart start punching his ribs again. The door clicked open. He slammed his eyes shut and feigned sleep.

"This him?" an unknown person asked with a slight Indian

accent.

"Indeed," George recognized Järvinen's smarmy voice in response.

"And you allow cat naps in this shoddy operation of yours, Jarven?"

"Dr. Sansor had an... episode. I can't use him if I push him too far. That's basic human resources, Mr. Shah," Järvinen said. George stiffened. The only "Shah" he ever knew was *the* Mr. Shah: Nathan Shah, CEO of EverCorp. The richest and most powerful man on the planet, and it wasn't even close. President Buynak answered to *him*. Wars were fought and elections were won or lost at *his* direction. *Couldn't be*, George thought. *Could it be? Are you dreaming this?*

"I'm not funding this for sunshine and snuggles, Jarven. If he can't run my operation, get rid of him and find me another nerd that can," Shah said.

"I can't just 'find someone else.' Dr. Sansor here has been instrumental in the execution of the Americans' piece of the project," Järvinen said.

"*Instrumental? I've seen more 'instrumental' pieces come out of a dog's ass than him*!" Shah screamed at Järvinen. "Look at him! I've got production lines waiting to start. *I'm* ready to begin on Mars. Are *you*?" Shah demanded.

"Mr. Shah, we are nearly completed with our task, and we greatly appreciate your-"

"-This is why I do shit myself," Shah continued, cutting off Järvinen, "because when you rely on others, you get amateur-hour garbage like CERN. I could just bring in my own scientists and make up for all of my time you've wasted."

"Kyllä, voisit," Järvinen said, obviously alarmed, "but it would be a tremendous waste of time and expenses. We're nearly at the finish of this and you want to begin the race once again, Mr. Shah. With due respect, I ask for your prudence."

"I'm running pretty low on 'prudence,' Jarven. Get this done or your funding is gone and I'll string you up on treason charges," Shah sniped back. "Now show me this hunk of shit that I'm paying you dearly for." The door clicked again as the two exited. George squinted one eye open as the door snapped shut once again. He exhaled loudly again. *Holy shit. EverCorp is deep into this. Järvinen's been keeping this. Kevin. Oh my God, where is Kevin?* He shot up off the bed and collected himself as he sat on the edge of it. Vertigo set in as his body attempted to regain homeostasis. He slapped his legs and climbed to his feet.

His body fought him instantly. The lights dimmed and hissed at him in retaliation for his disobedience. Pain shot through his brain stem and brought him back down to the bed. Tears welled in his eyes as became overwhelmed with fear and nausea. *We're fucked,* he thought, *the whole planet. We're all dead. I couldn't fight NASA. I couldn't fight CERN. I couldn't fight Järvinen. How could I even think about taking on EverCorp?* George began openly sobbing as he gave in to resignation.

The door clicked once again and he didn't care. *Let them know I'm up,* he thought. *We're all doomed anyway.* He kept his eyes focused between his feet as he listened to feet shuffle into the room. He sighed quietly as he sucked in his tears.

"Dr. Sansor? They're gone, I think," Kevin said meekly. He snapped his head up. Kevin was looking at him inquisitively, like a lab rat that had wandered out of a maze without the cheese. Betraying his emotions, he jumped off the bed and hugged Kevin tightly. The embrace was met with awkward recoil from Kevin. The two gauged each other once stepping back, George still in a mental cloud.

"It's over," he revealed. "Järvinen's selling us out. He's a corrupt fuck." Tears were still lingering on his cheeks as he looked at Kevin. He was met with a look of contemplation.

"What's over? The end of the world? I think that's still pretty imminent, Dr. Sansor," Kevin bit back.

"B-but Järvinen. He's selling us out to-"

"-To EverCorp. I was eavesdropping on them. I heard everything about their grand colonial government plans," Kevin finished for him. George flinched. *How long had he been out? A day? A week?*

Kevin saw the puzzlement on his face and dipped his head down. "You didn't hear that part?" George shook his head. "They've already got some shadow government ready to be installed on the first day they take over Mars. Of course, those selected bigwigs will have the first jumps there," Kevin said with a heavy eye roll.

"But we're nowhere *near* being ready to send people through that machine! We haven't even constructed the collision gate!" George hissed.

"Actually, construction has already started. I finished with my calculations, so I went ahead and finished the translation while I was... waiting on you," Kevin said. George froze in terror. *Did he see what I saw? Did I even see what I saw?* He pulled Kevin closer and searched his face, Kevin still being noticeably uncomfortable with the physical contact. George took on a hushed, lower tone as his eyes glanced around the room.

"Kevin, don't bullshit me. Did you see anything... *odd* in the translation?" Kevin pulled away from him, irritated and overtired.

"It's a plan for a teleportation device. It was *all* odd. Is that what this is about? What did *you* see, Dr. Sansor?" Kevin implored. *Good question*, George thought. He was trusting his senses less and less the more time they spent around the alien artifact. His sanity even less. Kevin checked George's eyes for answers but found none.

"Anyway," Kevin continued, "probably a half-second I completed it, EverCorp security rushed in. I didn't even have a chance to call Järvinen. I thought they were going to kill me or something," he said with a sigh. "They told me that I had to leave, and everything in the room was EverCorp property, and that I'd signed a non-disclosure agreement. Which I *know* I didn't, but whatever. I'm so over this project. I just want to go *home*."

"They're not letting us leave?" George exclaimed. He had anticipated that but had also been keeping a small, feeble hope that they would be released and could put the whole damned project behind them. Even if it meant putting the apocalypse in front of them.

"Not yet. I managed to get Järvinen to speak to me for a second. He said we still had to 'see this through with the pilot.' I assume that means whatever test dummy they tricked into going into the portal first," Kevin said.

"They're never letting us out of here. We know too much," George snarled. "Easier to just take us out back and shoot us like cattle." Kevin scowled at the dismal outlook. His cynicism was new, and not to the heights that George's was. He was still sensitive to topics such as his own murder.

"So what have you been doing since you got kicked off the ground floor?" George asked, mostly to change the subject.

"Wandering around, mostly. But there's not a whole lot

of space that isn't on lockdown from EverCorp now. *Armed* lockdown. They even took everything out of my room. Like, *everything.* They took my toothbrush!" Kevin said with a sour look. George shook his head in disgust.

"I guess let's go wander, then. Maybe we can give that rotten bastard Järvinen another crack and see if we can get any more answers," George suggested as he took a painful step towards the door. "Because I really don't understand."

"Understand what?"

"Why he was telling Nathan Shah that we were still needed on this. We did our part. EverCorp can handle everything from here on out," George said as he reached for the door.

"Oh, no they can't. Do you know what the *very* last words of the translation were?" Kevin's words stopped George instantly. His hand wavered inches from the door handle. His gaze stayed on the handle, as well, for several seconds. He finally looked up at Kevin in apprehension.

"They said 'only The Decryptor can open the Gate.'"

14

Saving Grace

Christopher bounced his legs around impatiently as he sat in the back of an E-856 jumbo carrier. He wasn't used to being flown anywhere, and had demanded when he learned he was flying to Europe to be allowed to pilot the aircraft. He received a "no" in a long line of "no's" since agreeing to the top-secret mission. *I never knew NASA was so secretive*, he had thought, *or based in Europe, for that matter.* His flight companions were hundreds of stacked wooden crates marked with EverCorp's logo. They were sneaking him in under the guise of a supply run, that much he knew. He never even saw the pilot of the plane. He had wormed his way between some crates and knocked on the door to the cockpit, but got no response. *They probably stuck me on an automated plane*, he realized. He hated that computer algorithms were replacing good men and women aviators, and had famously vowed to shoot down any AI planes in the middle of a combat mission, regardless of what flag they bore on the tail. Of course, that was after closing down a local dive bar, so his friends giggled along with his bombastic proclamation.

He snatched his phone up from his go bag and checked his notifications for the third time that minute. Still nothing of interest. More messages from Grace, which he didn't read. He opened his EverNews app, and was immediately showered with more images and headlines about Philadelphia.

"PHILLY "MAY BE BEYOND RECOVERING" PREZ BUYNAK SAYS"

"FOOD SCARCE ON ENTIRE EAST COAST"

"CITY CONTINUES TO SINK INTO OCEAN DESPITE EFFORTS"

"LESS THAN 10% OF RESIDENTS ACCOUNTED FOR"

"1/3 OF AMERICANS WITHOUT POWER"

He quickly closed the app with a shaking thumb and squeezed his eyes shut. *Commander Wendell, get your head in the game. This is so not the time for your cowardice!* he chastised himself. His phone buzzed again and he snapped his eyes open. Another message from Grace. He sighed and tapped on it.

Please? He scrolled upwards to begin from the first unread text to get more context. *I'm not mad at you. But we need to figure out what to do with Lunie and Mark.*

My oncologist says I have to make my final arrangements soon. They think it could be any day or week now.

I just want us to all be able to be together one more time before I go...

The kids ask about you all the time. I tell them Daddy's busy fighting bad guys in the air and that's why he can't be here.

I know you're a good man, Christopher.

WAS THAT YOUR SQUAD IN PHILLY?!!!?

PLEASE CALL ME AND LET ME KNOW YOU'RE OKAY

PLEASE OH GOD DON'T DO THIS TO ME

Please?

He sighed and wished he wasn't so bored. He tapped the phone icon and the line began to ring. As it did, he heard three distinctive clicks. He chuckled quietly to himself. *Ah, NSA, you never fail to disappoint. Listening in to see if I divulge the juicy secrets of this mission that I don't even know about...*

"Christopher? Are you okay?" Grace said as she picked up. She sounded weak, like it hurt just to breathe.

"Hey, Gray. Sorry I missed your, ah, many messages. I've just been super wrapped up in work," he coyly responded.

"But are you *okay?* The news said that Cerberus was the squad that had planes shot down in Philadelphia," she asked again.

"Yeah, we're fine. No one shot at us, I don't know where they got that. Erik and I just wanted to go for a nice swim. You know how he likes his cardio."

"He's always getting you into trouble," she said before regressing into loud, hacking wheezes and coughs. He heard the distinct sound of an oxygen tank being sucked on. It pulled his heart down into his stomach and filled it with instant regret about calling her.

"How are *you*, Gray?" he asked.

"Oh, you know. Dying," she bluntly cracked.

"I... I don't know what to say?" he offered. *Man, I hope you aren't asked to do the eulogy, you bastard*, he thought to himself. "Listen babe, I never meant for-"

"-Stop. Just stop. None of that. You're no good at it and I can't handle you trying," she pled. "I have the kids with my parents right now, but they'd love to see-" she stopped mid-sentence and began another round of convulsing hacking. The offer filled his chest with dread. He had no idea what he'd ever say to his children if he ever saw them again. He actively avoided thinking about it, and them. To him, they were better off with him as a deadbeat dad than a present, awful one. *You can't fail at something if you don't try*, he always rationalized to himself.

"I would, Gray. I really would. But I'm actually prepping for a mission as we speak. I go wheels up really soon."

"Don't tell me they're sending you back to Philly," she groaned. Three more clicks followed.

"Nope, not Philly. Something totally different. I think I might be training other pilots on this one or something. Nothing too scary," he lied.

"Okay." Silence fell between them. Nothing but the hum of the aircraft and more triplets of clicks from the phone tap.

"Okay then," she offered once more to break the silence.

"Okay. I'll call you whenever they let me loose," he lied again.

"I'd like that. Christopher?"

"Yeah?"

"Be safe with whatever you're actually doing. I do love you." He grimaced and dropped his head back. *Always gotta make this shit difficult, doesn't she?*

"Christopher?"

"Yeah. I love you too Grace. Take care of yourself, hear?"

"I will. Bye." He tapped the red button on his phone to hang up and tossed his phone to the metal ground of the cargo hold. He hated her for doing that. Making him say that. *What am I going to do, tell a woman on her deathbed to shove it and that I don't love her? Because I don't love her. Not one bit*, he lied to himself. *And even if I do, why should I have to say it? She really is a twisted bitch.*

"Beginning descent," a computerized voice announced through a speaker somewhere behind a crate.

"Crash yourself, you weakass excuse for a pilot!" he yelled

in response.

"No crash detected. Reporting diagnostics to Command for further analysis," it chimed back. He sighed and slumped further onto the uncomfortable bench he sat in. *This is literally the worst flight I'll ever have in my career, guaranteed*, he thought to himself.

15

Hard Landing

A loud, mechanical buzz filled the cargo hold, which Christopher recognized as the landing gear beginning to activate. *Final descent was an hour ago*, he realized as he checked his watch. One of his major objections to AI pilots was that their calculations and algorithms were written extremely conservatively, which meant that routine flights took twice as long. Enemy aircraft were avoided and followed but never engaged. *But computers don't piss their pants, you jackass*, he thought as he gritted his teeth.

"Approach for landing imminent. Please fasten all safety harnesses and-"

"Yeah, yeah, yeah, I got it, Hal," he grumbled as he clicked his five-point belt in.

"-ensure that all cargo is secure." Christopher paused.

"Secure?" he asked himself. A hard thud of the landing immediately followed, and the wooden crates were sent scattering. "Shit shit shit shit shit!" he yelled as he was swallowed up in an avalanche of them. Sharp pains hit him everywhere, and he was too pinned up against the wall of the hull to assess his damage.

"Arrival. All diagnostics report a completed and safe flight." Christopher groaned in misery. "Please exit. You will live forever, Wendell." His muscles tightened up in fear.

"What'd you say to me?" he demanded. Silence. *Shit, I know they taught us how to talk to these robots. What was that code word?* He cleared his throat. "Computer?" Again, silence. "Hal?" "Tango?" *Goddammit. It was something dumb. Something about Africa.* "Lion?" Simba?" "Zebra?"

"Go ahead," it chimed back at him. *Ah, there it was.*

"Zebra, repeat last transmission within the plane."

"Arrival. All diagnostics report a completed and safe flight. Please exit," it repeated.

"No, after that."

"No transmission reported. Sending error analysis to Command." He looked around suspiciously. *I know I heard that. What the hell...* The cargo door at the back of the plane opened, and brisk, cool air entered. The familiar, repugnant choke of airborne ash filled his nostrils.

"Commander Wendell? Are you in here, sir?" a voice called out.

"In here! Or, I mean, *under* here!" he shouted. Several footsteps clanged against the steel flooring and grunts echoed through the hull as the crates began to be moved. He felt the pressure on his body start to ease. Finally, a crate was lifted, exposing only his shoulders and head. He squinted as his eyes adjusted to the new lighting. Four military members, donned in full gas masks, looked down at him in bemusement.

"Aww, the Americans sent an oschterhäsli!" one said as the other three broke out in laughter. Christopher blushed in embarrassment.

"No oshterhollie here. I'm a goddamn United States Navy pilot, now would you get me out of here?" he snarled back.

"Yah yah, oschterhäsli, don't get your tail in a poofer," one joked as he moved a crate. Christopher was finally freed from his trap, and he stood upright. Ignoring the pain resonating through his body, he took on a machismo stance, standing nose-to-nose with the nearest soldier.

"Are you ready now, Commander Wendell?" the soldier said, a smirk evident on his face from behind his mask.

"I'm *always* ready," he growled back. He turned to exit the plane but was restrained. He looked down and saw his foot was still pinned under a crate. He looked back to the soldier, who hadn't moved or stopped smirking.

"Would you like some more assistance?" he said wryly. Christopher twisted his foot to escape, then came crashing down on top of another. He popped up quickly, puffing his chest out to project the same bravado as before.

"No... Nope," he responded as he moved toward the exit. The soldier sighed and rolled his eyes.

"Right this way, *Commander*," he muttered.

Christopher exited the plane, pausing before his boots hit the concrete of the tarmac. He glanced back at the aircraft. *What the hell was that about? Did I imagine it? Live forever?* The soldiers shoved some more crates out of the way and followed him. He saddled his go-bag firmly on his shoulder and proceeded on. A wide-open grassy field, which had seen better days, surrounded by short buildings met him. He immediately saw that this area was probably beautiful at some point, like seeing a turbotweaker with all her teeth and C-cups. "Where am I?" he asked one of the soldiers escorting him.

"Dübendorf Air Base. Right this way," the soldier responded

and directed him across the tarmac and into one of the many modest buildings.

"Dübendorf? So what, Germany? Right?" Christopher asked.

"Nej. Schweiz. Switzerland," the soldier responded as his group continued to navigate him through a maze of different hallways and rooms. Christopher quickly lost his sense of direction, with every new environment looking like the last. He felt like he was walking through a fun house at a carnival.

Finally, he was walked through what appeared to be a front lobby area, with a soldier sitting as a front desk receptionist. The soldiers suddenly stopped, and Christopher did as well.

"Out there," one directed him and pointed to the exit.

"Out where? Outside?" he asked. The parking lot was completely bare of anyone.

"Yes," the soldier responded.

"Am I just supposed to hoof it from here? *I don't even know where I'm going!*" he exclaimed in exasperation. Two of the soldiers rolled their eyes again.

"Your ride should be waiting for you. If not, tuff skit," the soldier who had been leading the way said as they turned around and re-entered the door they had just left.

"But what-" Christopher responded as the door slammed shut. He looked at the soldier sitting at the front desk in protest, but he ignored him. Christopher sighed and turned around. A small, black Volkswagen was now idling at the nearest crosswalk from the front door. "So is that my ride?" he asked the soldier. He was met with the same silence as before. "Forget this," he muttered as he left the lobby.

As Christopher approached the vehicle, the passenger side window slightly rolled down. He leaned in to peek an eye in and assessed the man behind the wheel: he was wearing a dark suit, small glasses, and lanky legs sat crossed behind the car's pedals. The man looked over at him in an unimpressed fashion and unlocked the doors.

"Are you my ride? I'm United States Com-"

"Commander Wendell. I am Jan Bachmann. Please get in."

"Where are we going?" Christopher demanded.

"To your destination. I am to take you there. Please get in," Jan responded, as drab as before.

"Man, I swear. I've had about enough European hospitality as I can take," Christopher barked as he yanked open the back door of the car and dropped into the passenger seat. "Fine Bachmann, just take me then. I'm guessing we're not going to Ibiza," he cracked at him sarcastically.

"No," Jan simply responded, and shot the car off to the base's exit. *Jesus*, Christopher thought as he tumbled in his seat, *probably would've been safer to walk!* He noticed Jan operating the Volkswagen in a way that brought reverence to him: manually. No AI or automation was visible in the old jalopy.

"If you don't mind me asking, Bachmann, how'd you get a car like this? I thought they were all illegal," Christopher asked. Jan drove onward in silence. "Oooookay..." he said to the obvious shun. He clasped his hands together and began to tap his thumbs together. *Dammit. Really wish I hadn't chucked my phone back there*, he thought to himself. "Hey Bachmann, where *is* everyone? This place looks like a ghost town. Is this some Swedish CIA shit or something?" he pressed on. Jan turned on the radio and rotated the volume knob, drowning Christopher out in classical symphony music. Christopher groaned and sank back further in his seat. *Why can't I say no to the weird operations?* he lamented to himself.

* * *

Grace, Luna, and Mark crossed Christopher's head for the umpteenth time when Jan turned into the parking lot of CERN. Lying in bed, playing with Luna's long, red hair. Throwing Mark higher than he probably should, causing looks of panic to cross his handsome boy's face, then immediate giggles when he caught him. Wrapping his arms around Grace's slender figure as she cooked dinner. He loved how she fit perfectly into the center of his chest and he could just envelope her. It was like their bodies were made to fit together perfectly. *What happened?* he wondered to himself as he gazed out of the window at the barren landscape of the mountain pass. A trio of sheep unsteadily surveyed their trek across the road next to the parking lot. They were so ashen that their eyes were almost completely obscured. *They know it,* he thought. *Everything is so different now. It all was so good, then. Now we're all just fumbling around in the dark like these goddamn sheep.*

"We've arrived. Please exit," Jan said as he cranked the emergency brake of the car. Christopher lazily looked at CERN Headquarters. Its large, bloated architecture loomed over him as if peering down on its newest visitor.

"Nice boob you guys got here," Christopher said as he opened his door and slid out. Jan sighed and glared straight ahead. As Christopher emerged from the car, he stopped and leaned into the driver-side window to address Jan. "So, where to from here, Bachmann?" Jan responded by slamming the vehicle into gear and speeding away, just narrowly avoiding running over Christopher's foot.

"Hey asshole!" Christopher yelled, smacking the car in frustration as it shot by. He watched in agitation as Jan twisted and weaved through the parking lot to the exit. His eyes rose to the remarkable round structure and felt its shadow grow longer over him.

It was all so good, then...

...then you chickened out.

He reached for the door and squeezed hard as he pulled it open. *And cowards don't live forever, Christopher.*

16

Within the Mountain

George tried the last door in the same hallway as the infirmary. Metal struck metal in denial, just as every other door had done. He looked up and shook his head at Kevin in frustration.

"I told you, Dr. Sansor. This place is locked *down*. I've been *trying*," Kevin said. Footsteps echoed down the hallway, and the two darted to the corner of the hallway intersection for cover. George peeked around it and waited as two men wearing dark camouflage uniforms, military-style hats, and carrying weapons passed at the intersection at the opposite end of the hallway. "EverCorp guards," Kevin whispered to George.

"So then, *not* the Girl Scouts?" George whispered back. Kevin breathed heavily through his nose indignantly, but George wasn't in the mood for apologizing. Aside from his very real new health issues, he recognized the stabbing pain behind his eyeballs as caffeine withdrawal. Old, grizzled NASA veterans were salty enough as it was. Take away coffee, and you could turn even the friendliest mail sorter into a menace. "Come on, there's only one option at this point," he said while straightening up, "we go find that asshole Järvinen." Kevin motioned further down the hall they had sought refuge in and led him through a snarl of cold, uninviting, corporate hallways. No doors were marked with identifiers. Every time George felt as if he was getting his bearings about him, he realized that he was entirely turned around. *This kid's smart*, he thought to himself, *learning this layout so quickly.*

After what seemed like eons to George, Kevin stopped in front of a door. Nothing of it stood out from the countless others they'd passed. Kevin put his head up to the door to attempt to listen.

"What's this?" George asked.

"Järvinen's office. Shhh," Kevin whispered back, putting his index finger up to pursed lips. The hair on the back of George's neck stood up. *This is the lair of the villain. Fuck, we're standing right in front of Snake Mountain.*

"Anything?" George whispered as he leaned his head in. Kevin shook his head in response.

"Hey, what are you two doing?" someone hollered from down the hallway. They turned to see an EverCorp guard, rifle at low ready, watching them. They shrunk back from Järvinen's door as if it was radioactive. "I said... *what are you two doing?*" the guard repeated his demand as he started towards them.

"Kevin?" George asked.

"Yeah?" Kevin responded.

"Run."

"Hey!" the guard exclaimed as the two pivoted and fled. George could immediately feel his heartbeat inside his own skull. He began flashing back to that momentous early morning at NASA Headquarters, racing through a subterranean puzzle towards uncertainty. Physically strenuous activity failed him then, and it was failing him now. Kevin was increasingly gaining space between them, and the EverCorp guard's footsteps were getting louder and louder. *This is it*, he thought. *That guard is going to shoot us and this is where we'll die. Right here.* His defeatist thoughts began to slow him down even further than his own body did.

Kevin suddenly swerved to the right and burst through a door that was surprisingly unlocked. He held it open and motioned for George to hurry. Flailing his arms higher in a desperate attempt at running, George complied. He tumbled through the door and fell to the ground, hyperventilating and aching. His eyes were fluttering, but he was still able to inspect his surroundings. Dozens of other legs, which were otherwise moving, stopped near him.

The door behind them slammed open with a loud thud as the guard made his entrance known, as well.

"*I said... stop!*" he screamed, bending over George's helpless form.

"What is the meaning of all tämä?" a voice called out. *There you are, you prick*, George realized with a grin. Kevin's arms slipped between his and began pulling on him. The two groused in pain as they tried to get him on his feet.

"I caught your little lab rats nosing around, and then they disobeyed a *direct order* from me. As EverCorp employees, they are not permitted-" George's face, already profusely sweating and red, hid his instant emotions.

"-Fucking *excuse me? EverCorp* employees? I work for the *god-damned United States federal government*! You're not *my* boss. You're not *his* boss," George roared, pointing a shaking finger at Kevin, "and you're not *anyone's* boss. Piss off." The guard stiffened up his large shoulders and took another step towards the two, and George held his breath.

"Big words for a little man," the guard growled at him.

"Enough. The both of you. Dr. Sansor, won't you please have a seat? Look at the state of you," Järvinen said as he emerged behind a slew of several workers. George looked around and discovered that they were back in the original room they'd entered CERN in. Where they had agreed to participate in Järvinen's tangled web of deceit. Only now the number of workers in the room had quadrupled. Some were resigned to sitting alongside walls, working on tablets. Most had lab coats or uniforms with EverCorp's three-dimensional "E" logo embroidered on the chest. Järvinen approached George with a smile and put a hand on his shoulder. George shrugged it off and glared back.

"Enough bullshit, Järvinen. We want to leave. *Now*," he demanded. Järvinen's eyes shot around to assess the conversation's privacy. Everyone was still frozen, watching the encounter.

"Okei, everyone! I thank you for your concern. Now, we have our work to tend to!" he called out. Everyone turned back to their work, unfazed and obedient. "As for these two," he said as he turned to the EverCorp guard, "please allow me to speak with them. They are not up to date on our newest, ah, security detail, and therefore could not possibly have known any infractions they could have been breaking, joo?" The guard, eyes still trained squarely on George, shifted his balance on his legs.

"Yeah, sure. Whatever. But I'm reporting this incident," he said as he turned and left through the door that the three had burst through.

"Very good, sir. Very good!" Järvinen responded with a smile.

As the door clicked shut, his smile immediately turned to a sincere frown. "What were you two *doing*? And Dr. Sansor, so soon after your health alarm?"

"We were leaving. Which we're still doing. *Now*, Järvinen," George responded steelily.

"Come with me. We can't talk here," Järvinen responded in a hushed tone. He started to lead them away from the mass of EverCorp employees.

"No! We've got nothing to say! We're *done*! That's *it*!" George yelled and slashed his hands through the air. Järvinen halted in mid-step, looking over at the two. Kevin sighed and bowed his head.

"Let's just go with him. Whatever we've got to say, better without an audience," Kevin said, motioning to the trove of witnesses in the room. People were still curiously glancing up from their computers, pretending to work but nevertheless eavesdropping on the sensationalism. George looked glumly at Kevin. *He's grown decades from this damned project*, he thought to himself.

"Fine," George said as he began to shuffle his feet.

"To my office, yes?" Järvinen asked.

"Sure. Fine. Whatever," George responded defeatedly. *Escape Velocity Project my ass*, he thought. *There's no escape from this.*

* * *

The trio wound through the hallways George and Kevin had just been sprinting down. The doors and halls looked the same at a slow pace as they did in the blur of cowardly flight. They arrived at Järvinen's office, which he opened with his security card.

Inside, George's jaw dropped as he marveled at the decor. It was decorated in the fashion of the days of CERN's past, triggering waves of nostalgic sentiments coursing through his head. The old statue of Lord Shiva sat as a backdrop to a large oaken desk at the far end of the room. Historic moments of the organization's success were framed and lined the walls. A large model of the Large Hadron Collider and Future Collision Collider sat juxtaposed in the middle of the room and had small steel marbles running in orbit along their elliptical shapes.

"I know, I know. I'm a bit of a fool for history," Järvinen said as he motioned to the chairs sitting in front of the large desk. "Please, let's discuss the project further." The two cautiously sank into the plush chairs. Järvinen perched across the desk into his with an upright posture and a warm, bogus smile. "My dear Dr. Sansor, how are you feeling? We were all quite concerned for your well-being. I was told you had no prior health matters reported to NASA?" he asked.

"I'm fine," George fumed through clenched teeth.

"Hardly. When Mr. Yim discovered you, he thought you were possibly deceased," Järvinen responded.

"I said I thought he'd had a heart attack!" Kevin whined. "Which wouldn't surprise me, with how hard you've been working us!"

"Regardless," Järvinen said dismissively, "I never doubted you two would complete your task. Humanity owes both of you a great debt."

"I think you mean *Nathan Shah* owes us something, isn't that right, Järvinen?" George stabbed back. "Just how much did he pay you off to *buy Mars*? What'd he offer you? Power? Money? Neptune?" Järvinen's face dropped to a fixed, emotionless gaze.

"Mr. Shah offered me something that I otherwise would never have been able to procure on my own: this project. He funded it, and yes, paid off the right governments to see to it that nearly every person on the planet has no idea it exists. Can you even begin to comprehend the sheer impossibility of that in the Neo-Information Age, Dr. Sansor?"

"Mazel tov," George said while returning Järvinen's deadpan, cold stare.

"What would you have me do? Let EverCorp run as lead on this?" Järvinen asked.

"Seems like they pretty much are," Kevin interjected.

"Roska," Järvinen said, snapping his eyes to Kevin. "This way, we had the best, brightest minds that the world could offer, in order to save itself, *for* itself! Mr. Shah wanted to bid it out to the highest offer. He's still in denial that the world is even in such a grave state. *I* convinced him to let CERN have a hand at it first because *I* knew firsthand how wrong he truly was!"

"And all it cost you was your soul, right? *Again.*" George leaned in, wrinkling his nose in pious scorn. "First terraforming, now this? 'Earth's biggest threat' isn't climate change, it's foolish bastards like *you* and *Shah* that play God with everyone else's lives on the line." He paused to catch his thoughts. "This wasn't your call to make. You're not any more important than the other eight and a half billion people out there," he said, motioning to the far office door.

Järvinen sighed deeply and leaned back in his chair, clasping his hands together and resting them on his chest. "Yes, my dear Dr. Sansor. You are correct. We have made mistakes here. *I've* made mistakes. But we have always proceeded with the interests of our species' survival at heart."

"There's a path to somewhere paved with good intentions, Järvinen," George replied. "You can't get in bed with the Devil and claim righteousness. He used you for power and his bottom line. If you're too thick to see even that, I guess we're done here." He had plenty more to get off his chest, but George was exhausted: both mentally and physically. "I'm done with these fuck-fuck games. Let us leave so we can at least watch this planet burn in peace. I'm not dying in a bunker with the likes of you."

"What about the last line?" Kevin whispered through the side of his mouth to George, as if Järvinen couldn't hear him.

"Ah yes, Mr. Yim. Indeed. Dr. Sansor, I trust Mr. Yim has informed you of the final instructions given? 'Only the Decryptor can open the Gate?' Would you really build this project to its finality, only to abandon it?" Järvinen asked.

"I'd burn the whole thing to the ground if you gave me some gas and a lighter," George said with a slight chuckle.

"And Shah would have you killed before you stepped out of the door," Järvinen responded flatly. "Gentlemen, do not take this lightly: this is not a person to be interfered with. He has started military incursions for a half-day stock market boon. To call him a sociopath would be quite an understatement."

George began to counter, words of ambivalence towards his own life shooting to his lips. He caught a glimpse of Kevin's feet, which began to nervously shake at the real threat of death. *Who the hell do I think I am,* he thought, *getting in a pissing match with our lives? How selfish are you, George?* He sat in embarrassed silence. The room took the three over, as no one knew the next words to say.

"Here is what I believe is the best proposal to our friend Mr.

Shah: you complete opening 'the Gate,' and he lets the both of you walk unscathed. I fear he thinks of you as 'loose ends.' If you would do this, I can return you to the United States to - as you said - watch the planet burn," Järvinen said.

"He'll do it," Kevin interjected without pause. The two looked at him incredulously. He returned their looks with resolve and purpose that neither Järvinen nor George was willing to challenge. George sighed and dropped his head into his chest. Silence overcame them again.

Järvinen's phone interrupted the gravity of the situation, piercing the room with a monotone hum. He picked up the receiver while motioning for the others to wait.

"Joo."

"Joo."

"Joo. I will be over." He placed the receiver back in its cradle and smiled at George and Kevin.

"Sirs... our pilot has just arrived."

17

Into the Mouth of the Beast

Christopher didn't know whether he was more annoyed or amused. The science nerds that were scurrying about like little bunnies definitely amused him. A couple of the females had that nerdy-but-oddly hot thing, which he appreciated. All of them treated him with the reverence of a rock star, which he relished. The swagger in his step was almost that of his stroll to his jet before a mission. He even had his own personal nerd escort team, guiding him around the facility.

But the military never ceased to do things ass-backward and without good reason. Cerberus had once spent three days locked and loaded, waiting on an aircraft carrier in the Pacific Ocean, readying for the green light on a mission that had been scrapped by the Pentagon a month earlier. He received two bouts of sea-sickness, a commendation in his jacket, and an STD from a petty officer for his troubles on the mission. He was getting pangs of that bitter, cynical resentment as he began to feel like he was wandering aimlessly through the lifeless corridors of CERN. *And where is the goddamn rocket ship I'm supposed to be getting on?* he wondered. *All I saw around this stupid building were goats and mid-twenties Camrys.*

He and his entourage passed through another door, this one leading to a new sense of environment: a large auditorium hall, which had been repurposed into a group office setting. He breathed a sigh of relief as he noticed EverCorp logos abound. On laptops. On coffee mugs. On hot nerds' B-cups. *At least SOCOM or this CERN isn't doing this amateur-hour style*, he assured himself. A man nearly half Christopher's size strode over to him, cutting through the chaos of the workspace, and extended his hand with a pleasant smile.

"Greetings, Commander Wendell. I hope your travels were suitable, yes?" he said while grasping Christopher's hand. Christopher gripped firmly and shook with authority.

"Yeah, they bumped me up to diamond class. Luxury truly befitting a king," Christopher drawled.

"Good good! We spared no expense in acquiring the best pilot the United States could offer us," he said, evidentially missing the sarcasm. "I am Dr. Järvinen. Welcome to CERN," he said, raising his hands to motion to the room for dramatic effect. Christopher coldly surveyed his surroundings, unimpressed. Järvinen's eyes opened wide in disbelief. He had rarely received such an apathetic response to his grand introductions.

Christopher cleared his throat, still inspecting his surroundings. "So... are you like, the head nerd around here, or something? Or can I speak to that guy? I... I gotta be honest, Jarg, I have no idea what it is I'm supposed to be flying around here." Järvinen's face fell and became stoic but quietly seething.

"Yes, my dear Commander Wendell, I suppose you *could* refer to me as the 'head nerd.' But 'Dr. Järvinen' will also do just fine," he rolled through gritted teeth. "Aasi..." he muttered to himself.

"What was that?" Christopher asked.

"As I was saying, yes, I will be your primary resource for this project. The Escape Velocity Project, as it were," Järvinen added as he turned and began walking to the far exit door. Christopher's escort group followed without him. After a brief pause, he saddled his bag and caught up. He jogged past a man, seated at one of the work tables, his face in his hands and only his shaggy salt-and-pepper hair visible. A pudgy Asian kid was sitting next to him, his hands clasped together on top of his legs that were rapidly bouncing in anxiety. *Yeesh*, he thought, *get one a Valium and get the other off it.*

"Escape Velocity, huh? So where will I be 'escaping' to? The moon?" Christopher said as he reunited with the group.

"Mars," Järvinen said flatly, suppressing a sigh.

"*Mars?* Haven't we already been there? I was kinda hoping to discover a new planet or something," Christopher whined. Järvinen stopped cold in his tracks. The rest of the group mindfully did as well. He turned and stared at Christopher.

"Didn't you... didn't you just ask... about the moon?" he asked, face contorted in confusion.

"Well, yeah. That was my number one guess for where I'd be going," Christopher responded with full sincerity. Järvinen opened his mouth to answer but found no words emanating. The rest of the lackeys looked at each other nervously.

"Allow me to... show you to your quarters," Järvinen said with repugnance. He turned and continued the path through the primary exit door, pinching between his eyes. "Typerä Amerikkalainen," he grunted as he felt his forehead sear in heat and pain.

After traversing several more hallways, Järvinen stopped and pointed at a door, not even bothering to turn around. "You may rest here until we are ready," he called out to Christopher, who was trailing behind him.

"Aren't there any mission docs I need to review? Flight specs? A Mars brochure? *Anything?*" Christopher demanded.

"No," Järvinen said as he and the other workers started to walk away. Christopher stood still, watching the group leave through a side door. As it clicked shut, he glanced around, discovering that he was all alone. He shook his head and rolled his eyes as he bounced the door handle to his room.

"Sure thing, Garland, I'd *love* to take a mission without knowing jack squat about it!" he dryly cracked as he entered the room. The door shut behind him with a modest clack. "What could go wrong?" Eyeing his surroundings, he saw a small, twin-size bed with paper-thin white sheets on it. A bare metal table sat beside it. In the corner to his left, a toilet, sink, and mirror occupied the corner with nothing but a curtain for privacy. Sliding the closet door open, he found a one-piece jumpsuit with the EverCorp logo emblazoned on the front breast. "Oh *hell* no," he uttered to himself as he slammed the door shut.

Defeated and tired, he sat on the bed. Stiff springs groaned under his weight as his butt made contact with the bed frame. He sighed and reclined backward onto the rigid slab.

He thought about Grace. He thought about the kids.

Dammit, does she ever consider how hard I tried? I tried and I tried and I tried before I just couldn't try anymore. But it was never enough for her, was it? He was combat trained to compartmentalize his thoughts, but his frustration was burning through his skull. *Most of the married sailors I know are way worse husbands than I ever was. And somehow their wives make due. Cheating. Terrible work schedule. Getting beaten. Alcoholism and drug abuse. PTSD. What'd Grace ever have to complain about? That I liked to sleep in on the weekends? That I didn't scream at the kids at the drop of a hat like her, which in turn pissed her off because I was somehow making her "look bad?" What?*

He had to move or he was going to crack apart at the seams. He jumped off the bed and threw himself on the floor, beginning swift, focused push-ups. *One. Two. Three. Four.* He panted as he counted each repetition, staring holes into the ground. His arms and chest began to burn. He surged ahead. *Forty-six. Forty-seven. Forty-eight.* Sweat was beginning to pool directly below his face on the floor. *Seventy. Seventy-one. Seventy-two. Seventy-three.*

"Um, Commander Wendell?" Christopher fell to the floor in surprise and looked up. An EverCorp employee was standing in his opened doorway, looking at Christopher's display with a perplexed look on his face.

"Yeah man, what do you need?" he asked as he slid to a seated position on the ground next to his bed.

"I have this for you," the worker said as he held forward a plastic bag.

"And it is?" Christopher responded with exasperation.

"I believe it is your test suit, sir. I think they're just about ready for you," the worker said.

"*Test* suit? You mean *flight* suit?" Christopher demanded, eyes squinting in suspicion.

"Sir, they just asked me to deliver this. I don't know *what* kind of suit it is. But you should get changed into it. It's almost time," the worker said as he set it down inside the doorway. He gave a thumbs-up sign, then left. The door followed him to shut.

Christopher returned the sign with a middle finger.

18

The Clothes Make the Man

lmost time. Sure. Christopher had heard that before, working for the government. He woke up for the third time to urinate and shook his head as if he expected something different. He hadn't heard even the slightest of footsteps outside his door. And despite the hours of sleep he'd logged, he spent the majority of his alone time tossing and turning on what he'd decided was the world's most uncomfortable bed.

The toilet looked like it was an exercise in marksmanship. *What barbarian designed this?* he wondered as he marked the seat and floor with sloppy splatter. He didn't care. He had been through hazing, interrogation, and promotional boards, but nothing compared to this mission. For the first time in his storied career, Christopher was willing to surrender. He'd seen other sailors at the end of their ropes turn in their commissions on formation lines because of the silliest things, and always tried to talk them out of their madness. "You've been through so much harder, why would you give up for such a bullshit reason?" he'd ask them. Their answer was always the same:

"I've had enough of this shit. I've just *had enough.*"

Christopher had enough. Maybe this was a Behavioral Health Institute experiment, the kind whispered about but never confirmed amongst grunts in Basic Training. The kind where the lab rats don't know that they're inside the maze. Either way, he was willing to concede defeat. He zipped up and didn't bother to figure out the commode's controls to flush. Strolling back, he inspected the suit.

It was a matte white and adorned with a modest CERN logo on the left breast and back. It was thick and unforgiving, like a tarp. Nothing that he could adequately control an aircraft with. The gloves reminded him of the ones the hockey players wore when he pretended to watch the Boston Bruins. Trying one of the silver ones on, he realized why the Bruins were so terrible. *How could you control a hockey stick wearing one of these oven mitts? This is such a farce*, he decided.

The white boots were obviously not designed for military use, as they were far too heavy. Since the Vietnam War, military boot designs had switched to a lighter, more comfortable shoe. These were possibly constructed for a trek through the Arctic region, he decided. A royal blue, velcro, nylon belt rounded out the ensemble, with no belt loops to secure to. He made due and pulled it tight like a makeshift rope.

Christopher looked at himself in the far wall's mirror. He saw a scared, embarrassed, wide-eyed Navy pilot that he didn't recognize. He expected to see Neil Armstrong or Buzz Aldrin. *That's not the stud that bagged the Vice President's daughter*, he realized. *Christopher Wendell, what the hell are you anymore? Look at this getup. This is some twisted joke. Erik's on the other side of this door, ready to punch you in the balls and laugh at you.*

They're all going to laugh at you after you die.

The door snapped open, and Christopher jumped at the intrusion. "I see you have received your suit, Commander Wendell," Järvinen said as he entered.

"Um, yeah. I have. By the way, have they invented 'knocking' over here yet? I could've been mid-strip into this amazing costume or something, you know," Christopher barked back, standing up straight.

Järvinen chuckled. "Oh my dear Wendell, I won't even be shameful about it: there are three cameras in this room that you never realized had existed. Believe me, I knew you were prepared." Christopher paused in an angry glare.

"You were spying on me?" he said, taking a step towards Järvinen.

"This entire facility is mine. 'Spying' is not an accurate word. If I so wanted, I could have your urine analyzed for protein biotics and DNA histrionics," Järvinen responded flatly. Christopher averted his eyes to the mess he made at the toilet. Järvinen breathed heavily out of his nose. "So, now that we understand each other, would you care to embark on the mission? If your modesty is not too humbled?"

"Sure. Let's just get this all done with," Christopher said with heavy contempt.

"Loistava! Please follow me!" Järvinen exclaimed as he opened the door. Christopher walked behind Järvinen like a chastised puppy. The two strode down the hallway: one beaming with energetic passion, one slouched over in a suit that rustled and crackled loudly with each push of his legs. They entered the main room, which was now deserted, save for one worker punching vexingly into a calculator, eyeing notes from three separate workstations.

"Smoke break?" Christopher offered up a joke on reflex.

"Hardly. They're all at The Gate," Järvinen answered as he briskly continued to the elevator access. He passed his access card in front of a black panel next to it and input the code. The door opened, and Järvinen stepped inside and turned around. Christopher hesitated, his instinct telling him to pivot and run. The door began to shut, and Järvinen caught it. "My dear Commander Wendell, it is time."

"Time for what? *No one* has told me jack or shit about what I'm doing here! I don't fly blind, man. You need to fill me in on this project of yours, and *now*," Christopher shot back as he crossed his arms. The door attempted to close again, striking Järvinen's outstretched arm.

"That is what the elevator ride is for. I promise you, there will be no tricks or surprises. You will be happy you took this mission, young man. Just by being here, you have cemented your legacy with humankind. Please come with me. Redemption awaits," Järvinen said.

The words struck Christopher like a sidewinder missile. He stood, rooted in place from uncertainty and contrition. He remembered Garland talking about "fight or flight" one day at a unit meeting after he had discharged a pilot named Chase Cleeard from Cerberus. Chase loved wearing the uniform and loved being a pilot, but the other guys in the unit quickly figured out that he loved the *idea* of being a pilot. When it actually came time to do the difficult tasks demanded of them, he simply froze. Garland's speech was expected and mostly intended to motivate the group than anything else. But he drove the point home that when people spoke of "fight or flight," they were neglecting a third action that arose from adrenaline dumps: freezing. Garland drove into their heads that freezing was even worse than fleeing, and was a one-way ticket to a dismissal from the squadron. "The worst decision you can ever make is no decision at all," he had lectured them. "Like a deer in headlights."

Like Christopher was doing that exact moment. *Move, you cowardly sunnovabitch*, he thought to himself. The door slid into Järvinen's arm again, triggering red lights to activate inside the elevator and a steady chime to begin. Järvinen glanced up, then at him. Christopher took a deep breath, nodded, and lumbered through the door. He turned around and watched the door close to the main room.

"Please allow me to explain the Escape Velocity Project to you, my dear Commander Wendell," Järvinen said with a satisfied grin.

19

Down to Get Up

As the elevator hummed to life, descending Christopher and Järvinen into the bowels of CERN, Christopher stood and watched above the door out of habit. Järvinen stood facing him directly. Christopher, feeling his gaze, glanced over, then back to above the door. No matter, as there were no floor numbers to monitor.

"I find it a matter of amusement, Commander Wendell, that in this particular elevator, humans succumb to even the most base decorum. We, as humans, have been instructed to limit, *confine* ourselves out of sheer decorum. I believe that is why we find ourselves at this particular point in human evolution. Don't you agree?" Järvinen said.

"'Escape Velocity Project.' Spill it, old man. Or I hit the emergency stop. Don't be a cock tease," Christopher responded.

"Joo. The Project. What do you, as a pilot, do when you are attacked by another aircraft?"

"I shoot it the fuck down. I wouldn't be standing here if I didn't. You ever serve, Jarg?"

"And... suppose you had no bullets in which to shoot it?"

Järvinen said, ignoring his posture.

"I don't fly without bullets, *Jarg*. You ever?" Christopher said, defiantly. He knew Järvinen was playing at a metaphor, so he was being difficult and disrespectful to a task. He'd once spent a week in the brig with Erik because Garland didn't appreciate their brand of sarcasm. 'Sarcasm is lost to the weak-minded and uninformed,' they chanted for the entire week as they endured manual labor befitting a slave. Their punishment was only supposed to be for three days until the command staff learned of their song. To be fair, Christopher had always argued, that particular conversation had started with Garland, a ranking officer, saying "Sup?"

"You would flee," Järvinen said matter-of-factly. Christopher's jaw clenched. Although retreat *was* a very practical military tactic, every cell in his body pulsated with madness when he heard the word. Retreat was a failure in his opinion.

"Permit me to be candid, Commander Wendell. Our planet is being attacked. We have no attainable 'bullets' to shoot. Our only alternative is to flee. We must leave Earth, vittu, and we must do it *now*," Järvinen said. The elevator hiccuped, if only slightly, as it entered the area of the Future Collision Collider. The bump stirred Christopher's brain out of its daze, and he turned to face Järvinen.

"I like this planet just fine, Jarg. It's you elitists that think everything needs changed on wholesale level. Nathan Shah's too rich? 'We need Communism!' World's a little polluted? 'Let's get rid of energy!' Easy to say behind your goddamn ivory towers. Some people like me still gotta fly planes so your little towers don't get knocked down," Christopher said as he took a menacing step towards Järvinen. The bully in him took over and Järvinen slid backward.

20

Vitam Immortalem

The elevator finally came to a rest at the base of the project. As the door slid open, Christopher, hunched over, spat up what was left of the bile upheaval that had come up during the descent. He didn't have much in his stomach to vomit to begin with. Järvinen stood proud and tall, his hands clasped behind his back, evaluating the work being done before him. EverCorp employees scuttled around before him like ants.

"This, my dear Commander Wendell, is where we become *legends*. Where we *save humanity's existence*." He turned around to face Christopher, who was unfolding himself to assess the labyrinth of machinery.

"The Escape Velocity Project," Christopher said, eyes fixated past Järvinen's head.

"An alien construct, in simple terms. It teleports objects to and from Mars in an instant. What was once a two-month trip to the planet will now be achievable in mere milliseconds. Come, let me show you," Järvinen motioned as he stepped off the elevator lift.

Christopher hesitated, but only for a moment. *This is crazy, right?* he thought. *There's no way teleportation is possible, right?* He considered what Järvinen had waxed poetic about on the ride down to the base of the project. *Immortality.* He glanced up to take in the full scope of the underground chamber. Dim fluorescent lights lined the top of the oblong dome carved out into the Earth. He estimated the ceiling of the pit was at least half a mile upward. *Sorry Grace*, he thought, *guess I lied again. This is extremely not safe.*

Immortality. The word ricocheted around Christopher's brain again as he stepped out of the elevator and followed Järvinen. *Why though? What kind of risk junkie has an aversion to dying? Why should your life count so more?* He walked by mindless EverCorp drones, most of whom paused what they were doing to quickly measure him up. Embarrassingly, most of their uniforms looked as gaudy as his. He wasn't special. Just another cog in the machine. *Immortality*, he thought. *How'd I get the golden ticket? I mean, I should. But shouldn't someone like Erik get this before me? He's much more of a pilot than me, right?*

Christopher realized that in his preoccupation, Järvinen had been talking the entire time: "...almost *three* decades!" he exclaimed. He turned to look briefly at Christopher, then frowned. "Something troubling you, Commander?"

"I don't understand. How does this whole... *thing*... fly? Or whatever? And how exactly does that save the planet?" Christopher asked.

"I thought that was clear, Commander? Who said anything about saving the planet? Ei, the planet will falter. I said we would save *humanity*. When we master teleportation, we no longer will require a planet to remain indefinitely hospitable. Rather, we can just move to the next best environment. Hopefully, on a continual basis," Järvinen answered.

"You're talking about a mass evac? Of a *planet?*"

"Indeed I am. A planet that will have men like you and me to thank for their survival. They might even name some holidays after us," Järvinen chuckled at his own joke as he continued through a hallway of servers and wiring. Christopher followed, attempting to process what had just been unraveled before him.

"Jarg. Wait up. So does *everyone* get a ticket, or is this a Titanic-like situation where only the turborich get on the lifeboats with their chihuahuas?" Christopher asked. Järvinen sighed slightly and dropped his shoulders.

"So it is, then," Christopher lamented.

"That is... not my decision," Järvinen hesitantly answered.

"Oh, so is that where your 'legendary' status ends? Picking who lives and who dies? Are you even going to let the 'plebs' know that they're on a one-way ticket while some social media star with a fat ass skips town?" Christopher bellowed. The machinery around them hummed and clicked with excitement as if part of the conversation.

"I am *trying*, young man. But it is difficult. My function here is to oversee the production of-"

"-Excuses are tools of incompetence used to build monuments of nothingness," Christopher interrupted. *Oh my fucking God*, he thought. *I'm quoting Garland. I've turned into Garland.* His eyes shot wide. *This is how Admirals are created. Top-secret government experiments. This is how Garlands are made.*

The two stood glaring at each other. Järvinen pushed his hands into his pockets in exasperation. "Commander Wendell, even your Noah was only permitted to bring two of every species aboard his vessel. You bring me the Arc, and I will try to get every single soul from this planet on it. You have my word. Now, let us continue."

"The rain has begun to fall."

21

The Gate

Christopher turned the final corner and stopped, astonished at what he saw. A behemoth of an arch, with the creases spiraling around its arms in a sterile way to the base. It wasn't an upside-down U, but it wasn't an upside-down V, either. Somewhere in between. He'd never seen anything like it. He was there when the Glorious President Putin Towers came crumbling down, courtesy of the Cerberus Squadron. When the Novi-Bolshevik Resistance had risen, he was there to personally see its monuments, swords and fists alike, fragment to powder. He'd been witness to more historic events than any other, in his eyes. So to say that he'd seen a monument or two would be an understatement.

The arch was a pristine white. *Too* white. Looking at it was near to looking at the Sun, to Christopher. He shielded his vision until he saw no one else doing so. He looked over to Järvinen, who was also marveling at the glory of it.

"What?..." was all Christopher could manage. There were so many questions that could follow. The simple question actually seemed to suffice his thought process. Järvinen, still flooded with emotion, peered up to him with excitement.

"I know what you're thinking, lad. But fear not, it's not a piece of divinity. As far as we know," he said as he pushed him forward. Christopher's instincts triggered, and he began surveying the rest of the area, looking for an exit. The two nerds he'd seen on his entrance to the facility, almost the only ones not draped in EverCorp apparel, were hunched over a table, which was illuminated at the top. They were staring into it and talking between themselves, pointing at certain items on top of the table. Flashes of light were bouncing off it so quickly and abruptly that it seemed like they were watching a tabletop rave. *Probably turbotweakers*, he thought dismissively with a roll of his eyes.

* * *

George watched the pilot prance and swagger toward the Gate, as if he'd built it himself. All eyes in the Project were on him, and from what George could tell, he seemed to be enjoying that. *What a cocksmootch*, he thought. *We're sending this man towards his death. Fuck, I'M sending this man towards his death. This is stupid. It's pure fantasy. THIS is the savior of humanity?* He looked over at Kevin, who acknowledged his feelings with an eye roll and a shrug.

"You think his death will be quick?" George asked derisively.

* * *

A set of metal grated steps were suddenly at Christopher's feet. He lifted a boot, which now felt like it weighed a metric ton, to the first step.

Clank.

He was afraid of looking ahead.

Clank.

He was afraid of appearing weak.

Clank clank.

He was afraid that Grace, Luna, and Mark would never know how much he loved them.

Clank.

He was afraid of dying.

Clank.

He was afraid.

Clank. Clank. Clank.

Christopher climbed the final level and stood in reverence of the white, pearlescent Gate. It hummed to him with beckoning enjoyment. Between the arches, bright flashes of neon pink, blue, and white sparkled so brilliantly they merged together in an electric purple frolic. Every instinct he had screamed to him that he would be electrocuted instantly if he touched it. The icon resonated with the brightness of a thousand suns.

"Jarg, talk to me," he whispered out of the side of his mouth. "What the hell did you guys actually build here?"

"V⬡✝C01⊛⌒⌐29.209△h͓hhhhhB%,ڿ \$pU≈⊟ ⊠ڿ▨ ▦■⌐ʟɛ̠ɪ̠9vD become Ξ∠|uo◖++R'⊠ڿ▨ ▨◩◪ڿₚ82588◪◩⇛|kWJʿ , the ₪y‰◖++R'TY1vXC◪◩ₚ82588◪◪₿▤ △◌◠...7.912.⊼◑++R'₿▤◉,◂◂n6. ⊛⌒⌐29.209△Sℙ◁ wor-{ζ~▷⊠₪y‰TY1vXC," Järvinen responded flatly. His voice sounded broken and encapsulated in static as if it were coming through a vintage MP3 recording.

Christopher stared at Järvinen, both in shock and anger. *Is he fucking with me? Right NOW?* he thought. Järvinen looked back with dubious trepidation, wondering the same about

Christopher. The Gate rang with fervor between the two, seemingly wrapping them in a charged hug of excitement.

"Commander Wendell," Järvinen said through the turbulence, "go forth to your destiny." One of the EverCorp minions handed a helmet, which had two small oxygen tanks affixed to its rear, to Järvinen. He circled around Christopher, then placed it over his head. He clasped the snaps down tight, and all the noise of the room suddenly muted. All except the static reverberations from the Gate. It shrieked and screamed even louder to him now that his thoughts were isolated. Christopher puffed his chest up in a ritualistic pre-flight bravado. *Who's ready to fly to Hell?* Erik's motivational credo poked through his attention and perked his attentiveness to his mission.

"Hooyah!" Christopher shouted, as he smacked his chest and marched into the jowl of the Gate. He disappeared into a frothy swarm of static light and high-pitched garbles. George looked down at the table monitor. It had subsided from a swirl of symbols and patterns to one solitary line, blurred between pink and blue letters on a black background:

Commander Wendell will live forever.

22

A Destiny of Mud and Rot

Dharavi, India. September 11th, 2001. 5:58 PM.
Six-year-old Muhammed Shah was kicking stones along the unpaved, jagged road as he pulled a cart loaded with his family's laundry. He had just finished washing them in the Mithi River, which was mostly a coalescence of sewage, toxic waste, and discarded animal byproduct. He had seen dead humans floating in the sludge more than once. What precious little water they could scare up couldn't be wasted on frivolous things like clothes, he had learned. Baths and drinking water were also sourced from the river in his neighborhood. He became accustomed early in his life to always being sick, hungry, and nauseated.

Muhammed twisted and swiveled, pretending to be the spaceship that adorned his favorite shirt. He narrowly navigated the lopsided shanties and tents with his cart, nearly losing its lone wheel on it with every turn. Adults bartered and quarreled at self-constructed shops over prices of commodities: mostly ragged clothes and rotten food. He noticed a thief take a piece of fruit from a stand and begin to run in his direction. The two made eye contact for a brief second, both wide-eyed and panicked. The shop owner, cursing and spitting, chased the man down with a large kitchen knife. Muhammed scurried out of the way, then sprinted, praying that the cart would keep with his tiny burst of speed. He heard a crash of confrontation, then the familiar screams of a grown man in his expiring moments.

Muhammed gained enough distance from the encounter, then stopped to collect himself. His chest was heaving up and down, but he didn't feel tired. He surveyed the area behind him and noticed he had lost scattered items of clothing in a breadcrumb trail where he had fled. Residents were already picking them up and collecting them for themselves without reservation.

"Aai ghalya," he swore under his breath. He rallied what he could without fighting - he'd already discovered his ineptitude in physical conflict years ago - and fled the area. After what seemed like a day's travel, he finally arrived at his home: three exterior walls built with defective Toyota minivan doors and tied together with nylon rope. The fourth wall was an ever-shifting monument of laundry, cookware, and anything else hung out to dry in the sun.

His siblings: Aabid, Farah, Saira, Yelda, Syed, Uzma, Urshia, all raced around the shack. Only baby Rasul escaped the command of daily chores, and tending to him was part of everyone else's. Yelda and Saira mostly laid claim to this role, as they began to learn and accept their maternal ordinations. His mother, Aasma, barked orders to the rest of them from within the abode. Recollecting the previous events of his laundry pilferage, a shudder traveled down his diminutive spine. *She might kill me*, he feared. *She's told me about killing me before. If she doesn't, Poppa surely will. They're going to kill me for losing some of the family's clothes.*

Farah emerged from the house's front "door," which was just a dirty opaque lining of plastic, and stopped upon seeing young Muhammed.

"What has taken you so long?" she hissed under her breath. She always was the "mother in absentia" to the rest of the children, keeping them in conformity with the rules when the watchful eye of their mother could not. Although she didn't have the decorum of their matriarch, she most certainly held the gravitas and wit. Muhammed froze in terror, with no explanation or answer. He held his body stiff, eyes trained on the ground, waiting for a drubbing or reprimand.

One never came. Farah snatched the cart from his motionless clutch. She turned and almost seemed to strut towards the shanty, cart wobbling behind her in despair. Their mother bolted out seconds later, like a bull being released from its pen.

"Farah! What are you doing with that laundry? It was supposed to be here hours ago!" she roared. Farah glanced at Muhammed and smiled briefly, out of one corner of her mouth.

"Maai, there was a large fight in the market. A disgusting man attacked me with his manhood and I had to release the cart to fend him off," she bluffed. Muhammed dipped his head in shame, for playing along with the deception, and for making his sister deceive their mother in the first place. Aasma narrowed her eyes in matriarchal skepticism. Her gaze fell upon Muhammed, whose mea culpa was all but scrawled upon his dirty forehead.

"So that is the story you weave. Then tell me, Muhammed, why was Farah doing one of *your* chores?" she pressed. He exhaled loudly and stared at the ground. He was not quick of the tongue, like his sister. "Muhammed!" his mother yelled, jolting his gaze upward. She stood, arms folded across her large bosom, and judgment shooting from her eyes.

"Mama, I beg you; forgive him. I finished my chores early, so I accompanied him to the river. We became separated in the market, just before I was attacked by that terrible man. I should have been watching him better." Farah leaned deeper into her lie, hoping to elicit a sympathetic response from their mother.

Aasma circled the two, scrutinizing them and the cart. Muhammed felt like he was on trial in the highest judiciary in all of the Republic. His inner organs shifted in tumult. He peeked over at Farah, who was looking straight ahead with an amused flash in her dark eyes. *How is it she remains so calm?* he wondered to himself. *I cannot do this!* He opened his mouth to pour out the sour confession that was acidifying his tongue when a scorching crack across the back of his head brought him tumbling to the ground. One more sounded off, and Farah was suddenly lying next to him, both dazed and unsteady. He was certain his neck was shattered. The maternal betrayal he felt twisted him into a thousand folds.

"You imbeciles! Half our clothes are gone! *Your father will beat you until you beg Allah for swift death!*" Aasma screamed at the pair. *No matter*, Muhammed thought, *I already do.* He looked over to Farah, who was inspecting the ground beneath her face and licking her teeth. Her tongue and bottom teeth were stained a bright ruby red from her biting her own tongue. He sucked in his own breath hard and inhaled dirt and rot with it.

"What is the meaning of this, Aasma?" a deep voice boomed from behind the two. Muhammed's insides went from sinking to frozen stiff in fear. The voice belonged to his father, Yusuf. He began to pray.

Muhammed's body suddenly lifted from the ground, with his limbs falling listless beneath him. As he was stood upright, he looked up at Yusuf, who eclipsed the midday sun. Yusuf released the back of his shirt that he had yanked Muhammed up by and bent over to bring his face closer to his son's. His beard, an amalgamation of gray, white, and black, wildly ran away from his face in all directions. His chestnut skin was leather and worn from too much exposure to the hot Indian sun. His clothes were a jumble of rags stitched together by Aasma. Behind him, she berated the two siblings further in Marathi. A slight, rare smile crept across Yusuf's creased mouth. So slight and rare, Muhammed questioned whether his eyes had deceived him.

"Come, Muhammed. I must speak with you about today's events. Your *Tai* can fetch the rest of our lost garments," Yusuf said as he shot a piercing look toward Farah. She responded by bowing her head, causing a line of blood to dribble out of her mouth. Muhammed felt guilt swallow up his fear as he left his sister to the abuses of their mother. He followed the large, brawny figure belonging to his father.

Yusuf walked not to their home, but past it. Curious, Muhammed continued behind at three paces. Winding, the duo headed north towards the Sion-Bandra Link Road bridge. He caught his breath upon seeing it: Yusuf strictly forbade the family from even approaching it, let alone crossing it. Crossing over a field of decaying woodland that seemed like rotting flesh, it was a symbolic gate more than a bridge. Instead of unifying, it kept people like Muhammad's family 'out' of the richer, more privileged Greater Mumbai. A full complement of armed federal officers and soldiers - all facing outward to Dharavi - saw to this. The imagery was intentional and quite clear: Dharavians were not welcome in the city. But cross the expanse was exactly what they did: Yusuf with steely resolve, Muhammed with jaw agape.

He always assumed one foot onto the beginning of the bridge's cement path would provoke a volley of gunshots. When Yusuf and he plodded onto the bridge, no bullets rang out. Inspecting further, he didn't see any large men with their equally large guns. As the two reached the crescendo of the bridge, they found no soldiers guarding the other end, either.

Instead, there was chaos. Cars wrecked into each other and continued on their way, honking in exasperation. People ran from block to block, yelling and motioning to each other. Of all the glimpses Muhammed had snuck of the area, he had never witnessed such disarray. It looked more like Dharavi to him. *What has happened?* he wondered about the "civilized" population. Yusuf looked back to check on his son. "This way. You need to bear witness to this moment."

Moment? Muhammed's head spun even madder. *What has happened?* He reached a moment of clarity as his foot hit the first paver stone off the bridge. Mumbai City. *True* Mumbai City. Dharavi was considered 'part' of the city, even though in reality it was its own autonomous zone to keep the poor - to keep Muhammed - out.

He looked up and took in a view he had never seen: shops with glass windows at their forefront. Functional electrical infrastructure. Even amid the shouting and panic, he felt like he had just stepped into another reality. Everyone's clothes appeared to be store-bought and freshly washed. *I do not belong here*, he quickly chastised himself. He trusted his father, but could not imagine such a scenario that would bring them to such a foreign spectacle.

Yusuf continued on, striding with purpose. Muhammed kept with him, eyes darting to and fro. That no one swept in to eject them from the area was a continuous suspicion and astonishment to him. It was almost like everyday life for him on the other side of that bridge: he felt invisible. They walked with the desirables without any mistreatment from anyone. Everyone was too concerned with leaving the area.

Muhammed's stomach started to sink into his bowels as he understood the circumstance of their leisurely stroll. *No one cares that we're here because this is somewhere no one wants to be.* Shops that held cell phones and pagers were laid barren and deserted. Metal sheet gates were down in front of grocery marts. Amongst the rubble and smoke of the vehicle crashes, he saw doors slamming shut as if expecting Yusuf's and his arrival. *Do they hate us this much?*

Yusuf suddenly changed course, crossing the street at a forty-five-degree angle. Muhammed diligently followed. They approached a cafe, long since abandoned by its staff and clientele. Spilled cups and overturned tables littered the metal upholstery of the front part of the store. Yusuf took a seat at the bar area of the diner and slightly patted the stool next to him. Muhammed obediently sat, apprehensive about every move he made in this unfamiliar territory.

"My son, bear witness," Yusuf growled as he pointed to a television monitor behind the service area. Muhammed gazed up and was instantly perplexed: giant buildings he never would have been able to imagine engulfed in flames. The chyron below the moving images read "अमेरिकेवर दहशतवादी हल्ला" (Terrorist Attack on America). Muhammed looked upon his father for perspective and found him staring coldly at the television. He turned his eyes back to the monitor and gasped aloud.

One of the buildings, larger than any in Mumbai's skyline, was crumbling like a sand and mud pile he would sometimes build outside his residence. *What massacre is this?* he wondered. *The mighty Americans could never be invaded. Could they?* He snuck a look up at Yusuf, who was watching, wide-eyed. His lips were pursed, and his face twitched at every cut from the cameras. Studying him for just a moment longer, it almost seemed as if he was silently cheering on his favorite football team. Encouraging the next play to succeed. Muhammed's eyes slowly crept back to the television, as if in dread.

Who am I rooting for?

The channel seemed to be on an automated timer to change. Now, the two were watching a Western news anchor. She was fair-skinned, blonde, and pretty, even though she was choking back obvious tears. He looked upon his father and felt what he saw. Betrayal.

"Some buildings were just damaged, and you're sad? Where are your tears for us?" Yusuf screamed. Muhammed turned to survey outside the diner. Few people remained, but the destruction sat as a monument to the fervor. *Where are the tears for us?* he wondered.

He returned his focus to his father. "Baba, what will become us?" he wondered aloud. Yusuf slowly turned as if he had just heard the wildest accusation in his life. His eyes were frenzied, and his breathing was uncontrolled. Muhammed reflexively shirked backward, expecting a drubbing. He'd seen that look before. No words needed to be spoken for him to know that he'd overstepped his bounds.

Yusuf inched deliberately close toward his son like a trained assassin. Muhammed shrank and stiffened up, waiting for his pummeling. Instead, a tight, firm hug absorbed him for the first time in his life. His arms flailed outward, unsure of how to respond to the unknown embrace. *He's crushing me to death*, was his first thought. *Goodbye, Baba. I'm sorry. I love you. I'm sorry I wasn't better. I'm sorry for everything.* His breath became shallow and he started to disassociate himself from his body.

As if an echo to that thought, Yusuf relented in his squeeze. Air jammed into Muhammed's thin lungs like an ancient balloon getting its final aspiration before bursting. Customary pain ignited into his entire body like a bonfire. He gasped, then moaned into a whimper as his father ever-so-slightly released him from the hold. He still held him close, though, in the embrace. An embrace Muhammed was not accustomed to. He only knew pain and thrashings from him. He trembled and waited for the punishment to begin.

It didn't. For the first time in his life, he felt a true loving affirmation from his guardian. He leaned in and cradled his head sideways into Yusuf's meaty chest. *We must be all destined for death. I love you, Baba. I love you, Maai.* Just as he felt his paternal heartbeat thump into his right ear, he was pushed away. He looked up into Yusuf's eyes, feeling both fortunate and disoriented. *Did I do something wrong, Baba? How do we do this?* Embarrassed, he understood that he didn't know the proper way to show affection towards his father and that he might have crossed an unknown line.

Yusuf pulled Muhammed's face close to his; close enough for his burly beard to scrape and scratch at Muhammed's. In a voice that was both firm and trembled, he informed him: "you are leaving here." Muhammed's brain scrambled with astonishment. *Where is he sending me? Where could I possibly go?*

"Just me?" he blurted out. Yusuf, as if to answer, pulled him by his hand and yanked him toward the diner's exit. He stopped just outside the door and appraised the disarray in front of them.

"The Americans are about to wage a holy war. Their king has already promised it. He will rain down missiles upon us, and we will be dead," Yusuf declared. Muhammed felt nausea unlike any he'd ever experienced before at the curt statement.

"But Baba, we had nothing to do with that, right?" Muhammed pled. Yusuf shot an indignant glare at his son. "Did we?"

"Blame matters not in war, son. It does not matter who burns the house down, it only matters if you are in it when it crumbles. The Americans tend to not worry about this when it comes to destroying other parts of the world," he said as he clenched his jaw, keeping his eyes fixed ahead. His eyes suddenly darted upward, as if anticipating the very bombs he spoke of to be raining down. "Come, Muhammed. We're getting you out of the burning house."

The two walked for what seemed like days to an airport. Muhammed never even knew of its existence until he saw the large sign with a picture of an airplane that read the airport's title: "छत्रपती शिवाजी महाराज आंतरराष्ट्रीय विमानतळ (Chhatrapati Shivaji Maharaj International Airport)." He had never actually seen where those huge planes went off to. They just seemed to rumble and tremble his family's home with the greatest fervor - especially when they were landing. At times, he believed Allah himself was dropping down into their residence, only to find it was an overhead flight filled with foreigners. He was both overwhelmed and disgruntled at their daily intrusions. *Who gives them the right to challenge Allah's might? No one should have that kind of power*, he always worried.

The structure of the grand airport loomed large in front of the two: a huge behemoth of a disc bigger than Muhammed could ever dream, squatting fat upon the earth. Everyone seemed to be in a frantic hurry in and around the gates.

"They know, too. They're escaping, as well," Yusuf exclaimed. Muhammed paused to take in the view. No one was *leaving* the building. Everyone was filing inwards as if completely sucked in by the mammoth saucer. People jammed up violently against the doors as backups spilled beyond the main lobby.

"Baba. Are we leaving the family behind?" Muhammed asked. The thought tore at him once he spoke it aloud, but he couldn't bear what Yusuf had told him. That only *he* was leaving. He barely went anywhere in their neighborhood unaccompanied, let alone somewhere that a plane would need to take him. He had never even been on a plane, either.

Yusuf stopped and collected his thoughts. Turning to Muhammed, he towered over him and looked down upon him. "Only you will be leaving. I saved what little rupees I ever could for a moment such as this. I only have enough for one ticket and to pay the extra to the security agents."

"Why do you have to pay the agents?" Muhammed asked.

"That is needed to allow you onto the plane without documents. Most of this is done through trickery. Otherwise, none of us would be able to leave," Yusuf informed him as he turned to proceed toward the front gates. Muhammed scurried to keep up with his father's long strides. As he caught up to his father, Muhammed blurted out the question that had been churning inside his mind ever since the diner.

"Why me, father? Why not you? Or Farah? Or Maai?" he pled. "Why should I go without you all?" Yusuf grunted in disapproval as the two turned and made their way to an unassuming side door. To the casual observer, it appeared shut. As Yusuf pulled it open, a broom - which had been wedged into the jamb to keep it slightly ajar - fell down with a sharp crack. The two entered and allowed the door to close behind them.

"You will go where I tell you. When I tell you. I cannot send a *woman* off to the far reaches of the world unsupervised. They would be dead within a week. I am too old: my time to expand the family has come and has gone. No. You, Muhammed. You, are going to leave this cursed land and conquer anything in your way as you do it. *You* are the future." Yusuf's words roused more confusion than answers inside Muhammed's mind as the two continued down darkly-lit hallways and through doors that had "करूमचारीच" ("Employees Only") spray painted on them.

Yusuf approached a security agent, clad in camouflage and carrying a large rifle. The agent's eyes darted around, then he cupped his hand out low, near his outer thigh. Yusuf stuffed a large wad of rupees into the agent's hand and spoke in low tones to him. The agent looked down at Muhammed, then nodded at Yusuf.

Yusuf bent down and looked sternly into Muhammed's eyes. "You cannot use your given name anymore, son." Muhammed was appalled.

My name? It is the Prophet's! I surely cannot abandon it! I'm leaving everything!

"It will be used against you now in this crusade. I will not send you away just to see certain death. Every little boy named

'Muhammed' will be lined up and shot on the streets. You understand?" Muhammed nodded, tears welling in his eyes.

"You will be known now as 'Nathan.' It will serve you well in England."

"Where is England, Baba?"

"It is far from here. But the Americans will not invade it, as they are subservient to the English king. You will thrive there. Now go with this man." Muhammed paused and looked at the agent. He was peering down stoically at him with no emotion. Muhammed looked back at his father. "Go, son. Now!" he ordered. Muhammed left with the agent, quietly sobbing. He looked back for Yusuf before he and the security agent exited through a series of double doors.

He was gone.

"Goodbye, Baba..." he quietly whispered.

"Come now," the agent said, inspecting a ticket he retrieved from his bulletproof vest, "your plane departure is right ahead." He handed Muhammed a one-way boarding pass. Muhammed snorted in a line of snot dripping from his nose and inspected it closely: he had never seen one before. DEST: LHR. NAM///SHAH, NATHAN.

Thirty-seven minutes later, Nathan Shah left India and never returned.

23

D⍰emons of Mars

Static filled Christopher's helmet. His teeth. His sinuses. His eyes were pressed tight, but he was still blinded by fuchsia and aqua lights that seared his retinas. His ears screamed from a raging shriek that had no end.

He braced and waited for death. There was no other outcome. All his training had led to this.

Always thought we'd eat shit on the same mission together, Erik. Sorry, buddy, he thought as the hellscreams penetrated his frontal lobe. Within seconds, the pitch inside his head was so high that he went numb to the pain. It felt like an eternity to reach.

He cautiously opened his eyes. Retinal flashes still pulsated and fogged his vision. Pink deepened to a burnt red-orange beneath his knees, which he was curled down over. Aqua was swallowed overhead by an obsidian sky.

I'm in x⊙⚧iK⚧☽++R'{ζ~▷⌧{ζ~▷⌧, he thought. I never –

His eyes narrowed in focus and his brain widened in suspicion. This wasn't Hell. Very surely, this was his destination.

Mars.

The Red Planet sprawled out before him in an unholy exhibit. Mountains fell into vast craters. Sandswept plains fled away from him to the end of the horizon. Everything was racing at light speed and unshakably still at the same time. Large boulders - bigger than a football stadium - were discarded left and right in a haphazard manner. Rocks in every single size between those and fine dust littered the sanguine terrain up until it met the horizon.

To his left, in the distance, a large chasm opened its maw an unknown canyon. Above it, a sandstorm had gathered. The gale pranced and frolicked within itself as if it were the only toy on the planet. It suddenly plummeted downward into the fissure, escaping from Christopher's slight amusement.

The sky was something he thought he would be prepared for. He assuredly was not. The sheer immensity gave him chills of reverence. Looking at it, he'd never felt so truly small in his entire life. He couldn't determine if, compared to the best view from Earth, the sky was blacker or the stars were more radiant. He suspected both were true. He searched for Earth in the astronomical dreamland, but could not. He immediately understood infinity, because it was the exact number of radiant diamonds strewn across his view.

Amidst the jarring collision of red and black, a teal light shined from a distance. Not a light, but a glimmer, like a reflection from a swaying mirror caught in an azure sunset. He peered closely at it and stepped in to move closer. His legs, unaccustomed to the new gravitational force, failed him and he soon found himself on his back, staring at the void.

He pushed his radio transmitter to report his status. Nothing came out of his mouth when he tried to talk. His transmitter click was the only thing that broke the dead silence of space.

He began to panic, his chest heaving up and down. No fog materialized on his helmet visor, and that's when he realized: *There's no oxygen. My oxygen tanks aren't working. Did they even give me oxygen tanks? Oh God, I'm suffocating.* His breathing became desperate efforts for his lungs to claw themselves to the surface.

No matter. His chest began to burn a searing pain up his windpipe. The more painful it became, the more valiantly he tried to breathe. He wasn't thinking. He wasn't reverting to his training. He was simply flailing and grabbing at his equipment that he'd received no training on.

As his strength faded, he turned his head to gaze at the planet once more before he met death. *No parachute to save you this time*, he thought. He peeked to his left, not even able to move his head. The blue light was now within feet of him. The red grit and sand had blackened to powdery soot. The splatter of stars that had been overhead had even abandoned him. Everything had lost color but the blue light. It moved right. Down. Up. He rolled his eyes upward to meet it with the last bit of strength he could summon.

Death? God? What ⊙Δ*g*∜Ɠ*F.*97▣φ*j*↤ᴘ\J *you?* he thought. As he became blinded once again, he heard - or thought he might have heard - a response: "Commander Wende{ζ~▷⊠{ζ~▷⊠! Can you hear me?"

Christopher fell backward into emptiness as his eyelids fluttered shut and his heart pumped one last feeble beat.

24

Factory Reset

Beep.

"...don't call it a 'failure,' you gutless fuck."

Beep.

"...not like we get another shot at it anyw-"

Beep.

"...probably just tell us to kill him so what's the p-"

Beep.

"...vegetable probably won't need his yogurt, right?"

Beep.

Beep.

25

The Road Home is Paved with Nothing

George stared glumly out of the plane window at the churning Atlantic Ocean. After being summarily excused from the project, he and Kevin were removed from the building. They were not provided transportation to the airfield, or even a flight home. He was forced to pay for both their flights from his own bank account, after convincing the cab they had waved down on the road to take them to the airport on George's good word that he could pay at the destination. At three weeks' pay equivalency, the two were soaring across the waters towards Washington, D.C. on a shoddy E-988 puddle jumper.

Neither man spoke to the other. There was probably nothing to say. There was definitely nothing either wanted to hear. George assumed that he would probably kill himself when he finally returned home. He was unsure of the gun laws in the District, so he didn't know if he could possibly buy one illegally. *How would one even go about that?* he wondered. *You're out of your depth*, he scolded himself, *as usual.*

Pills? No. You don't have the right kind to do the job. You're back in the same predicament as the gun. Since vehicles had been made completely autonomous and electric, they had been rendered incapable of being used inside closed garages for suicide. *Why did you think you could pull off this project? You can't even kill yourself. You're as impotent as they come, George Sansor.*

He glanced over at Kevin. He was mindlessly swiping through his phone, although at the rate he was pushing, George knew he wasn't reading or focusing on anything. It was a coping mechanism, pushing human interaction in front of him. Human interaction with the outside world, which a young man like Kevin had been deprived of for too long. *Are you happy with how badly you've broken him?* George thought to himself. *He was your responsibility and you failed him, too.*

What can't you fuck up?

The plane hit a patch of turbulence, and the windows suddenly went ashen. George gripped the armrests and held his breath. A soothing ring chimed out, and the cabin's intercom activated.

"Good afternoon, ladies and gentlemen. This is your captain. Um, due to a rapid rise in sky spouts, we're rising to orbital altitude. You may experience dizziness or fatigue for a brief moment. If that occurs, please tap your 'call attendant' button on your EverCorp E-Fly app, and we can provide you with a complimentary Astrobalance pill. This should decrease our flight time by an hour or so, and we'll get you to your destination safely. Flight attendants, please prepare for orbit entry."

Sky spouts - colloquially referred to as "devil dippers" - were deep-sea typhoons that rose up to ten times the size of normal twisters. They appeared without considerable warning or storm, seemingly rising up from the oceans like tentacles. A college friend of George's had died on a cruise in the Caribbean when one cut the ship into shreds. It was two weeks before they'd ruled out terrorism and he got any kind of closure on his friend's death. There was never a funeral for any of those lost that George knew of.

The sky near George's window wisped harshly, and suddenly the cabin turned calm. His ears pressed into his brain and he started swallowing to ease the pressure. It didn't matter: they felt ready to explode inward and turn his brain into a creamy mush. He felt a tap on his arm and looked over. Kevin was mocking him like an idiot.

Kevin was holding his nose and pressing his cheeks out firmly like a monkey. *Very hilarious, asshole*, he thought. *Yeah, we're just monkeys in the experiment. How truly meta of you. You win the Most Clever Asshole in the Fire.*

Kevin thumped his arm again, this time much harder. He exaggerated his actions, pointing to his face, which was turning red from forced blood flow. George stared, dumbfounded. *Good God, man. What did you DO to this kid?* he wondered. Kevin exhaled with frustration.

"Plug your nose and breathe out, goddammit!" he yelled as George's hearing began to dull.

Oh, shit. Oh yeah. That actually makes mathematical sense, George thought as he obeyed. As he shot oxygen bubbles from his brain to his nasal cavity and back, he sat in admiration at Kevin. *This kid had every reason to crumble,* he thought as he watched Kevin focus intently on his own cranial pressure.

He didn't.

You did.

George kept pressing on his inflated nostrils, but it was no use. Within a minute, he had passed out.

A fitting exit to a terrible failure, he thought, as his world faded to black.

26

Conjuration

Christopher Wendell woke up annoyed and confused. He knew exactly where he was. Andrews Hospital. The dated wallpaper and stench of slow death were ones he'd experienced before.

Beep.

Beep.

Beep.

He checked his surroundings: an empty television stand, with connection wires still exposed, stared back at him from the opposite wall. Two nondescript men sat in chairs mindlessly thumbing at their phones. From their bland suits and defeated attitudes, he could tell they were government employees. He tried to raise his legs to climb out of the bed but found his limbs unresponsive.

Oh, fuck. Oh, fuck oh fuck oh fuck. You're a cripple. You cripple you're a cripple!

His stirring caught the suits' attention. Both shot their phones to their ears and began chattering into the devices. He rolled his eyes. *Can't even scratch my nuts without getting in trouble*, he thought. One of the suits scrambled out of the room, motioning wildly with whoever was on the other side of the conversation.

"...I don't care what meeting he's in, go get him!" the stiff yelled as the door closed. Christopher didn't care who "he" was, there was only one person he wanted to see right now.

Erik. The one who'd seen him through his darkest and brightest days. The one who would make fun of his dead legs the second he walked through the door. Or Grace? The kids? *How have they not seen you through better and worse? Who's really your best friend?*

Who's really got your back? Has anyone? Ever?

He paused his thoughts as he made eye contact with the agent still in the room. His body language was off. He was...

He's surprised, Christopher thought. *This is not a part of the plan.* This was not good. Things that ran this deep like the Escape Velocity Project, unplanned outcomes were not dealt with kindly. He had dropped plenty of bombs onto populations with an expected death toll of innocents. But that was okay because it was "part of the plan." Unplanned results had much more unforgiving consequences. He was now a liability to the United States Government, and worse, EverCorp.

Beep beep beep beep beep.

Christopher tried to climb out of bed again. His legs shifted, if only slightly, but still without use or purpose. The suit kept his eyes on him, squinting slightly, and murmured into his phone. *Fuck you if you're going to kill me in this shitty bed*, Christopher thought. He shoved his legs over the edge of the bed, and gravity took him by force. He landed on his stomach on the cold, harsh, laminate floor. His back was to the agent and his head to the wall. He'd essentially turned his rear end to man.

He breathed heavily and tried to push himself to his feet again.

Not even a push-up by Air Force standards. He lay there, groaning at the pain that shot through his body.

"Wendell, would you cover yourself up? I've seen just about as much of your ass as I'd ever like to," a familiar voice gnashed at him. In all fairness, Christopher's bottom was indeed completely exposed by his hospital gown, having been pushed up to his naval in the tumble.

"Sir, I have exactly one written reprimand fully detailing me exposing my ass. That they know about," he said as he grunted and flopped himself over, "I'm starting to think that the United States Navy wants it more than it lets on."

Rear Admiral Garland was mid-eye roll when Christopher finally locked eyes with him. When he first came into Garland's radar, he used to fear him. Now, that look of desperation and admonition felt more paternal and venerable than ever. He'd take fear any day over this level of humiliation. He was a goddamn fighter, the best of the best. And here he was, splayed out across a cold linoleum floor, flashing his penis to his commanding officer like some common turbofreak. His penis curled up into his abdomen, which had retreated somewhere into his chest cavity. His throat had retracted to an air-tight barrier. He was completely helpless.

"Get him up," Garland growled as military personnel entered the room.

"Oh sir, I don't need help getting 'it up,' you know what I mean?" Christopher shot back as he was crassly hoisted off the floor by the military grunts. He held in any moans of pain that he might have growled as they heaved him back onto the bed, purely out of egotistical pride.

He landed with a hard thump onto the unforgiving hospital

bed. As he did, he eased into the excruciating pain that resonated through his entire body. *Travel through the pain,* he remembered from OCS. *Don't dwell on it.*

Garland strode towards the bed. Christopher tried not to wriggle, much as he wanted to. His body burned against the constraints of the stone slab the Andrews Hospital characterized as a mattress.

"You just refuse to die, huh Wendell?" he snapped with a slight gleam in his eye.

"I'm... old-fashioned like that, sir," Christopher replied as he continued to catch his breath. The two men gauged each other.

"I'm recommending a full honorable discharge for you, Commander. After I finish your recommendation for the Congressional Medal of Honor. You have served with valor, young man."

The words hit Christopher like an atomic bomb. He slowly sunk back into the bed, partially unaware that he'd arched his back in response to the news. Tears began to well in his eyes that he immediately blinked away. He searched his bedside as if the answers would be there, waiting for him.

Garland sensed his trepidation. "This is the highest honor you can achieve in the military, son. What's the issue?" he demanded.

"You're... you're kicking me out? What did I ever do besides be your absolute best fighter?" Christopher said, his eyes rising to Garland's. "What more do I have to prove to you? I gave you everything!" His voice began to rise in fury. "Why is it never good enough for you, old man? Do I actually *have* to die before you'll give me a lick of credit? Is that when I'll prove myself? When I *die*?" His jaw had steeled and his gaze had heated to a firestorm. Garland shuffled his weight in his stance, taken aback and defensive.

"Who in the exact hell do you think you are, *Commander?*" His tone began to match that of Christopher's. "I've had hothead sons of bitches like you before, and I'll have them again." He took two steps toward the bed. "I know this may be a foreign concept to you, but your mission is no longer to blow shit up. When you are awarded the Medal of Honor, you are officially an arm of the public relations division of the United States military. Your fucking task is to win hearts and minds now, *squid.* Your glory days are *over.* You're going to be giving speeches in high school gyms and E-meetings. Congratulations. You're a *fucking celebrity,*" he growled as he neared Christopher's bedside. "You're also very *welcome,* by the way."

Christopher kept his eyes locked with his superior. Underneath his convicted exterior, Garland's words shot through him. *Neutered,* he thought. *They couldn't contain me, so they're neutering me. Throwing a bullshit citation on me so they can put me on the sidelines. The Navy just never runs out of ways to stifle success.*

"If there's nothing more, *sir,* I'd like to see Commander Stormer," he breathed through his teeth. He hoped it was the last thing he ever said to Garland. He noticed his breathing had become more rapid and started combat breathing to calm his agitation.

Garland's eyes moved in slow motion towards the floor. The soldiers who'd previously manhandled him, standing at the opposite wall of Christopher, went from an at-ease stance to at-attention. His eyes slanted in suspicion at the room as he surveyed their body language. *The fuck kind of trouble did Erik get himself into this time? And without me, no less*!

No. Something was not right in his gut. He had been in enough formidable situations to have a sixth sense for peril. It shot the hairs on his neck straight back and turned his stomach into a pretzel.

"Chris..." Garland began.

The pretzel turned into a nebulous DNA strand, spinning into infinity.

"Erik. He's, well he's not coming."

"Bullshit. He can be mad at me all he wants, he'll still-"

"-He's dead, Chris."

27

...And Now Untwined

Christopher pushed one waterlogged boot after another onto the steps toward his apartment. Every try felt soggier than the previous. The rain pounded down upon him from above like reverse uppercuts. His peaked cap absorbed every blow and sent a concussion jolting inwards toward his brain stem. He deserved more punishment. He kept his eyes on the ground and gnashed his teeth together. He couldn't feel the oral pain – or much else – through the haze of the alcoholic inebriation he'd put himself under. He had started with liquor and then moved on to wine. By the time he was late for Erik's funeral, he was chugging hard lemonade in his bathroom between violent fits of vomiting and crying.

People had come and gone by his side during the event. He couldn't tell who. It had been a dimness wrapped around him, blanketed in a blur. He had just kept staring at the coffin, draped with an American flag. At one point, he'd managed the fortitude to lurch forward and tug the flag to the ground. However, his feet failed him and he foolishly fell to the ground. He was just as quickly yanked back up to his feet – likely by other sailors - and brushed off. The twenty-one gun salute soon followed, sending rattles of sobriety stabbing through his saturated brain.

Erik had killed himself. A coward's death. Garland had tried, in his own way, to explain the circumstances of it to Christopher. After so many curse words and berating from Christopher, he'd finally thrown his hands in the air and given up. Both knew it was likely their last conversation with each other. But neither would admit it to the other.

He peered closer at his uniform. Disheveled and muddy. His ribbons and name tag were crooked. *A poor excuse for any serviceman*, he thought. His eyes slowly moved back upwards and scoured his environment. Doors. So many doors. No clue which one was his.

He pitched his keys in a childish outburst, attempting to add some dramatic flair to his circumstances. Always one for a show. Always acting as if cameras were upon him. The move took his breath from him and he fell to his knees, breathing with his whole body.

Fucking.

Hate you.

I fucking hate you, Erik Stormer.

A door creaked open and he shot his head up from his ridiculous crawl. A blurry vision of a human form turned its head at him in confusion. He blinked twice and the form took a sharper image, showing his next-door neighbor, Janice. B-cup, at most. He kept his distance from her even at his most desperate times for pleasure, because he was fairly certain she was a turbotweaker. He didn't have hard proof, but enough suspicion that he didn't feel like contracting hepatitis. She pointed towards the door to her left with worry set in her eyes.

He groggily followed the signal without objection towards the door she'd motioned to.

* * *

After Christopher left, without so much as a goodbye to his closest battle buddy, Erik floated without purpose. He had flown another reconnaissance mission shortly after Christopher's departure but had nearly had a mid-air collision with a British fighter jet. He was quickly scuttled to training exercises. When compulsorily moved to a specialized position like this, it was like being sterilized. Someone should have been closely monitoring Erik's mental health. No one did. When he acted out in constant, and severe insubordination, Garland added a disciplinary notation in his service record and informed him of such before having him escorted off Andrews by military police.

No one checked on Erik. If they had, they would have found that he had a co-dependent relationship with Christopher. A cursory check of both their backgrounds would have revealed that they encouraged each other to insubordination and rebellion. Even when one would be hesitant to rebel, the other's commitment to misconduct would spur the other to participate without hesitation. More often than not, there was no hesitation between the two in this regard.

But no one checked.

The first, urgent clue that something was wrong was when Christopher's locker at Andrews was defaced. Custodial staff had reported it at 0332 hours while doing a routine mopping of the room. *DESERTER* was carved into its face. Across the five lockers spanning left and right of them, *HOH* was jaggedly, and more swiftly etched below it. Garland received a phone call about it at 0351 hours. By 0438 hours, a new locker door had been installed for Christopher. No other official investigation was undertaken into the matter. The *H* and *H* remained on the other unfortunate pilots' bins.

I fucking hate you.

Erik had put on his full dress uniform in his apartment after a one-night stand. An unnamed female had been strewn out in his bed: naked, turboed out of her head, and spinning downward from the supplementary red wine. He had choked her in a way that had given even him pause, but she was too stoned to offer up a resistance. He played with her breathing, toying with her life in a twisted gamble. He'd lost interest, and the ability to maintain an erection, hours before.

He gazed at his reflection in his bedroom mirror. His eyes were sunken into his head, and spittle was gathering at the corners of his mouth. Whatever drugs he and the prostitute had shared were beginning to wear off, leaving only overwhelming depression in its place.

Fucking.

Hate you.

Just bounce off to your cushy new training job? Leave the rest of the squadron behind?

Leave me behind?

His date stirred restlessly behind him. As her nipples crossed the path of the lone moonlight peeking in through the curtains, his brain pushed out fluids of rage and humiliation that he hadn't been able to please her. He hadn't been able to please anyone. Her. His squad. Garland. Least of all his "best friend," who couldn't even be bothered to tell him that he was transferring units. Now he didn't know who he was anymore.

He didn't know if he was going to kill his date or not. He was still mulling it over.

Everything suddenly made sense. Clarity swept over Erik in an astounding way that he'd never felt. His eyes crept towards the pulsing glow surrounding his military-issued E226 pistol, laying on the dresser to his right. Christopher always had pushed him to never question his gut. He wasn't about to start again, not now.

Erik picked up the firearm and welcomed it with a passionate kiss. Not the first time he'd done so. He squeezed the trigger hard as if he was embracing the hand of a long-lost love. He was still alive to feel the freedom of his brain matter decorate the ceiling of his apartment in sanguinary hearts. His date was screaming in sudden confusion as he blurred to nothing.

I fucking hate you, Christopher Wendell.

No one checked on Erik before he killed himself.

* * *

Every lunging wriggle across the common area of Christopher's apartment complex felt like a monumental leap. Vomit kept pushing up and down his larynx like teasing fire. A demon trying desperately to both escape and stay. A curse and a blessing.

The demon ended up spewed out upon his doormat, affectionately labeled with "COME BACK WITH A WARRANT." His cheeks slammed down onto the mash and swill of alcoholic beverages and cheap fast food menu items.

The door crept open and a foot stood by Christopher's floundered face. He pushed his legs into his abdomen and began sobbing uncontrollably as he was gathered into his residence. Whoever was dragging him was having trouble with the ordeal, and Christopher made no attempt to help. Finally, after ample carpet burn had been applied to both involved, the door slammed behind him with an unceremonious *thud*.

Fucking hate you, Erik Stormer.

28

Autopsy

Nathan Shah stalked the bowels of the Escape Velocity Project with petulance and rage. He had heard the words "can't" and "impossible" more times than he ever cared to. His scientific lackeys cowered behind turbocomputer terminals and screens to avoid him. They were cowards and would inevitably hold him back in his mission. He stopped his warpath as it fell directly in line with the Gate. It stood still and dark, a monument to the failure of epic proportions.

"Every one of you has told me why this machine *can't* do what it's supposed to do. Tell me again, what exactly do I pay *any of you* for?" He pushed forward towards the nearest scientist. "How did George Sansor and his child figure out what you all couldn't with a fraction of the equipment?" The scientists shuffled in nervousness and glanced at each other. Nathan surveyed the lot of them and found his target: a scientist half squatted below his terminal. Ducking so low he might as well have been on his knees. A lamb to the slaughter. He strode towards him with his figurative claws bared.

"Answer me, you dope!" Nathan screeched as he towered over him. The scientist recoiled at his outburst as if a sword had just been skewered through him. Another began forcibly vomiting in a far corner from the two.

"Sir," the scientist murmured, "you sent Mr. Sansor home." Nathan stood over him, astounded.

"Yes, how *dare* I assume that the lot of you would be able to get this machine working with *thirty* times the budget of the United States military! George Sansor is just *one man*! You can't do this just because of one man? *He cannot be that powerful!*" Beads of sweat began to form on Nathan's forehead. "I've spent more on this than your entire bloodline is worth!"

"Sir, we can't in good conscience move forward with this project anymore. It is too unstable," the scientist said, his face to the floor. "How many lives..."

"As many lives as it fucking takes!" Nathan shot back. "I'll throw all of you on the tinder to get this functional, do you understand me? *Are you hearing me?*" The trembling and scuffling of the grunts in the basin of the project came to an immediate halt. He'd gotten their attention. While all of their spines stiffened at the threat, his became exceptionally relaxed.

"What do you need?" he pressed. The gallery stood still, no one daring to be the next target of his ire. His eyes darted around, surveying his prey. At his fiercest, he was the most focused. ECorp's stock portfolio reflected that.

No one accepted his offer.

"Fine," he responded to the silence. "Make due with your graves, traitors," he spat at them as he began to climb the nearest set of stairs.

"Sir?" a scientist asked of him.

He stopped instantly and looked down at his underlings.

"Out with it, chap," he responded.

"Maybe we need a *willing* pilot?" the scientist responded. The stillness of the area was palpable. "I'm just saying... perhaps Commander Wendell resisted the G-Pull by a fraction? That would line up with the diagnostics we've seen so far."

"You're saying we need a pilot to buy into this project more?" Shah asked, intrigued.

"It may be an issue worth exploring, sir," the scientist responded. "But finding such a subject... that may prove difficult. But given this trial run... another body into the fire won't work. I believe our work here has already been leaked to the outside world."

"I'm well aware of the happenings of the outside world," Shah hissed back. His lackey was correct, though. Every military operation under his thumb had already made excuses as to why they couldn't proceed with the project. Some of them hadn't even been officially aware of it before informing him of their cowardice. But his mind was turning to future profits. *There's only one person who could go into this without resistance...* he thought. "It's obvious what I need," he declared. "We need Commander Wendell to go back into the void. Willingly." He grinned as machinations began to evolve in his thoughts.

"I need to make him *believe*."

29

Spotlights

Christopher woke up on the floor of his apartment's living room. The hard surface had done no favors to his back or right shoulder. He squinted as he gathered in his surroundings. *How did I end up here?* The familiar stench of vomit saturated his nasal cavity and caused his stomach to begin churning once again. He needed greasy breakfast food and any pain meds he could get his hands on.

His ears perked as he heard movement from the kitchen area. He tactically began planning his attack, only for his body to reject him. Everything hurt and attempting movement made his nausea increase tenfold. He'd been here before, but it had been a while. The last time his gravity and vertigo had interchanged so fluidly he had been on a Caribbean cruise with...

He shot up reflexively and began to forcibly dry heave. Bile collected in his throat to satiate his retching.

"Oh honey, let's get you into the shower. I've got sausage and egg muffin sandwiches almost done for you," a familiar voice floated over to him through his waves of disorder. *Grace.*

Dammit why would you be here? You don't need to see this.

Not again.

Footsteps approached him and he felt a tugging at his armpits. He pushed past his ailments out of boldness and machismo. Grace guided him as he lurched through the hallway to the bathroom. He collapsed again as he reached the cold tile near his shower. She began to undress him, evoking sexual nostalgia from him even in his debilitated state. Even though he hated her, even though he felt near to death, a woman undressing him spurned a reaction of preparedness for screwing. He felt both elated and reduced to emptiness. He both wanted to die and wanted her to start blowing him.

She finally stripped his military garments off of him without any sexual advances. His dress blues lay in a neatly constructed pile near his bathtub. Rising, he strode confidently into his shower, before smacking his nose directly against the tile wall of it. Humiliation burned through his face while he tried to feign his composure.

As the cold water and blood began to drench his face, his eyes rose to meet hers.

Fuck.

Her genuine concern ran chills down his spine past whatever the water could ever aspire to. He was accustomed to being tossed into a shower - in their former familial house - by Grace with contempt. It had become almost commonplace to him at one point in his life. But that had been long ago and even longer since he had seen this measure of his maturity. It humbled him further than he already was: naked and afraid.

Grace tried to yell something through the glass partition to him before he slipped to his ass, but he didn't hear it. He cracked his head on the rubber matting of his shower, which saved him from a severe concussion. He turned away from her instinctively, not wanting her to see him in pain.

After a few minutes, the door ripped open and the water turned off. His eyes opened wide to gather in his senses. "⇸⇸□⇛|kWJ′ ℬ▤◉,‹‹n6.▦TY1vXC◨◪⌀ₚ82588◪◪

⊛⌓⍑29.209△▢7ri,9.+⇛|kWJ′ ◗⊥⊥R'ℬ

▤◉,‹‹n6., come on. You're flopping around on the floor, and the world is in flames," Grace scolded him. Her castigation confused him, piquing both anger and intrigue. *What did she say? She used to be so obedient*, he thought. The chill and electricity of the air matched her gaze.

"What?" he argued.

"I love you, Christopher. The world will love you, too. But it's in flames. It needs you. Come on, let's get you dressed," she cooed as she helped lift him to his feet, then dropped to her knees to dry him off. Her face sat just mere inches from his member. He felt another bout of sexual provocation as she did. *She's... she's smiling, right?* he thought. *This is how blowjobs usually begin on ehub...*

She ignored the obvious erection near her as she dried him down with his parachute Turkish towel. He tried to nudge his penis closer to her body as if it were a magnet and a positive connection was all he needed. She sidestepped him, subtly performing her marital duties. To him, it rang louder than the E-Corp Liberty Bell. His member lulled to a slight softness that he was unused to. He stared at it, then onto Grace.

The fuck...

Grace smiled at him, clearly aware of his sexual weakness. Her face was mere inches from his genitals, and she was unquestionably aware of it. *All she had to do was be obedient*, he thought. She snapped the towel as she finished wiping him, standing and spinning towards the bathroom's mirror. His gaze drifted down to her rear end, still excited from their nearness.

She leaned over the counter, exposing her rump even more. Even in her mom jeans, he could delight in the curvature of her behind. *Is she?* he thought. *She'd never been one to flirt so blatantly like this, bending over and showing off her ass like a porn star...*

Grace started navigating Christopher's mirror computer interface, tossing menus to the left and right with authority. She didn't seem to have any difficulty, despite not ever navigating his personalized system. He stood in awe as she bypassed several apps that required E-IN codes without pause. Her arms waved frantically as she pushed menus and windows up, down, and to the side. Various news feeds caught his eyes as she did.

"MASS EVACUATION OF AUSTRALIA UNDERWAY"

"ANOTHER SUPERVOLCANO ERUPTS IN BRISBANE"

"MILLIONS FEARED DEAD"

"REFUGEES HUDDLED IN BEACH ENCAMPMENTS"

Eventually, she zeroed in on a specific menu.

DatrApp. Where he'd been busiest in his life after leaving her. His eyes drifted to the floor as she turned around and clenched the edges of the countertop. Images of women younger than her, flashing their thongs, littered the mirror screen. Her clenched fists began rapping the countertop in a furious cadence. She started screaming in disgust, but he didn't hear a thing that he hadn't heard before.

"Whore!"

"Traitor!"

"Selfish prick!"

"Narcissist!" She was just getting warmed up when he

stopped her.

"Gray, what are you doing here? Why are you here? Where are the kids?" he shot back. He didn't realize how legitimate his arguments were until the words left his lips. He'd stumbled upon a series of accidental cogent questions. *What did he have to explain to her? About anything? Did she just love to bleed him like her personal punching bag?*

She squinted her eyes as she clenched the countertop tighter and pushed off. She was within inches of his face in a fraction of a second. He'd never experienced this level of hostility from her, even at his worst in their marriage. It caught him off guard.

"What do you think this all is, Christopher?" she demanded as she motioned back to his mirror. "Just another chance to score another bimbo? With everything that's on the line here?" She punctuated her statement with a crisp slap to his left cheek. It was the first time she'd ever struck him. She leaned in closer as he slowly took in the disbelief of the attack.

"After all you've been through with the Project, why in the hell do you think you're still alive, Christopher Wendell? This isn't a rhetorical question!" she implored. He took his time searching his thoughts. He found nothing. From his experience, he knew that meant...

"Luck," he bumbled out. "Pure, unadulterated, blind, stupid, luck." He'd never been more honest with anyone, let alone Grace. She searched his eyes, scanning for his typical deception. She only saw complete collapse. A slight grin crept up her thin lips.

"No, Christopher. Nathan Shah doesn't believe in 'luck.' You're here because of him. And he has amazing plans for us. Get dressed."

His towel dropped as she turned and left him naked, cold,

baffled, and alone. DatrApp autoscrolled pieces of shameless skin in a whirlwind as if sensing the tension of the room.

What the hell just happened?

30

Dead Hooks and Knots

Nathan Shah had tired of the games. He had tired of the excuses. He'd certainly tired of the incompetent presidents, kings, and generals that had laid their pity upon him while kissing his ring. Sometimes he felt like he was the only one in control of the wheel of a vehicle that was careening off the road, and everyone else was tugging at the steering.

His driver pulled them into a terrible apartment complex. The mere sight of children playing in the parking lot - unattended - made his skin crawl. *Off to learn about life without any adults guiding the way. Gutter trash. All of them.* Every fiber in his body yearned for his driver to run the nuisances over, but he knew the cleanup would only bring him greater stress. He could accomplish so much more if he had even one person below him that worked as hard as he did. No matter how deep he sliced into his subordinates, he never pulled back up the excellence he expected. It was a constant trial and error that always fell short. *Simpletons*, he thought. *Can I not escape them?*

His car finally pulled into a parking space. He shuddered as he felt the suffocating constraint of other vehicles surrounding him. *Simpletons*, he reiterated to himself as he waited to be saved by his driver from the smothering. He hunkered down as he waited for his rescue. The door nearest to him popped with commanding dominance. He took a deep breath as he mentally prepared his entrance to the outside world.

Humid, gray, smokey, air crammed his lungs through the fake smile he put on out of reflex. He looked at his driver in intense hatred, blaming him for every particle he breathed in. The man, who had introduced himself with some boring name – John or Jørn, he couldn't remember or care – stared stiffly back at him. He was the first employee Nathan could remember in years that didn't appear deathly afraid of an obvious mistake.

He peered up at the building they stood in front of. Terrible plastic siding lined it. Once white, it was now brown and coated in a thick layer of dirt and ash. A dog was busy licking the grime from a window from one of the lower units, seemingly enjoying itself. He straightened himself up and marched up a set of dingy wooden steps to a door marked "C2." He looked over to John; after all, he wasn't going to knock on the door himself. However, Jørn wasn't anywhere to be found. He lurched over the railing of the landing, being careful not to touch it, to see that his driver was seated in his car staring straight ahead.

You very much wish that I'm only going to fire you, he thought as screams from within the apartment caught his attention. His eyes flicked to the door as he recognized the familiar sounds of a domestic argument.

"...the fuck gives you the right?"

"...swear I'll cut that little prick right off from your balls!"

"...you'd probably have to touch it in order to do so!"

A confident grin crept over Nathan's face. He was most

certainly at the right address. He snuck closer to the door to further eavesdrop.

"...even know *why* I left your useless, pathetic ass?" There it was. That was his cue. He knocked on the door, however hesitant he was to touch the repugnant surface. The screams abruptly stopped, and he heard hasty shuffling. *Probably hiding their turbospeed and pipes*, he mused to himself.

"Who is it?" a voice demanded from inside.

"Housekeeping," Nathan responded with indignation. More fumbling followed inside the dwelling, adding to his irritation. Finally, the door's lock cracked and it crawled open. Christopher Wendell peeked his head barely around the partition and surveyed his meddler.

"Unless you have a message from the President, get lost," he mumbled.

"I have a message from someone much more important than that buffoon, Commander Wendell," Nathan replied with conviction. The door, which had already been shutting, paused. He waited.

"State your name and your business, asshole," Wendell growled from behind the door.

"I'm here to debrief you on the Project, son," Nathan replied.

"Pass," Wendell responded as the door slammed shut. The lock clicked back shut.

"Commander Wendell?" Nathan called through the door. "I'm also here to read the final will and testament of Commander Erik Stormer." He assessed the monument of his words.

Silence. Absolute silence.

Nathan stood in reflective stillness as well. He checked his watch. *Ninety seconds. I'll give him another minute and a half. This could still work.*

Sixty seconds.

Seventy.

Eighty. *Shit*, Nathan thought. *Plan B is much less suitable.*

Just as Nathan was about to turn to exit his stay, the grimy door shook inward. He watched triumphantly as the archaic lock plunged towards the open position. Wendell opened the door, wearing nothing more than underwear briefs. His physical appearance made Nathan take a step backward in distress.

"Lord son, are you... are you *okay?*" Nathan asked. Never one to take into consideration another person's well-being, he was genuinely astonished. It was a reflexive comment, but exceptional nonetheless.

Wendell stood before him, barely. He used the door as support. His skin hung limply off his bones and organs like shapeless tumors. He gazed back at Nathan through sunken eyes like he was staring through him. Every piece of information Nathan had received about Wendell was that he was the best-of-the-best the U.S. military had to offer from its pilots. His fitness regime was celebrated amongst those in the know. Now, he wondered if he should've inquired more discerningly with Israel or Canada.

Wendell lurched as the door he hung on pivoted on the hinge. It was a flawed excuse for a brace. His withered legs, grayed and dilapidated, shook as he tried to hold himself steady. Nathan gazed down at them in awe, then back up to Wendell's glower, which hadn't moved.

He looked like the *vetala* his mother used to warn him about. "Wander over to the Sion-Bandra Link Road bridge, and you will be feed to the vetala! She will feed upon your sinful blood inhabiting a body of the dead!" The threat alone kept him unconditionally absent from the area of that particular bridge. As a child, he used to experience nightmares about reanimated corpses, with eight arms, sucking blood from his head.

Grace appeared from behind Wendell and wrapped her arms around him.

"Come on honey. Let's get you set down. Come on, sweetie," she cooed as she led him away from his support pillar. She fired a brief look back at Nathan as she did and nodded her head away from him, inviting him into the apartment. Inspecting the cleanliness first, he enthusiastically followed. *I suppose it could be worse*, he thought to himself. Although the stench from the dwelling was fetid to his nostrils, he anticipated much worse. No feral animals attacked him, and there were no overdosing turbofreakers in sight.

Grace coaxed Wendell over to a stiff, fashionable couch. He hobbled and labored along, even with her help. The two finally reached the furnishing, both exhaling loudly as he fell into his rest. Grace rested her thin hands on her knees, breathing deeply from the unaccustomed physical exertion. *She's really selling this 'housewife' facade*, Nathan thought.

Nathan processed the mess in front of him. Wendell grunted and groaned as he tried to find a comfortable space to lie in. Grace tried in vain to prop him up to a respectable position, to no avail. After enough struggling, he waved her off. She took no notice of his command.

"A-hem." Grace ignored Shah and continued her efforts to move Wendell to a seated stance.

"Ack-HEM!" he shouted, infuriated with a disobeyed order. Grace's head snapped back to him. He pointed her to the back of the apartment, finger shaking in indignation. *How dare she make me ask twice*, he thought as she slunk away. He turned back to Wendell.

He was leaning halfway up the couch, as best as Grace could manage to get him. A shell of a man. *For fuck's sake, this wretch is supposed to get me into outerspace?* he thought.

A sigh crept through his mouth, but reflexively just as a sham symbol of compassion. Much as he hated to, he slid onto the cushion beside Wendell. He stared ahead to the stark kitchen that lay beyond the living room they sat in.

"I won't bullshit you, Commander," Nathan began. "This planet is not long in survival. It needs a hero. It needs *you.*"

31

Turtles Upon Turtles Upon Turtles on an Elephant of the World

Christopher sat in weary shock. *Why is Nathan Shah in my house?* he wondered. He would probably have delved deeper into that thought process, but his brain wasn't completely operational, even for his standards. He felt the heavy fog of a hangover, with the consequent stomach-churning nausea.

Jarg. Mars. Erik. Grace. And now Nathan Shah? His life had been flipped inside out in a matter of a day. Or a week? He had no idea how much time had passed since he had foolishly accepted Garland's offer for the project. His ignorance spurred instinctive anger as he scrutinized his uninvited guest.

Shah sat next to him, his legs clamped together as if he were wearing a skirt. He wore a crimson suit lined with black trim, a black shirt, and a red tie. Against his dark skin, the outfit was impeccable. Christopher wasn't well versed in men's attire but could determine that the ensemble probably cost more than his annual salary. His hands were laid down on his lap in perfect posture, holding a single file folder.

Erik. He said something about Erik.

"Tell me… how does an asshole like you get Stormer's will? Last I checked, you weren't enlisted," he spat out through chapped lips. Shah chuckled ever so slightly.

"Son," he began, "I *fund* the United States military. At your rank, I think you probably know that. Can we skip the formalities and get down to brass tacks?" Shah countered with a glower and grin.

"You came all the way down here to read me Erik's will? You?" Christopher replied.

"Absolutely. After we watch some television together," Shah said. Christopher was unprepared for that comeback.

"Television?"

"Indeed. I don't think you know what a celebrity you truly are," Shah said. "Grace? Could you be a dear and come work the television, please?" he called into the back of the apartment.

"She's not a kept woman. I'll fucking get it," Christopher said as he leaned forward to the coffee table to retrieve the remote controller for the TV. Shah waved him off, captivated by Grace's obedient entrance into the room. Christopher paused, watching the both of them incredulously. Grace floated into view with a look of pure delight on her face, retrieved the remote, and surrendered it to Christopher. He sat frozen in dumbfounded awe, hand still extended. *Is this a trick?* he thought. *When did she become Miss Homestead? Who is this woman that will just bow down like this? Who is this man that can make her?*

Shah snatched the remote controller from Christopher's outstretched hand and turned the television on. "Look, son. They're talking about you." Just as she had entered, Grace drifted out of view, like a phantom without a purpose.

The Evernews chyrons all read the same:

"*NAVY CDR WENDELL FIRST TO REACH MARS*"

"*NAVY PILOT WENDELL HAILED AS HERO TO EARTH*"

"*USA WINS SPACE RACE – AGAIN*"

"*CDR WENDELL ENSURES HUMAN RACE TO SURVIVE*"

"*AMERICAN PILOT FINDS MARS – FIRST IN HUMAN HISTORY*"

The captions continued as Shah kept scrolling through the channels. They began blurring together. It was everything Christopher had ever wanted, and nothing that he deserved, fused together. He had finally brought his name to prominence, as it rightly warranted. People were uttering his name in every conversation.

But not like this.

"This fucking mission was a *failure*," he said, turning to Shah. "Why are they talking about it like it was a success?" His tongue, swollen and blistered, failed him with the last word of his attack.

"Because they know what you don't, Commander," Shah cooed. "They know that you were the first to step foot on our next inhabitable planet. That alone should merit you a monument built in your name. I told you: this planet is not long in survival. It was built upon a mountain of turtles, sitting on an elephant. We are down to the elephant. And the elephant is dying."

"Sounds like we still failed then," Christopher shot back, cynicism running strong in his veins.

"Tell me, Commander. Why are you in this state? Look at the sight of you. Does the VA not take care of its veterans?" Shah said, evading. The question made Christopher laugh until his lungs raged with heat, and he bent over his knees, gasping for air.

"I knew a... little about... you," Christopher said in between spats of hacking and rough lung movements. "But I... never... knew ab... about your... sense of... humor," he retorted.

Shah looked at him with faux concern. He plucked his phone from his pant pocket, a model Christopher had never seen before. A small antenna crept up from the side on its own as Shah placed the device to the side of his face.

"Why hasn't Commander Wendell been receiving his Everdine treatments?" he implored to the other end of his conversation.

"None of that should concern me. Yet here I am, deeply concerned about it. Do you see the problem with this, Janis?" he said. He looked up at Christopher and gave a slight thumbs-up. "Fine. Turn in your resignation after it is done." He clicked the phone call off before an answer to his order could be received and stood up.

"A courier will be by shortly with your medication, Commander. I will rectify the serious mistake made by the VA, rest assured. Be sure to take the medicine they deliver. It will help you recover from this grave condition and back to your usual readiness," he said as he stood to leave.

"Wait a goddamn minute!" Christopher exclaimed. Shah slowed, then stopped his exit. "You said you had Erik's will to read. Only reason I let you *in here*. So out with it," Christopher demanded.

Shah nodded and smiled. "Fair enough. Grace? Could you come set the EverTable up for reception?" Grace, almost expecting her cue, was upon the two without notice, punching a code into the side of Christopher's EverTable in front of him. He stared at her in bewilderment.

How does she know the code to my table? he thought.

"Honey, do you really have to ask?" she answered as if reading his mind. "Your passwords have all been the same for years: 848856." *Damn it, she's right*, he thought. The last three numbers of Erik and his Department of Defense numbers combined as one. She was one of two people that knew that. The other was Erik.

The table, which appeared as a solid piece of sandalwood, shimmered with an operating screen on its face. Shah smirked and approached it, placing his phone on a corner resonating with a flashing beat.

RECEIVING FILE... a notification read in the center of the screen.

FILE RECEIVED... StormerLastMessage.edoc

Shah removed his phone and slipped it back into his pocket, looking over at Christopher.

"As I said, Commander. Be sure to take the medicine the courier delivers. Grace, will you ensure that he stays on his recovery plan?" he said as his gaze rose to her. Her fists tightened as she shut down the EverTable's reception module.

"Yes, Mr. Shah. Christopher will be ready," she responded. Their conversation was a distant hum to Christopher. He leaned in closer to the table's screen, absorbed in its contents. Shah left without another word to him, escorted out by Grace. The two chatted briefly at the door before he did, but Christopher's attention wasn't broken.

FILE RECEIVED... StormerLastMessage.edoc

32

By One Thousand

Christopher stared at the file in his "Table Downloads" folder. He found himself hesitant to open it. He glanced up at Grace, who was sashaying back into the room after seeing Shah out, swinging her hips and ass at Christopher with every step. She grinned with a smirk as she did, taunting him with her vivacity.

Where'd this assertiveness come from? The Gray I knew never even knew how to shake her ass, he wondered to himself. *Even more: how is she even ALIVE? She was on the doorstep before I took on this assignment...* He looked back down to the monitor below him and shakily pushed on the selected file. It shimmered up to a near-3d form off of the table in a translucent aqua hue.

* * *

Where could I possibly begin? Christopher recognized Erik's speculative nature immediately. *You're reading this because you want answers. I get that. But step outside yourself for just one brief moment and ask yourself: if Erik Stormer had all the answers,*

196

would we really be here?

Mom, Dad, I'm truly sorry. I know how proud you were of my successes. You never wanted anything more from me than to be happy and content in my own life. As I've grown to learn, that's probably the most challenging task for humans. None of this is your fault. I'm sorry for being a failure to you. I'm so sorry for ALL of this.

I know how pissy that sounds. I realize I have a mission and duty that most would only dream of. Still... do they know the burden that they dream of? It's not at all what they're being sold on. Certainly not what I was. Fuck the Navy. Fuck the entire military complex.

Yeah, I said it. FUCK. THE. NAVY. You'll find my Naval OCS letter of recommendation in my apartment building's dumpster. I should've lit it on fire.

The Navy gave me everything and took it all away. They used me like a cheap hooker and threw me away after they'd had their fun. I was the BEST until I WASN'T.

How dare they? That's more fucked than any other kind of rejection. Oddly enough, I think the whore I had for tonight is currently overdosing on the floor over there while I write this. Funny, this has come around full circle...

"Not self, but country," is our motto. No, not a motto. A belief. An ideology. We lived these words day-in and day-out in the service. Putting the mission of our country's defense before our livelihoods, before our personal safety, before any sense of normalcy. I could never get married or raise a family of my own because that would have interfered with my career. Hard to be a husband or father if I'm busy dropping bombs on husbands and fathers on the other side of the planet!

A motto is a shitty PR catchphrase. And I guess in my naivety, I fell for it: hook, line, and sinker. They convinced me (with little effort), to sign my life away so that people like Nathan Shah and the rest of the 1% could move their money from one country to another. I truly wonder if I ever fought any wars that were on the up-and-up, like they were sold to us all. Because I have serious doubts about almost every mission I flew for these corrupt bastards.

Which brings me to the missions. And the person who was ~~seemingly~~ *there with me through all of them: Christopher Wendell.*

Killing myself is easier than being your friend.

Christopher stopped reading and shut his eyes, pinching at the bridge of his nose. The two of them had traded barbs daily in jest. But reading them now had no satisfaction of sarcasm or wit. Just bitterness and malice. He paused enough to collect his bearings, sucked in what breath he could, then forced himself to take in more of the abuse.

When were you gonna tell me i▦◪◪ᴅₚ82588◪◪ was all a lie? The words hit Christopher like a bomb. He sat, mouth agape, pressing on, if only to open the wound further.

From what I hear, we're actually "best friends." What kind of "best friend" throws someone under the bus just to advance his career?

I was there for you through it all: Grace, Mark, Luna, and your inevitable fuckup of all of that. Do you know how many nights I spent on the phone with your wife, consoling her? Defending you to the ends of the earth, and sympathizing with her because you're the biggest asshole we both know? At first, I thought she was just trying to fuck me. And I wasn't going to, because I ACTUALLY CARED ABOUT YOU. You're welcome. Then I found out it was much worse.

You're just that horrible of a person. You're actually worse than I even knew.

She wasn't looking for some new dick. She was genuinely scarred from entering your life. And God help her, she procreated with you. She had to find out the hard way something most of us know: anyone that gets sucked into the shitstorm that is Christopher Wendell is worse off from it.

<u>*You destroy people just by knowing them.*</u>

When you went off to Houston to be an astronaut, I knew I'd never see you again. No one needed to tell me that you were never coming back. I deleted your number out of my phone that same day. Because if you had ever planned to keep in touch, you'd have told me about your new assignment.

But you didn't. Gee, I wonder why?

Pretty easy to figure out when I heard Garland pissing in the locker room one day. He was on the phone with someone high in the chain of command. He didn't know I was there to organize my locker. Normally, I'd give someone a courtesy cough to let them know their conversation wasn't secure. But when $pU≈▫ heard your shit name cross his shit lips, I didn't. Because fuck all of them. And you too.

Listening to him sent chills down my spine as to how disloyal and traitorous our supposed "commanders" are supposed to be. He had plans for you. For me. For the whole squadron. All that was news to me. The way he so nonchalantly talked about it – about our fucking LIVES – made me want to put a knife in his neck while he pissed. You don't know the bullshit you've signed up for, and I honestly hope you never do.

* * *

Christopher took another pause, breathing heavily. His pulse was rapidly approaching a dangerous level, even for a combat pilot. He surveyed the room, and looking up, found Grace in the kitchen. She stared at him, then eased into a half-hearted smile. Her pants were off now, wearing just a tank top - no bra - and cotton panties.

She's just stripping unprovoked now? Who is this woman? he skeptically wondered. His brain and his libido were at odds. A beautiful woman wearing exactly what she wore was his - hell, *every man's* - biggest weakness. But she never knew this during their marriage.

He took in her body like he never had before.

The tightness of the garments she still had on accentuated her best features: her flat stomach, pelvic bones that rode high into her curvy hips, and perky breasts that sat high into her chest. He'd seen enough fake breasts in his days as a bachelor to appreciate a true natural chest form like hers, slightly leaning to each side of her body and nipples protruding through the shirt - just enough - to suggest their overall dimensions.

She sauntered towards him, emphasizing every step with her hips as she did. As she was halfway across the room from him, his brain sparked into a frenzy. *Erik. Erik's letter. Erik's letter I'm not done with it Erik's letter.* She tried to decline into his lap, but as her bottom brushed his thigh, he refused her, rejecting her to his side. He heard a slight grunt of disapproval as he did, but he ignored it.

He dove back into the confessional.

* * *

Did you know that there was a "list?" Ranking us by importance - who would die last - in this little mission of yours? And wouldn't you know? You were tops, number one, like always. And like always, putting in the least amount of effort to get the most amount of results. Most of the guys in Cerberus hated you for this exact same reason. Only they thought you were getting special treatment because of "Daddy." I knew it was something worse: you were trying to OUTDO him.

You always acted like your Daddy was some kind of burden upon you, while the rest of us had to climb out of poverty, homelessness – and worse – to get to where we were on the squad. How fucking dare you. You had everything given to you, and then some. To say that you'd be the least likely to die is only because the Navy would never allow their "golden boy" to see serious harm. You'll be a GREAT Admiral one day.

I'm pretty sure the hooker I've been doing turbo with all night is dead. I tried to fuck her after she went unconscious but my pecker wouldn't work anymore. Some farewell, huh? If not, she's pretty close. But hey, just another day in the life of Cerberus, right Christopher? Maybe I should tell ◤◤ↄₚ82588◢◢⇛|kWJʿ ◑+̰+̰Rʿ hₔhhhhhB%,ﻪ⊛◠˗29.209

△Ƀ☰◉,◅◅n6.{ζ~▷⊠ﬅy‰,

CHRISTO4,n₌˙˙>q//8HER?!?!

END OF FILE... StormerLastMessage.edoc

* * *

Christopher sat in frozen shock as the file minimized automatically, pinging a quiet tone as it did. Time around him moved differently, but he didn't pay attention to how. He dipped his head down into his arms, which were clasped together by his hands. He couldn't find any thoughts to grapple with the flood of vehemence he'd just withstood. Tears began to flood the cradle his hands made for his face.

Slender arms wrapped around his sunken shoulders. For the first time in what seemed like ages, there was someone to comfort him while he sustained trauma. His entire adult life he had spent suppressing it: when he saw terrible things, and when he *did* terrible things. The Navy had set up a token "crisis incident support system" for servicemen before Christopher had ever joined up. During Recruit Training, a slide show was shown to the sailor recruits about its existence. Muffled laughter filled the classroom when it did. From that day forward, the standard was set: *if you need mental health help, you're too weak for the United States Navy.*

Christopher wrapped Grace in the tightest embrace he'd ever given. His sobs quickly turned into full-blown wails, as he broke down emotionally and mentally. As she calmed him with maternal purrs, she turned her gaze to the EverTable's fisheye lens. She winked at it and gave a "thumbs up" behind Christopher's back.

33

Life Sentence Fragment

Weeks had passed since Christopher's return home. Seconds bled into hours. Hours bled into days. His waking time was broken up by sporadic nightmares of hellfire and infernal images. Falling, it seemed, for eternity into a dark watery void. Static crowded his ears. He tried to suffer watching the news - but only briefly. It was nonstop coverage of the Escape Velocity Project.

He was acutely aware that she had miraculously healed from her terminal cancer. And now, shuffling around his apartment like a walking corpse, he could only find the humor in the situation. He used to have a silent, morbid smugness in his relative health over hers when she first got sick. He never purposely let it show, but never let an opportunity pass to contrast their physical capacities. Asking why she was tired in the middle of the day. Loudly sighing when her coughing fits became too intense on phone calls.

He never questioned her seemingly divine cure, because she was handling the role reversal with more dignity and decency than he ever afforded her.

Grace made sure that he took the medication that Shah had insisted upon, whether or not he was acquiescent. The medicine made him both foggy and lucid at the same time. He was more perceptive of her movements around his apartment, however, he had still barely moved from the living room's couch except for when Grace had forced him off it to shower.

Every shower had included Grace in it. In the very first one, she had shed the "tease" principle. He'd been led to the shower and stripped naked, as usual. But within seconds of groggily reaching for his HairSplode shampoo, the door re-opened, and Grace slipped in, completely nude. They came together without hesitation.

It had been years since he had genuinely loved a woman. It hadn't been since her in the first place. Midway through, he began to think about the argument they'd had before Shah had paid his visit. *This is actual love*, he felt with each push. The two had fallen into a heap on his bed afterward, breathing hard in reflection. Most times had been hushed, both of them staring at the ceiling. After the sixth shower episode, Grace turned onto her side toward him and rested her head on her hand, watching him.

"What?" he finally asked.

"I wonder about you, Christopher."

"Oh, is that what all this has been? *Wondering?*" he said with a laugh. She glowered with contempt at his crudeness.

"Don't be gross," she said.

"Well, what do you wonder, Gray?" he responded in a challenging manner. She had played the part of a humble housewife for so long. Despite his skepticism, he had still subconsciously grown accustomed to her newfound formality. He struggled against his fatigue - he was barely able to stand in the shower by himself, let alone the activities Grace had introduced - and sat up against the headrest of his bed. He suddenly felt on guard from a typical marital attack. Grace sat up as well, bringing her knees up to her chest. She rocked slightly as her gaze wandered around the room.

"Why don't you ask about Mark and Luna?" she asked.

He felt like the question hit him harder than anything he'd taken throughout the entire Project. Partially because he had been purposefully avoiding the topic of the kids. To him, if he broached the subject, at least one of two things would be discussed: his failure as a parent, or hers. It quickly dawned on him after she surfaced in his apartment, and stayed there endlessly, that she didn't have them as a primary responsibility anymore.

Who's watching the kids? Does she care? Are they in protective services? Are they even alive? She's still a mother, yes? He took a moment to collect his thoughts before answering.

"Are they... are they okay?" he finally bumbled out. *How do you delicately ask a mother if she's taking care of her own children?*

"They're good. Great. They're really good kids, Chris..." she trailed off in thought of her next words.

"Listen, Grace."

"I know."

"No. You don't."

"You-"

"-I'm *sorry.*" He paused, knowing that the words had landed. She stopped rocking, looking over at him. He had never apologized to her. At least not sarcastically.

"For what?" she pressed.

"For fucking up their lives. For fucking up yours. For fucking up *everything.*" He sighed deeply as he sunk further back into his custom Egyptian down pillow. "My priorities have always been to the Navy. Not you guys. I put my career before my family," he prodded along in his confession.

"That's the military life," she offered up as an excuse.

"That's completely fucked up," he countered. "I wasn't there before. I hate myself for that. And I can't take that back, what I've done. But I'm *here*. *Now*. I want us to be a whole family. I can't ask for forgiveness..." he trailed off to solicit leniency.

"I can't see forgiveness," she snapped back at him. His head sank down to his chest, like a fatal strike to his frontal lobe. Her hand suddenly grasped his.

"But I can see redemption." His sunken head was suddenly turned out of both confusion and intrigue. She leaned closer to his face, putting their cheeks almost together.

"I want *us* to get better before we bring the kids in and give them false hope. *We* need to get better before we *all* get better," she said. He raised his head to respond, but she placed a finger on his lips, hushing him.

"There are plans for us. Amazing plans..." she whispered in his ear just before she slipped out of the bed.

34

Drag Coefficient

Grace had, once again, saved Christopher from himself. Although she refused to talk about their children – it was an absolute nonstarter – she had made him feel more confident in himself than he'd experienced since Philadelphia. He had equated it to a second attempt at dating one night as they snuggled under a blanket. She had pulled tighter into his chest and kept her eyes on the movie they were watching.

His apartment was filled with laughter for the first time since he'd moved in. The pills Grace kept feeding him almost certainly helped. The only lull in the elation was when they would turn on any television program that wasn't a movie service: any news or live programming would inevitably show Christopher's face.

Pictures and videos of him with his jet. His squad. His military identification photo. One news agency had even found a picture of him with Grace, Mark, and Luna. They all pulled him out of the clouds from which he felt he'd never come. They all used words dripping with lies and deceit.

"HERO"

"PATRIOT"

"REDEEMER"

"WENDELL 2056 US PREZ?"

He knew a government propaganda program when he saw one, and this was an all-out blitz. He'd quickly change the channel whenever the topic showed. The awkward silences that followed between Grace and him pierced through an otherwise happy, domestic home.

Grace prepared dinner every night. He was feasting on far too many stuffed shells on a late Thursday meal when his phone rang. He looked at the caller ID, then glanced up at Grace. *Martha Wendell (Mom)* scrolled across the top of his screen. He slid the phone over to her and kept chewing.

"Uhnt-uh. Answer it," she replied, pushing the phone back with a shake of her head. He stared at her, then dropped his head, continuing to chomp.

"Christopher! Answer your mother," she demanded. He sighed through his nose and picked the device back up. Rolling his eyes, he picked up the call.

"Hi, mom."

"Christopher? It's your mother. Are you okay?"

"I'm fine."

"What does that mean?"

"It means I'm fine, I dunno!"

"I just got a call from your great-aunt Julie, you remember her?"

"Never heard of her a day in my life," Christopher lied.

"She's my cousin on my dad's side's mother. You remember my fence I had repaired last year from the turbo winds?"

"Yeah." He put his fork down to pinch the space between his

eyes as he felt a migraine rapidly approaching.

"Well it turns out she is friends with the fence company's owner's wife, Amy! I was like, 'wow, small world,' right?"

"*Uh huh.*"

"Well anyways, Julie said she just heard on the internet that you're going back into that Escape Project thing? Please tell me that isn't true!" The hairs on the back of his neck began to tingle and he felt his face flush.

"Mom, what have I told you about what you read on the internet? It's bullshit."

"But *would* you go back in?" He looked up at Grace, who was quietly scraping her plate with her fork, avoiding eye contact with him.

"Christopher?"

"I... Mom, as far as I know, that thing is shut down. It's probably at a museum by now or something. You probably know more about it than me. Hey I gotta go, you called right in the middle of dinner."

"But Christopher..."

"Yeah mom."

"*Would y⊛◠⌐⁻29.209△u?*" He pulled his phone away from his ear and quizzically looked at it. *Martha Wendell (Mom) [4:14]* scrolled across.

"Hey mom, I gotta go. I dunno. Far as I know, I'm out of the military life. Love you." He hung up and tossed the phone across the table.

"So how's Martha..." Grace asked with a slight grin. Christopher let out an exasperated sigh. Doing so, he realized he'd been unintentionally holding his breath.

"Same old same old. Politics or something. Buynak is literally Hitler, you know," he said as he turned back to his dinner.

"And the Gate?" she asked. He stopped, not taking his eyes off his plate.

"Christopher?"

"Yeah, Gray. The Gate. She heard that I'm going back into it. You know she reads crazy shit on the web because there's nothing better for her to do. You don't have to-"

"-Are you?"

"Am I *what*?"

"Are you going back in?"

"You're testing me, aren't you?" he said as he looked to the sky and chastised a god he didn't believe in. He added a fist shake for a comedic effect. Grace didn't laugh. He froze, knowing he was cornered.

"I think we need to call Mr. Shah," she said, sternly eye-balling him.

"Why? Why call that asshat? He just wants to point me to the sky above and blast me off this planet for his own little amusement. Nothing more. That's how those rich fucks are, Grace."

"I really don't think so. I think this is more about him-"

"-Why?" he cut her off.

"Because. I talked to him. At the hospital. He wants - no, he *needs* to get to Mars. Off of Earth. He has this... compulsion? Like I haven't seen before. To take us all up off this... *rejection*. Don't you ever just feel like we've, I dunno, gotten a raw deal with this planet? Like it's just not *fair*? I think he's trying to right that injustice."

"All the more reason not to trust him. He sounds like a fanatic. Maybe too wrapped up in this thing to see the bigger picture," Christopher countered. Grace lowered her head and raised an eyebrow, smiling at him.

"Yes, we'd hate to see someone wrapped up in their career now, wouldn't we?" she taunted him.

"Okay, okay, keep it above the belt," he said, holding his hands up in surrender. "What do you want from me? You really want me to go back into that thing?"

"Let's just call him tomorrow. That's all I think we should do," she said as she stood up and gathered their dishes. "What's the worst that could happen from just talking to him?"

"You're right," he said as he stood up to help her. She waved him off and took his plate out of his hands.

"Go get ready for bed. You need a shower first, though." A smile spread across his face and he almost tripped, scurrying past her to the bedroom.

35

Cactus

Christopher tapped on his thighs, drumming at a furious pace. He kept checking out each window of the vehicle he was in the back seat of as if expecting some sort of attack. He was almost always like that when he went outside these days. Especially sober. He tried to limit his alcohol intake by limiting his exposure to publicity. It was even harder with Grace dictating his intake of spirits, lest he fall into withdrawal in his dilapidated condition.

But whenever Nathan Shah personally sent a private car to pick someone up, there was little room for objection. So there he and Grace were, crisscrossing through the streets of the District, avoiding barricades that seemed to shut down every other block.

Grace grasped his hand to settle him down. He looked over and gave her hand an appreciative squeeze in return. The driver kept notice of the two through his rearview mirror but had to constantly shift his attention back towards the road. The vehicle would have been illegal if not owned by EverCorp, as it was completely nonautonomous. The driver, an old, stern-looking man was familiar to him, but he couldn't remember where he'd seen him.

"Hey old man, did you happen to serve?" he asked, leaning forward. It was unlike him to chat up a stranger he wasn't trying to bed, but he needed more distraction than holding hands could provide.

"No," the driver replied. Christopher sat in anticipation, waiting for more to follow with the response. Nothing further did.

"Have we... have we met before? I feel like we've met," he pressed on.

"No," the driver replied again. *This fucking guy*, Christopher thought.

"What did you say your name was again? Charles? Reginald? Diana? I know it was something royal," Christopher said, sliding forward to look at the man closer. He responded by turning on the radio and tapping the onboard screen, drowning Christopher out in classical symphony music. It suddenly clicked.

"*Bachmann!* Holy hell! Babe! Babe this is *Bachmann!* I know him from work!" Christopher exclaimed, tapping Grace's leg like an excitable child. "Bachmann! Did you ever find true love in Switzerland?" Jan hit another button, and an acrylic glass partition rose up between the front and back seats, humming along until it completely blocked off all sound between the two compartments.

"Friend of yours?" Grace cooed as Christopher flopped back into his seat.

"He ditched me on the side of the road in the remote hills of Switzerland," Christopher puffed with a scowl.

"So he knows you pretty well then, huh?" Grace dug further,

rolling her eyes and grinning.

* * *

The vehicle pulled into EverCorp's Washington, D.C. head-quarters a little after 1:00 PM. It was difficult to tell because sunlight was still mostly scarce in the tri-state area. It had been weeks since the forecast hadn't been "overcast." Government officials had tried to spin it as just another random "weather phenomenon," but people knew better. The hell that had broken and swallowed Philadelphia was still churning out magma and ash at a deadly rate.

Christopher and Grace looked out their respective windows as they coasted into the front turnabout. The company's logo, three unremarkable E's posited at separate angles to suggest three dimensions, glowed bright white through the haze at the top of the plate-glass monolith. It stood significantly taller than any other building in the city at 2,560 feet (something that Nathan Shah had to have snuck into a Congressional funding bill to circumvent Washington, D.C. building code).

As the two climbed out of the car, Jan began revving the engine. No sooner had Grace slipped out of the enclosure than he started jetting out of the complex.

"Jesus!" she yelled, pulling her attire closer to her. As she adjusted, she demonstrated to Christopher her disdain, expecting him to intercede.

"Yeah, he... does that..." Christopher replied, eyeing the sedan that was screeching and sliding out of the terminal like it was being chased.

The two were greeted at the facility by nine facility staff, which were all young, fit, perky women in snug attire. Champagne glasses clinked as they were led through the front lobby area. The glass panels inside were a sheen black, reflective and cold. It captured the perfect corporate energy of lifelessness but still seemed to hum with energy as if it were a living organism.

The two were led to the main elevator terminal alcove: four on each side, and one on a far adjacent centering wall. The first eight had the standard "up" and "down" buttons, but the last one was barren of any interface. The group stopped there in awkward silence.

"Do we swap power rings or something?" Christopher jested to break the stillness. Grace shifted her balance, looking to her side in indignation. He looked around for anyone to laugh at his joke, but it fell flat with his crowd.

The elevator doors finally swung open to break the awkwardness permeating the area. Everyone entered, with Christopher last. He surveyed the entrapment. All silver sheen mirrored glass. Button controls, handrails, and advertisement screens were utterly absent from the cell. The doors closed, and everyone stared straight ahead as the elevator began churning upwards. Christopher tried to gauge the floor count. After what seemed like minutes, he gave up. He was certain that it was speeding up and slowing down as a security measure to not allow someone to anticipate the arrival of the vessel. It might have also traveled horizontally, but he couldn't be sure.

The cube finally eased to a stop. Nothing happened. Awkward seconds crept on as the anticipation of the doors opening began to eat at Christopher's psyche. He looked around at the rest of the group, but no one else seemed to be bothered by the delay. As usual, he was the only one not in the loop on the situation.

Eventually, the doors snapped open. Christopher, Grace,

and the attendants moved out in silent decorum. He took the room in. It was likely the top three or four floors, merged into one large colossal space. The large glass paneling had looked jet black from the outside, but he could see out to the city from within through the dim light that came in. Smoke and emergency lights blanketed the vista. The site stretched back hundreds of feet to a large metallic desk, behind which Nathan Shah waited with his arms crossed behind his back. Christopher couldn't tell if he was glaring or smiling.

The group started forward. Against the obsidian of the darkened walls, shades of brown and tan struck out in juxtaposition. Shields, swords, and suits of armor spanning the history of mankind were laid out on display as they shuffled past. Christopher noted shinobi armor, Knights Templar armament, and operator turnouts from the Korean War. A single white light shone down upon every display, highlighting every battle-inflicted blemish upon them. Christopher noted there were no aviator uniforms as he ducked his head and shuffled past. They finally approached where Nathan Shah awaited them.

"Commander Wendell, Mrs. Wendell, welcome to EverCorp Headquarters! Is there anything I can trouble you for?" he belted out. The pair looked at each other, then back to the entrance of the room. Their escort battalion of jades had halted some fifty feet back as if stopped by an invisible shield, leaving Christopher and Grace along on their own. They turned back to each other, as Grace clasped Christopher's hand tightly.

"Nice place you have here, Shah. Really captures that Death Star vibe," Christopher reflexively shot back in candor. Shah smirked in mock appreciation.

"Commander, I find it hard to believe you have such little veneration for a historical view of battle armaments. Such is the way of man, no?" he said as he motioned to the military relics. "We have *always* adapted, evolved! We are a testament to the harbingers of desolation, are we not?" Shah leaned forward and pushed on his desk as he made his point. "We have been building to this moment for *millennia*! Just as the caveman would have been astonished by the spear, so too will these apes be baffled by our ascension!" His dark eyes flashed against the dim lighting of the room as the fervor in his voice rose.

"But history is not written by the wretches, is it?" Shah continued, as he moved around the desk. Christopher, acutely aware of his surroundings, noticed the corporate maidens shuffle in response.

"I didn't come here for a sales pitch. What do you want, old man?" Christopher needled back. Shah sat back on his desk and folded his arms across his chest.

"Same thing as you do, Commander. Eternity. Timelessness. When mankind looks back on this era, I want two things to be unquestionable: that our very lives were on the brink of collapse, and that men like you and I stood for something - stood in the face of death and said 'no.' That men like you and I didn't waste our time praying to the stars to save us: that we went and grabbed ahold of the stars and saved *ourselves*." He clutched an invisible galaxy in front of him as emphasis, clanging the expensive jewelry that adorned his hand and wrist.

Christopher raised one eyebrow. "I'm sure this plan of yours in no way lines EverCorp's pockets, either." Shah nodded to himself, then retrieved a folding tablet from his jacket pocket.

"Money doesn't make me wicked, Commander," he said as he began scrolling through the screen in front of him. "It makes me productive," he said as he turned to Grace. "Mrs.

Wendell, you have, what, two hundred thousand dollars in unpaid medical expenses, yes?"

"Yes," she murmured as she looked away in embarrassment. Christopher looked at her in amazement and humiliation. She had never told him anything about her treatments or their costs.

Not that he had ever asked.

I'm sorry, she mouthed to him as their eyes met.

"Ah yes, two hundred and *forty* thousand dollars. And rising. The interest on those debts are just, well, *terminal*, aren't they?" Shah interjected.

"You got a point?" Christopher barked, looking back at Shah.

"I do," Shah said as he turned the tablet to face them.

*Thank you for your EverPay transfer *** TOTAL ACCOUNT BALANCE: $0.00*

Grace gasped and put both hands over her mouth. Christopher squinted his eyes at the screen, searching for fine print, and then taking in the significance of what had just occurred.

"Like I said, Commander. Not wicked. Productive." Shah said. "I can do this all day. Your mother. Your friends. Your children-"

"What about them?" Christopher asked.

"I can make sure they all live like kings and queens. I can make your enemies live in sewers. There *are* benefits to working with me," Shah explained.

"So, that's what your offer is. You're just buying me off with a bag of money," Christopher countered.

"Money, power. Those are all fleeting to a man of your stature. I'd never insult you as much. Look at it this way: I'm providing you with a *legacy*. I'm providing... Mark and Luna?" he said as he glanced down at his tablet, "a chance to read about their father in their classroom history books. To be able to go to Wendell Square and tell people 'you see that building? It's named after my dad.' That's worth more than all the money in the world, isn't it?" Shah set his tablet down on his desk with an emphatic *thud* as he made his point.

Christopher stared at Shah, who returned the view. He surveyed the room again, almost reflexively. Nothing moved. Time stood still.

"That Gate almost killed me last time. What good will sending me back in do, besides finishing the job?" Christopher asked.

"I haven't stopped working on this project for one second since we got you back. Rest assured, it's operational now. You let me worry about the finer specifications. For now, all I need is you to say yes," Shah said with a wide grin as he extended his hand to Christopher.

Uncertainty flooded Christopher's head as he considered the offer. He glanced over at Grace, who took his hand again.

"It's okay. We're okay," she whispered to him as she squeezed his hand tightly three times. Just as she always did before he went on missions. Three squeezes for three *I love you*'s

One from Mark.

One from Luna.

And one from her.

His cheeks rushed red as he let go of her hand and grasped Shah's, delivering a clap of a handshake. Shah smiled wider, flashing his dark eyes wide again.

"Rest up and take that medicine, Commander. You no longer fly for the United States of America. You now fly for Earth," Shah said as he motioned to the staff to whisk the two away.

Christopher looked back before the entourage reached the elevator again. Shah was seated at his desk, only observable from his waist up. He had propped his elbows upon a glass screen built into the desk in front of him, staring down into it with his chin resting in his hands.

36

God Loves Hell

Christopher was already tired of the day. His eyes had glazed over before lunch (which he skipped). He'd been woken up by car alarms in the parking lot - multiple car alarms. Checking the situation, he found a swarm of children jumping on cars beneath his bedroom window waving American flags. When he exposed his face, the crowd of juveniles cheered with jubilation.

It was no secret to his apartment complex who he was and what he did for a living. Nine times out of ten, it garnered nothing more than a slight head nod as he plodded towards his residence in a drunken walk of shame. His privacy was never an issue, until today.

Grace had a hot breakfast waiting for him as he emerged from the bedroom. She stood picturesque like a mannequin, poised by the biscuits, gravy, and bacon prepared for him. She had a checkered apron on, and her hair was curled in an elegant way only reserved for special occasions. As he sat down and began eating, he felt a creep up his neck. He looked up and saw that she hadn't broken her poise, still standing like an old marionette and grinning like a fool.

The hell is she doing? he thought.

"Grace..." he began.

"Yes, dear?"

"The hell are you doing?" he asked.

"Celebrating, dear," she responded through a clenched smile. "You're saving the world today."

"Oh, yeah. Sure. *That*," he answered as he mixed the food into an ambiguous mix of morning slop. She moved in closer without responding.

Christopher paused mid-bite.

"Gray."

"Yes, dear?"

"Seriously. What the hell are you on about? You're being creepy." She sat down at the chair next to him, delicately placing her hands on the table. She breathed heavily before offloading her exhilaration.

"EverCorp has arranged for the kids to be there when you go to Mars!" she exclaimed. "I don't even know how they did it. I didn't make the plans for it. But they're *here*, Christopher. In *D.C.*"

He froze. Fear, anticipation, and guilt swam in his stomach, greeting his food with a gurgling battle.

"Oh, just wait until you see how big they've gotten!" she continued. "Mark, he's... well... he's the spitting image of you, babe. And Luna, her hair is down to her butt now! She's so proud of her spaceman daddy!" Adrenaline kicked in with fight-or-flight, and Christopher began to sweat. He stood up, tossed his fork onto his plate, and wiped his mouth with a napkin.

"I have to go get ready," he mumbled as he walked to the

bedroom. As he went to pass her, she suddenly grabbed his wrist.

"Don't ever leave us alone," she whispered as she pulled his hand to her cheek and rested her face in it.

"Gray…"

"We *need* you, Christopher."

"Apparently, so does everyone else," he said with a sigh.

"Just come back to us."

"Right after I save you, I will, Grace. I promise. I'll come back." He pulled his hand from her cheek, which was now wet with her tears. Despite their tumultuous past; the ups, the downs, and everything in between, lying to her never got easier. He went to the bedroom and shut the door with a quiet click. Dishes began rattling in the sink as he finally caught his breath.

* * *

No one had told him there would be a parade in his honor. *But then again, why wouldn't there be?* he thought. *The idiots in charge can never waste a perfectly good dog-and-pony show.* His face was painted in murals along the parade route, which he viewed from an armored E-71 Vectorkat helicopter from thousands of feet above. The sky was burnt orange as the sun was steadily racing towards the western horizon, but he could still read most of the signs and billboards.

HERO OF HUMANKIND

GODSEND

CHRISTOPHER WENDELL, BROUGHT TO YOU BY EVERCORP®

He hadn't even seen a New Year's Eve festival as large as what was happening below him. Clouds of confetti rained down on the hundreds of thousands of screaming lambs. Video projectors telecast simultaneous demonstrations around the world. London. Dubai. Sydney. Tokyo. Fireworks shot off across the sky for as far as he could see.

He wished Grace had been allowed to ride with him to EverCorp. The two of them would have had a laugh, however subdued, at the pretentiousness of the spectacle. He wished Erik was still alive. No matter where from, he knew Erik would've been laughing at his face being broadcast to the world as some sort of icon. *Do I really have to do this by myself?* he wondered. *Can I even do this by myself?*

A procession of cars equipped with emergency lights escorted a larger envoy of floats, billboards, and dancers. He gazed down on them with disenchantment. *They don't even know the half of what they're cheering*, he thought. *People are going to die. Hell, I'll probably die. And they're cheering me on. They're celebrating my death.*

"Do they think we're in one of those cars down there?" he'd yelled to one of the EverCorp goons that accompanied him. The stiff shrugged as fireworks began to explode directly beneath them. The craft shuddered with each explosion but held its elevation.

"Who cares?" the man responded.

Fair, Christopher thought as he slid back into his seat. He peered up into the cockpit. Empty, just as he'd anticipated.

"Couldn't get Jan for this gig? What a shame," he shouted out to no one in particular with a pout.

"Huh?" the EverCorp man said. Christopher buried his mouth into his hands, glaring towards the floor, holding back any more smart-ass banter.

The chopper hovered for close to a half-hour above the festivities before finally settling at the top of EverCorp headquarters. The sun had fully set as the aircraft made its touch down on a large white circle that surrounded the EverCorp logo, designating the landing zone for the craft. Flashing ground lights motioned from the area to a small encroachment from the roof with a door leading into the facility.

"Arrival. All diagnostics report a completed and safe flight," an automated voice rang into the cabin before the side door slid open. He rolled his eyes and willed himself onto the rooftop. He ducked down and hastily made his way along the illuminated path with the other EverCorp occupants of the chopper.

They entered a small cabin of a room, no bigger than a closet. A set of elevator doors stood directly in front of them. As Christopher's eyes adjusted, one of them scanned a card from their wallet onto a dark console to the left of the doors. The console glowed green in acceptance, and the doors quickly opened. He glanced up and noted a security camera watching their movements.

"This way, sir," one of them motioned to him. He groaned in disapproval.

"Something the matter, sir?" the man asked.

"Nothing. It's... nothing. Just had a bad experience on an elevator with Jarg," Christopher explained. The man looked back at him in stoic confusion.

"Jarg? You know? Short guy? With the ears? The first go 'round at this?" he continued impatiently.

"Oh... you mean Järvinen?"

"Yeah, sure. Him. Was sort of expecting him to be here to give his usual elevator pep talk." The man began laughing as the group filed in.

"What's so funny?" Christopher demanded.

"Dr. Järvinen is... no longer affiliated with this project," another employee in the group coyly announced. Christopher looked at their smirks in the reflection of the elevator doors as the machine hummed to life.

What kind of assholes did you get into bed with, Christopher? he wondered to himself.

* * *

The elevator finally came to an abrupt stop and the doors slid open. A long, narrow hallway greeted the group. EverCorp's logo was affixed to the left of every door down the row, and a thin line connected them all. The rooms were numbered "EVP-1" and "EVP-2," continuing in succession.

"This way, sir," Christopher was ordered as they shuffled around him onto the office carpeting. He followed in drone-like subservience. His insides were screaming to demand answers; question every corner they rounded; implore about every designation to every closed door. But he had stopped caring a long time ago when it came to EverCorp. The best response he ever got was a riddle packed inside an enigma, wrapped up in a pile of bullshit. Fighting and clawing for answers was like punching water with this institution.

The group arrived at room "EVP-Conference." One of the employees passed his access badge in front of the door's security lock, and a green light accompanied a soft click before the man opened it. The room was sterile and low-lit, save for some ceiling lights highlighting the conference room's centered table. It sat empty until the end of it, where clothes lay neatly folded.

"You can get changed in here, Commander. We'll give you some privacy," someone in the group said as they shuffled out.

He grunted a tepid response to no one in particular.

Click.

The door closed again, leaving Christopher and the pile of clothes in the room with each other. He walked over to them. Apprehensive. Uninstructed.

Get your shit together, you, he scolded himself.

He unfolded the clothes. It was his flight suit. Pulling it up to look at it, he saw that Shah had made some modifications to Järvinen's vision.

The fabric was something he'd never quite seen before. It was obviously meant to be moisture-wicking but had the durability of a winter coat. The modest CERN logo had been replaced by large, gaudy EverCorp logos on both the front and back. Where EverCorp hadn't taken up real estate on the suit, they had sold out space to other subsidiaries of theirs. Corporate sleaze dripped up and down the arms and legs in the vilest of manners. There was hardly an inch that wasn't a tackle-twill advertisement to the highest bidder for him to exhibit.

He rolled his eyes and dropped the suit onto the table. The helmet and boots had been situated beneath the suit. He picked the helmet up and inspected it. Gold, and mostly opaque from the outside. When he placed it on his head, he gasped out loud. There was an onboard HUD with an overlapping augmented reality AI, scanning the environment of the room everywhere he turned his head. *TABLE [DIMENSIONS UNREADABLE * SCAN AGAIN].* He looked at the suit. *EVERCORP®.*

"Holy shit, they made me Iron Man," he said in awe as he took the helmet off, gazing at it with astonishment. He sat down in the chair next to him and took in the suit. *It's terrible and amazing, all at once,* he appraised. *Does Shah realize the irony?*

The door popped again, perking his attention. Grace, Mark, and Luna walked in.

37

Dekonstriksyon

"**D**addy!" the children yelled as they ran to him. Tears swelled into his eyes as emotion took control. They devoured him in hugs that he reciprocated with clutches hard enough to break all of their bones together.

Mark had a haircut with the sides of his head shaved. He looked even more like Christopher with an adult haircut. Luna's long, flowing red hair had curls at the bottom that bounced every time she moved. There were strands of blonde hairs in between the red that he couldn't determine if they were dyed or natural. Both of them looked like giants compared to the last time he'd physically held them in his arms.

How much have I missed?

Grace stood behind them in a supervisory fashion. As he looked up at her, a wash of shame rolled over his brain that he'd never experienced before.

Too much. I've missed too much. That's how much you've missed, Christopher. This is what it's been about the whole time. What she'd been trying to get me to see. God, I'm such a piece of shit.

But Grace wasn't giving off her usual look of judgment and displeasure with his paternal interactions. She was most definitely content and happy with the meet, for the first time that Christopher could remember. It filled him to completion like he'd not felt in years - maybe ever.

"Okay, kids. That's enough. Can I talk to Daddy for a minute?" she said. Christopher squeezed higher. *No, no you can't. You won't take this from me. Not now*, he thought.

"*Mark. Lunie. Let's go*," she commanded in a stronger voice. The children let their grips on him begin to slide, and he responded with even more force into his embrace.

"Come on, Christopher. Let them go. There's plenty of time for this later," she mewed to pacify him. His shoulders heaved up and down as the children's bodies covered up his sobbing. She started prying arms and fingers off each other, and finally separated the three.

He looked up at her like a lost puppy while she ushered the kids toward the far side of the room.

Click.

And just like that, they were gone and out of his life - again. He looked down at his hands, which were trembling and wet from tears he'd already wiped from his eyes. Grace's feet - always in EVTek Balances - stood in his peripheral vision after a few moments.

"What the hell, Gray..." he said, still overwhelmed by emotion.

"Do you remember when Mark was born?" she asked as she took a seat to his left. Christopher was confused. *Of course I do. What's she getting at? This is obviously a trick, so what's the right answer here?*

"Of course," he responded. "Why?"

"I don't really remember much. I mean, I remember going to the hospital. I thought you were going to be arrested for driving your car like that," she said with a sentimental grin. "And then we get there, all for him to take another day to get to us! I remember the waiting... God, the little shit sure took his time, huh?"

"I remember. What's this about?" he implored.

"Because it was the last time you were truly, and I mean *truly*, honest with me," she said, staring at him coldly.

The weight of her words crushed him. *Oh, so now is when we're gonna re-hash this shit, is that it? Right NOW? Typical fucking Gr-*

"-It wasn't anything you said. Because neither of us said much," she continued. "But when they decided they had to do the emergency C-section..."

"Grace. I thought we'd already dealt with this," he tried to interject.

"It was the first time - hell, it was the *only* time - that I've ever seen you truly afraid."

He sat and considered her words for a moment. *If only she knew*, he thought, *how chicken-shit scared I am on a daily basis.* He looked her in the eyes and examined her face. She was petrified. Only she was never afraid to show her emotions, unlike he was. *Christ's sake, Christopher. You're scared to show that you're SCARED.* His defense mechanisms rose up, and he became agitated.

"I don't understand, Gray. What do you *want* from me?" She took a deep breath and wiped a wayward tear from her cheek.

"That look. The fear I saw in your eyes. It was the most honest you've ever been with me, and you didn't even say a word. I need you to be honest with me again. Honest like you were that day. When you didn't want to be. Like you don't want to be now."

He shifted uncomfortably in his seat. Silence overtook the room. Finally, she couldn't hold back the tears any longer. She leaned forward and gave him a kiss, one unlike she'd ever given him before.

A kiss so pedestrian, he didn't recognize it at first.

The kind of kiss he gave his grandmother, who still insisted on kissing him on the lips as a grown man.

Not the kind of kiss to say "I love you."

The kind of kiss to say "I'm sick of your shit."

The kind of kiss to say "Goodbye."

* * *

Minutes later, Grace was gone. Mark and Luna were gone. Christopher was being led by EverCorp goons down more hallways, stairs, and locked doors than he could ever hope to count. If his first flight suit made him feel like an asshole, this one made him feel like the whole ass. Every reflection he caught of himself drove him deeper into shame.

He remembered one night when he was younger, probably the same age as Mark: his mother and he were sitting on the couch after dinner, watching television. As his father walked in the front door of their small brownstone house, a familiar advertisement began to play.

As Mrs. Wendell rushed to meet his father, Christopher became entranced with the jingle playing into his brain. It was so... *catchy*. Like it just *made sense*.

"*.... For food, folks, and fun!*"

Before he knew it, Admiral Wendell was standing directly

beside him.

"Remote," he growled.

"Dad?" Christopher had responded.

"*Remote now!*" his father bellowed back. Shaking, and oblivious to what had angered him, Christopher produced the television remote to him. Admiral Patton inspected the device and sighed. Then, with all the violence he could muster, launched it at the television screen.

The remote landed in a dozen pieces on the ground with a loud, sharp clanking. The screen's image played on, distorted and warped from the jagged protrusion of the glass that had broken.

"*.... For food, folks, and fun!*"

Christopher had to suffer an endless night of lecturing - and at times ranting - from his father about the "commercialization of America" that night. How Christopher was somehow being taught at school to be nothing more than something to work and consume, how his brain was being rotted from corporate greed, and that he was willingly being led into a machine to be a cog. Christopher fell asleep mid-speech from exhaustion. But his father had left an irrefutable mark on his psyche.

And here he was, as the physical embodiment of corporate indecency. His father would be utterly disappointed, as usual.

He lifted his head from his embarrassment as he entered a large, busy, all too familiar room. Sleek black-plated glass lined the floors, walls, and ceiling. Turbocomputer terminals with workers stretched for hundreds of feet. And beyond that lay an ominous ivory shape: an upside-down curved V. Not an arch, but not a triangle: somewhere in between. The empty mouth shot static and vibrated the visuals behind it with a force that dwarfed the CERN form. Variable aqua, pink, and purple shapes pulsed between the electric charges that his brain couldn't discern but attempted to decipher at the same time.

The Gate.

It hummed to him. Called to him. Teased him.

"Commander Wendell! Are you ready to live forever in glory!" Christopher's eyes drew from the effigy and located Shah, standing to its side with his arms folded behind his back. Shah was beaming, exuding confidence that was so prominent, it was unsettling.

Christopher marched up to him, meeting him within inches. The EverCorp lackeys trailed him every step of the way in conformity. He'd never noticed before, but Nathan Shah stood several inches shorter than him. Typically, he would use this to his advantage to intimidate another man. He looked down at Shah, who seemed to welcome the advance.

"Well, Commander? Are you ready?" Shah said with a relaxed smile.

"You promise me. Right here, right now. Before the chick-flick vibes," Christopher spat.

"Promise you what?" Shah responded, almost slyly.

"You promise those three will be cared for and looked after," Christopher said, beckoning to the door he'd walked through. "Whatever happens to me, they live happy, full lives."

Shah breathed heavily through his nose, searching Christopher's face. He seemed frustrated with the request.

"My dear Commander Wendell: do you think I would put so much faith, so much time, so much *acclaim* to a hero such as you, and you only? A man is only as good as the family that supports him. Grace, Mark, and Luna are just as much of humanity's treasure as you are. If not more," he said with his face turning solemn.

Christopher stood silent for a moment, assessing Shah's words. He didn't trust him. There weren't many people left on the planet he did. The Gate both whispered and screamed, telling him to do something he couldn't understand.

But he didn't have much of a choice. He knew that. Shah knew that. The Gate knew that.

"Fine. I'm ready," he finally relented from the confrontation.

"Splendid! Men, prepare Commander Wendell for travel," Shah barked to the workers. Minions swarmed him, strapping his suit tighter. One grabbed his helmet from his arms and fixed it onto his head, patting it as it seated firmly against his skull. He looked at The Gate through the helmet's visor.

Fd✖&6.3o1x◎⇧iK⇧φj↩ℙ\J –ℕm^^1_φj↩ℙ\Jhb□5x, T̈N⫩⌉♎◉ nhV⬡†Co1Ξ∠|uo.

Nearly unbearable weight suddenly encroached on his back, and he whirled around in alarm.

"Sorry, sir. Just attaching your auxiliary thruster pack. Top-of-the-line R&D stuff," one of the EverCorp stooges said with a smirk, working on an enormous pouch behind Christopher.

"Thruster pack?" Christopher yelled through his helmet.

"Well, sir... basically, it's a–"

"*–I've got a jet pack?*" Christopher yelled, even louder. He didn't even try to hide his excitement.

"Well, I guess you could *call* it that, sir. There could be terrain on Mars that could be troublesome. But I must warn you, sir, this is not for performing stunts–"

"*I do my own stunts!*" Christopher crowed, placing his hands on his hips. The room fell disturbingly still, gawking at him.

The Gate murmured to the lowest hum it had since Christopher had entered the room. He suddenly became aware of his surroundings, and he broke his pose.

"Who's ready to fly to Hell?!?!" he bellowed as he cinched his gear tight to his body. Slight shuffling from the employees was the answer to his call. He glanced over to Shah, who still stood proud as a peacock. His dark eyes were like two black holes, swallowing the room in.

Christopher marched to The Gate, absorbing the energy spilling out from it like a sponge. While everyone else kept their distance out of precaution, he embraced it. It swallowed, shook, and enveloped him, like a warm blanket in a hurricane. The pink and aqua charges pushed out from the void's emptiness and pulled him ever closer.

"How long will Heaven wait for our shadows?" he wondered out loud as the colored tentacles pulled him the rest of the way in. His limbs flailed out as a bright blue light flashed, bursting most of the computer monitors in the room.

And Christopher Wendell was gone from the planet Earth.

38

Re-Entry

Static went beating through Christopher's skull as he grimaced and held his eyes shut. Bright pink light flooded his sight even through clenched eyelids. When the mix of hissing and buzzing stopped, he peeked one eye open.

The void of outer space greeted him. There was no planet here: Not Earth. Not Mars. He began flailing about; grasping at nothing, grasping at anything. The unforgiving gravity held him in check. Through his panic, something immediately shot to the front of his thoughts.

I can breathe, he realized.

"Not a bad upgrade from the last go-round, Shah," he muttered into his helmet.

My helmet! he thought. *Radio back to EverCorp!* He tapped on the push-to-talk button the nerds back at The Gate had shown him.

Nothing but empty clicks echoed in his head.

"Hello? Anyone? Shah? Do you copy this?" he bellowed.

Nothing.

"Anyone? Help!"

"I need help..."

Still nothing.

The severity of the situation began to inch into his psyche when three small arrows in the bottom of his helmet's display caught his attention.

»>

He jerked his head to the right, but couldn't see anything. He couldn't move his body around with anything to secure onto. *How the hell am I supposed to move?* he thought. He wiggled like he was doing the funkiest of dances when he felt something slap his butt.

The jet pack.

He fidgeted with the sides of the otherwise cumbersome attachment. He found short handles on each side near his waist. Jerking on one, he immediately found himself spinning, the billions of stars in his view becoming a blur. He sucked in air and narrowed his eyes, focusing on the equilibrium rate, just like he'd learned in advanced flight training. Within seconds, he had control. He rotated the thrusters from the pack until he aligned with the arrows guiding his way. And there, undeniably, it sat before him.

Mars.

His breathing picked up with anticipation and he raced the thrusters forward. His head leaped in front of his feet, and he shot toward the fiery red planet like a rocket.

Holy shit, I'm actually going to make it, he thought to himself. *This dumbass mission is actually going to work.* The laundry list of people he'd planned to apologize to before he died left his attention as the planet slowly became larger in his vision. And there were so many: Erik. Grace. Mark. Luna. His parents.

His squadron. *Everyone you've ever come in contact with*, he surmised. *Erik was spot-on.*

THRUSTER LEVEL: 30% suddenly projected across his helmet's HUD. He assessed his flight path.

"No, no, no no no!" he screamed. Thirty percent wasn't going to get him anywhere remotely close to landing. He pushed forward in defiance. "No! I'm so close!"

THRUSTER LEVEL: 20%

"Come on! Get there, you shitty-"

THRUSTER LEVEL: 10%

PLEASE REFUEL THRUSTERS FOR FUNCTIONALITY

His breathing picked back up and he didn't even attempt to slow it down. He was so close to Mars that he could reach out and touch it.

THRUSTER LEVEL: 5%

He could pick it up and hold it.

THRUSTER LEVEL: 1%

THRUSTER LEVELS DEPLETED

He eased off the jet pack as he felt the death rattles of the acceleration. When it came to a halt, his HUD scanned the planet, no longer preoccupied with the dead jet pack affixed to him. Shooting a bouncing line back and forth for longer than anything it previously had been pointed at, it finally gave a reading:

TERRESTRIAL PLANET: MARS

ESTIMATED DISTANCE TO SURFACE: 18.561391 KM

Christopher floated, taking in the data and the serenity of his view simultaneously.

"Well, Shah, at least we got a little closer, eh?" he said with a laugh. "Hell of a view to die to, either way."

He couldn't decide if there were septillions or octillions of stars. *Could there actually be octillions? Can I see an octillion of things at once? Is that even possible to do?* He took in the scenery for all it was worth. As the list of people he needed to apologize to re-entered his mind, the illuminations in his eyes began to shimmer and fade.

39

Broken Men Build Broken Things

Christopher was smirking. It had been a half hour - at least - and his oxygen still hadn't given out. In fact, his HUD hadn't even warned him of any exhaustion from his oxygen tank.

↬↬▭⊠ڣ▨▩⌋⌉⌉∔∨∔∔Ss'◪◩ᴆₚ82588◩◩ NO◬◍∭∭↧L)h.9iTY 1vXC◪◩ᴆₚ82588◩◩

{ζ~ᐅ⊠◕±±R'◪◩ᴆₚ82588◩◩ ▪⌜⌞ε̲ɩ̲9vD◕±±R' ₪y‰▦◕± ±R' ▦⌋⌉⌉∔∨∔∔Ss ⌼7ri,9.⍭

◕±±R'⊠ڣ▨ ▩)◒◕±±R', ◕±±R'⇶|kWJ⌌ ? he thought.

b&≗jjJ⌔⇶|kWJ⌌ ⊠ڣ▨ ▩◪◩ᴆₚ82588◩◩ ◪◩ᴆₚ82588◩◩⇶|k WJ⌌ ◕±±R' SⱣ◅↧L)h.9i)◒⍣ɩρ⊠

w7?

b&≗jjJ⌔ x◎⇮iK⇮ ⊙Δg Fd⊠&6.301 Fd⊠&6.301 x◎⇮iK⇮ φj↫ᑭ\/ ⨚F◚f⸿ n⨚. ↬↬▭ ₠\₣10⦚01?

He'd lost his mind. This was obviously the last step in the dying process. He was thinking in a language he didn't speak.

"x◎⇮iK⇮ ◕±±R' {ζ~ᐅ⊠ {ζ~ᐅ⊠ ⇶|kWJ⌌ ⍟ᑫ≟29 .209◬ ↧L)h.9i ⌋⌉⌉∔∨∔∔Ss ₪y‰ TY1vXC-" he began to wax poetic on a final statement, only to stop himself short in terror.

b&≗jjJ⌔⇶|kWJ⸢ ⊠ف▨ ▩◪◩⌀₈82588◩◩ ◪◩⌀₈82588◩

◩⇶|kWJ⸢ ◕+̰+̰R‘ SⱣ◁↧L)h.9i)◒ ⋆̈ιρ⊠

w7 ▦ TY1vXC ⇶|kWJ⸢ ⊠ف▨ ▩ ◘7ri,9.+ ◘7ri,9.+ ◕+̰

+̰R‘ ⌋⌉⌉∔∨∔∔Ss ▦ ⌋⌉⌉∔∨∔∔Ss

____RGr₩ⁿ ◪◩⌀₈82588◩◩⊛⍾∸29.209⍙ ▪⸢⌞ε̲ι̲9

vD◕+̰+̰R‘? he wondered. He raised his hand in front of his helmet.

$pU≂⊟ TY1vXC ⊠ف▨ ▩ ⌋⌉⌉∔∨∔∔Ss ⌂⌂...7.912.⌅ ⊛

⍾∸29.209⍙ SⱣ◁ this real?

His hand began to fade slowly, exposing Mars behind it. He screamed in panic, flipping his arms around in a convulsive freestyle swim. No arms fell into his view.

⸙iiiiii⇚⌂⌂...7.912.⌅ arms. What ⇶|kWJ⸢ ⊠ف▨ ▩◘7

ri,9.+ ◘7ri,9.+ ◕+̰+̰R‘⌋⌉⌉

∔∨∔∔Ss◕+̰+̰R‘₪y‰ ◪◩⌀₈82588◩◩⊛⍾∸29.209

⍙ my arms? Ξ∠|uo⊛⍾∸29.209⍙ $pU≂⊟

⇶|kWJ⸢ ⊠ف▨ ▩▫₲G,4. ◕+̰+̰R‘ my legs? How does this happen

⊛⍾∸29.209⍙ ↧L)h.9i ◪◩⌀₈82588◩◩ here?

He stopped thrashing. Stopped fighting.

"Whatever this is: I submit freely. I am ฿▤◉,⯇n6. ◕+̰+̰R‘⊠ف▨

▩₪y‰⌂⌂...7.912.⌅," he spoke into his helmet.

The stars and the ruby-red planet ahead of him sparked and flashed aqua and pink as if to answer him. The light from all the spatial essences danced and blazed around his view, making him dizzy. They culminated in a cluster in front of him. Not making a certain shape, but not in a disorganized fashion, either. Something was out there. It moved and it shifted together, even if Christopher couldn't identify it.

"We see you, Christopher Wendell. You will live forever. hb▯5x,⍑

⊛◠⌐29.209⌂ ↧L)h.9i

_h̦hhhhhB%,ﻪ ▦ {ζ~▷⊠ {ζ~▷⊠_{ζ~▷⊠ ▦ ▫ℭG,4. ◓±+R' SP◁

⊛◠⌐29.209⌂ ℬ▤◉,◂◂n6.

◓±+R' ▫ℭG,4. ◓±+R' ℬ▤◉,◂◂n6.," a voice droned into his head. He snapped his head around to check his peripherals.

"Who are you? Where are △△...7.912.⤬ ⊛◠⌐29.209⌂ ↧L)h.9i?" he cried.

"We forget: we were once like you. Allow us to take forgiving: ⊠ﻪ▨ ▦◻7ri,9.⤲

⊛◠⌐29.209⌂{ζ~▷⊠⊛◠⌐29.209⌂____RGrW̅ⁿ▦◓±+R'TY1vXC," the voice responded. The cluster of lights in front of him condensed further. Hardly a star remained outside of it. A torso and head suddenly shaped. A large snout, like a tail, formed from the front of what would be a face. Blackened eye sockets peered downward onto him, reducing him to a tiny bug in the scheme of the endless void the two occupied. It shifted and moved in an unnerving way that chilled Christopher's spine.

"You're like *me*? x◎⇕iK⇕⊛◠⌐29.209⌂h̦hhhhB%,ﻪ?" he responded.

"We were advantageous. We could sustain. y54◠〳▽〳 ▦ SP◁ ◓±+R' h̦hhhh

hB%,ﻪ ⊠ﻪ▨ ▓

TY1vXC ⊠ﻪ▨ ▓ ▽∟ↄwEs ↧L)h.9i |⌉⌉⤒∨⤒⤒Ss ◫y‰ ⊠ﻪ▨ ▓ ⌋ ⌉⌉⤒∨⤒⤒Ss ◩◪⍺ₚ82588◪◪.

And then, all of that went away. Much like your planet: φj↩ᑭ\J ⊠ﻪ▨ ▓ ℬ▤

◉,◂◂n6.

◩◪⍺ₚ82588◪◪ ⇶|kWJ´ ," the voice said.

"Who even the hell *are you*?" Christopher shrieked, not

caring about his composure. The voice gave out what could only be interpreted by Christopher as laughter.

"You can call us The Entity. Yes, hفٍhhhhhB%,فٍ ◕+̰+̰R‘ ⊠فٍ▨
▩ ฿▤◉,
◂◂n6. ◕+̰+̰R‘
⊛ᑬ⍊29.209⍙ ⌋⌉⌉∓∨∓∓Ss ◕+̰+̰R‘ ⊛ᑬ⍊29.209⍙ SP◁ ▪⌜
⌞ꜪꝆ9vD ⊠فٍ▨ ▩ ⌋⌉⌉∓∨∓∓Ss ⌂⌂...
7.912.ㅈ," it responded in a preposterous tone.

"Well, what do you want with Earth, *Entity*?" Christopher snarled back. "How many of you are there in there, exactly?"

"We have found a way to survive. We are but many. Very many. Fd⊠&6
.301 ⊛ᑬ⍊29.209⍙
⊛ᑬ⍊29.209⍙ ▪⌜⌞ꜪꝆ9vD ⊠فٍ▨ ▩ ⌋⌉⌉∓∨∓∓Ss ⌂⌂
...7.912.ㅈ. Have you not learned of our planet's history, and how it parallels yours?" the Entity asked. "We once had waters flooding our entire orb, like yours. Ah yes, ⊠فٍ▨
▩)◒ ▦ ฿▤◉,◂◂n6.)◒ {ζ~⊳⊠ ◕+̰+̰R‘
⊛ᑬ⍊29.209⍙ SP◁ ⩔⌞≚wEs{ζ~⊳⊠ ◕+̰+̰R‘ TY1vXCTY1v
XC◕+̰+̰R‘₪y‰)◒ {ζ~⊳⊠ ◕+̰+̰R‘
⊠فٍ▨ ▩ ฿▤◉,◂◂n6.." Christopher was getting frustrated.

"So I get it: Mars died. What's that got to do with me, or Earth for that matter? Are you invading, is that it?" he shot into the starry emptiness.

"What did you think the Escape Velocity Project was, Commander Wendell?" the Entity asked. The question caught him unprepared.

Shit. It knows about the Project, he thought.

Of course we know about the project, Commander Wendell, the Entity vibrated into his entire body. *How do you think your planet ever got the directions to it?*

"What the shit!" Christopher cried out. He shook his body as if to exorcise a demon, only to look around and see that he had nothing of a body to shake anymore. He could only see from his own perspective, and nothing outside that existed.

"We apologize, Commander Wendell. Were you uninformed?" the Entity said.

"Uninformed? I'm in the United States military. We're *born* uninformed," he retorted.

"Commander Wendell... we must ask... what is your last living memory on your planet?" the Entity asked.

"Last memory? I dunno, looking at Shah with that shit-eating grin on his face? At EverCorp headquarters? And before that... seeing Grace? And Mark and Luna?" he said, trailing off.

"We said *living* memory. Fd⊠&6.301⇛|kWJʹ ◑+̰+̰Rʻ {ζ~▷⊠⊠ﻓ▨

▨TY1vXC◨◪◭𝒟ₚ82588◪◪

⌂⌂...7.912.⼂ ⊛◠⌐͟29.209◬↧L)h.9i TY1vXC◑+̰+̰Rʻ◑+̰+̰Rʻ ⊠ﻓ▨

▨TY1vXC ⊠ﻓ▨ ▨

■⌐∟ɛ͟ɩ9vD⊛◠⌐͟29.209◬₿▤◉,◂◂n6. ◪◪𝒟ₚ82588◪◪⊠ﻓ▨ ▨{ζ~▷⊠," the Entity scolded him.

"I told you!" Christopher spat.

"Unfortunate. We thought you were above the guises of your fellow planetarians," the Entity said, shifting its shape and sound as it bristled.

"What the hell are you talking about? Like you know-"

"We know that you never reunited with Grace Wendell. Or Mark Wendell. Or Luna Wendell," the Entity interrupted. Christopher lay silent, drifting in the space he was caught in.

How dare he, Christopher thought.

How dare b&°jjJ◌ φj↩⌐\J, the Entity shot into him. *The first* *time you attempted to reach Mars was your last,* it bellowed.

How do you figure? he replied within thought.

You never even left your planet. The planet you call φj↤ᴘ\J ☒ فِ▨

▨ ₿≣

◉,◂◂n6. ◩◪ᴆₚ82588◪◪

⇛|kWJˊ . *But you were still needed, by the ones in control. Grace Wendell has been dead since before you started this endeavor. Your offspring: sent to other sides of the planet."*

"Bull-fucking-shit," Christopher said. "I held them in my arms. Touched them. Connected with them. They were all as real as they come," he said.

"Your company: EverCorp. Fd☒&6.301 ⇛|kWJˊ ●⁺⁺Rʻ Ξ ∠|uo ●⁺⁺Rʻ ▫ԌG,4. ▦ {ζ~▷☒,"

the Entity said. "It has limitless resources – for a dying planet – and used all of them. The tribe that you encountered was false: ☒فِ▨ ▨)

◖ ◩◪ᴆₚ82588◪◪ ⊛|◌|˱29.209△

₿≣◉,◂◂n6. TY1vXC." Christopher grew hot with rage.

There's no way EverCorp could use paid actors for my family. No fucking way. I'd see it. There's no chance I couldn't know my family from some strangers. They couldn't fool me.

Could they?

They would use whatever means they had, Christopher Wendell. Even the foulest ones, the Entity spoke to him. Fd☒&6.301⇛|kWJˊ ●⁺⁺Rʻ ●⁺⁺Rʻ|]]⁺

∨⁺⁺Ss▨y‰TY1vXC,

◩◪ᴆₚ82588◪◪⇛|kWJˊ ●⁺⁺Rʻ ▪⌐ʟᴇιϙvD●⁺⁺Rʻ☒فِ

▨ ▪|]]⁺∨⁺⁺SsTY1vXC. The weight of the truth began to bear on his body that he no longer felt in reality.

Everything Grace and I overcame? All the shit she bested? It was really all for nothing? Why?

"To get you to this moment, Commander Wendell. You will live forever," the Entity growled. "Nathan Shah deceived you because this cannot be done involuntarily. Fd⊠&6.301

⇟|kWJ⌐ ◗±+Rʻ eξ7.03△⅝Dmm⊠ۭ▨ ▩◪◪ⴄ82588◪◪

◗±+Rʻ ⊛⌒⌐―29.209△⌡⌉⌉

⊥∨⊥⊥Ss{ζ~▷⊠△△...7.912.⤬ hۭhhhhhB%,ۭ◗±+Rʻ{ζ~▷⊠)◖⊛⌒⌐―29

vXC ◪◪ⴄ82588◪◪⇟|kWJ⌐ ◗±+Rʻ

hۭhhhhhB%,ۭ▦{ζ~▷⊠{ζ~▷⊠▦⌡⌉⌉⊥∨⊥⊥Ss____RGrW^n."

"I still don't understand: what am I supposed to do? Die here in the middle of space? How is that achieving anything?" he asked. The Entity pulsed and shifted again, taking more shapes than Christopher could comprehend.

"You have not been told what the Escape Velocity Project is, Commander Wendell. Yes, △△...7.912.⤬ ⊛⌒⌐―29.209△ ⤓L)h.9i

Ƀ▤◉,◂◂n6. SƤ◁ ◗

±+Rʻ {ζ~▷⊠ {ζ~▷⊠ ⊛⌒⌐―29.209△

hۭhhhhhB%,ۭ ▢7ri,9.⤲ ◗±+Rʻ ⊛⌒⌐―29.209△ ▢7ri,9.⤲ {ζ~

▷⊠ ◗±+Rʻ {ζ~▷⊠ ▦ ◗±+Rʻ

▽L⤳wEs △△...7.912.⤬ ⊛⌒⌐―29.209△ ▪⌐Lεⱺ9vD ▦

TY1vXC TY1vXC ▦ ⊛⌒⌐―29.209△ ⌡⌉⌉

⊥∨⊥⊥Ss," the Entity said. "This was never to transport your people. It was to *convert* them."

"Convert them to what? *You?*" Christopher shouted. The Entity buzzed, faded, and reappeared simultaneously.

"Waves of energy. Limitless. Unending. ∫F▬fˢ⊛⌒⌐―2

9.209△Ƀ▤◉,◂◂n6. ◗±+Rʻ▫ɢG,4.

◗±+RʻƀȐ▤◉,◂◂n6.," the Entity said. "It is the way we survived. It is the only way Earth will survive, as such.

∫F▬fˢ⊛⌒⌐―29.209△Ƀ▤◉,◂◂n6. ⊛⌒

―29.209△⌡⌉⌉⊥∨⊥⊥Ss◗±+Rʻₗ

▦TY1vXC ◪◪ⴄ82588◪◪⇟|kWJ⌐ ◗±+Rʻ

⊛◖⊙⌐29.209△◪◪♧82588◪◪⇟|kWJ˹ ◑⁺⁺R'ℬ☰◉,‹‹n6..”

“Waves? Radio waves? *You want to turn me into a radio wave?!?!*” he screamed through his helmet. The thought seemed too preposterous, even for where he found himself at.

This was always the only way to live forever, Commander Wendell, the Entity hummed in his head. *As waves of pure energy. Immortal and forever surging forward in space until a hospitable space is discovered.* It shifted and turned in Christopher's view, as the stars obeyed it like drones. The large snout of stars reached out to him as if to touch his mind. *Your planet is in decay, much like ours was.*

“You can stay and rot as a corpse. Or you can travel to Fd◙&6.301⇟

|kWJ˹ ◑⁺⁺R' –

₪m∧∧1_◑⁺⁺R'△△...7.912.☌ ⊛◖⊙⌐29.209△⌡⌉⌉⁺∨⁺⁺

Ss₪y‰ with us. Or, if you so choose, there is another path,” the Entity offered.

Why me? he thought. *What made me so special for this? Isn't this why we have world leaders and shit? Why did he choose me?* he thought.

“We most certainly did not choose you. ⊙△gTY1vXC TY1vX C⊥L)h.9i)◐⇟|kWJ˹ , your oligarchs didn't, either. Your *species* did. Such a ₪y‰◑⁺⁺R')◐▦TY1vXC▦⊛◖⊙⌐29.209△⌡⌉⌉

⁺∨⁺⁺Ss cannot be left to the corrupt,” the Entity explained.

Why would THEY choose me? he wondered.

Maybe they were wise. Maybe ◪◪♧82588◪◪⇟|kWJ˹ ◑⁺⁺ R'△△...7.912.☌ h¡hhhhhB%,

¡◑⁺⁺R'ℬ☰◉,‹‹n6.◑⁺⁺R' *foolish.* hb☐5x,T̈◑⁺⁺ R'TY1vXC, *a species chooses its own heroes,* the Entity said.

“What about the third option?” he asked.

"You can bring your fellow planetarians with you to Fd⊠&6. 301⇛|kWJ՛ ●++R' -

Ɱm^^1_●++R'⌂⌂...7.912.⺂ ⊛◖ᒥ-29.209⌂⌡⌡⫫∨⫥⫥Ss◫y‰. Yes, they can live eternally with us," the Entity responded. Christopher fell silent. He looked around as if the answer would be out in the black void somewhere.

Kill... everyone? To save them? he considered.

No, Commander Wendell. Not to kill. To free. Death is ∇∟⫽wEs⫯ *L)h.9i⊠⊠⫯ₚ82588⊠⊠*

⊠⊠⫯ₚ82588⊠⊠⇛|kWJ՛ ●++R' ∇∟⫽wEs●++R'__ _RGrₚ"⊞⌡⌡⫫∨⫥⫥Ss⌡⌡⫫∨⫥⫥Ss⊞⌡⌡ ⫫∨⫥⫥Ss__RGrₚ".

"But they *will* have to die first, yeah? Just like me?" he argued.

"They must leave their planetary bodies, yes. This much is true."

"And you want to make us all... waves of energy? To get to this '-Ɱm^^1_●++R'⌂⌂...

7.912.⺂ ⊛◖ᒥ-29.209⌂⌡⌡⫫∨⫥⫥Ss◫y‰?'" he pressed further. "Where is this place? Tell me more about it." The Entity shimmered brighter and pinker beyond the color spectrum of Earth.

"It is not of your way of thinking to know. Ah, the limits of ⊛◖ᒥ-29.209⫯L)h.9iℬ⊟●,⫪n6. ▪ᒥ∟εℓ9vD⊛◖ᒥ-29.209⌂ℬ⊟●,⫪ n6. ⊠⊠⫯ₚ82588⊠⊠⊠⌇⧄

▦{ζ~▷⊠⊞⊠⊠⫯ₚ82588⊠⊠⌂⌂...7.912.⺂," the Entity coyly shot back.

So he doesn't know, Christopher thought.

We know far greater than you could ever comprehend, Christopher Wendell. We know you lie before us a broken being, traveling on a road of self-hatred that has ended with an unceremonious death outside of your natural habitat. How is that? Why is that? the Entity rasped in his thoughts.

Because. Erik was right. I destroy people just by knowing them. He was fucking right the entire time and the further I get away from the people I love, the better I can be at protecting them, he thought.

Protecting them from whom? the Entity asked.

Me. Protecting them from me. He breathed heavily and pushed his eyes upwards to the Entity.

"Just me. Just take me," he proclaimed.

"Are you sure, Commander Wendell? There is no return from this transformation," the Entity warned.

"I'm sure. This is the only way I can make them safe." The Entity began to swirl and glow aqua, pink, purple, and navy blue. Novas started exploding as it began to envelop and swallow him.

"Grace... eξ7.03⨺5/8Dmm฿▤◉,◂◃n6. ⊠ڤ▨ ▩)◒◕±̰±̰R'..."

"Mark... ᛃiiiiii⇚ ⊠ڤ▨ ▩ ฿▤◉,◂◃n6. ⋆̈ιρ⊠w7..."

"Luna... y54ᑭ⋁⋁⊽⋁⋁↧L)h.9i⌋⌉⌉∔∨∔∔Ss⊠ڤ▨ ▩..."

"I love you ⊠ڤ▨ ▩ {ζ~⊳⊠ {ζ~⊳⊠."

Epilogue

George groggily opened his eyes as the daily prayers began broadcasting over the intercoms at Hearts Alive Recovery Center. He wasn't religious, but it was probably the best alarm clock he'd ever had in his entire life. Plus, the soothing British voice that read the passages was about the only thing that could pierce his drug-induced sleep. He'd literally slept through the first two days of Hurricane Alissa.

Not that he minded. When he first checked himself in for "stress/anxiety," they tried to turn him away. Luckily, between some high-level phone calls at NORAD and the White House, some strings were pulled and he was admitted. It didn't hurt that on his questionnaire, under "*what do you hope to gain from this experience?*" he answered, "I just want to *sleep*." Some took that as a thinly-veiled suicide threat, but it wasn't. He truly just couldn't function anymore. His memory, thoughts, and even depth perception were fried. He didn't want to die, but being awake had become an inescapable torment.

George swung his legs off the bed and rubbed his eyes. Breakfast would be served in a few minutes. He preferred to eat alone in his room, so he tried to get to the cafeteria before the boors were wheeled in. Most of the other residents didn't even know he lived there, which was exactly how he preferred it.

He peeked out of his room. Completely quiet, except for

a tall, friendly orderly lumbering down the hallway. George thought his name was Leroy, or Roy. He wasn't sure. *Why even pretend you care*, he chastised himself. He slunk out of his hideaway, allowing the door to push closed, and darted toward the cafeteria.

Runny scrambled eggs and oatmeal. Burnt toast and Eggos. He shoveled enough to feed himself for days and hurriedly returned to his quarters. He skipped the boxed milk, hearing other doors begin to open. He'd just drink out of his faucet.

George paused as he reached his door. The only door void of greeting cards, pictures from grandkids, or doorway decorations. And it was slightly ajar. The staff was under strict orders *not* to enter his room if he was not in it, or did not answer. His medicine was usually slid under the door in a plastic sandwich bag.

He began breathing heavily. He had kept his anxiety levels down with routine, even if most of that routine was lying in bed. This was out of routine and it terrified him.

"Sir? Dr. Sansor? G... George?" a voice drifted through the door. George's eyes widened with disbelief. Another strict rule - this one from his therapist - was no contact with anyone from work. *Especially* anyone associated with the Project. He hesitantly nudged the door open with his foot to find Kevin seated at the room's desk, beaming from ear to ear. George shuffled in and closed the door behind him. He plopped down on the bed and began shoveling the cafeteria's gruel into his mouth, staring at Kevin. The two men sat in silence for minutes. Eventually, Kevin became uncomfortable with George's glare and looked around the room.

"Nice setup you have here. Are you getting along okay?" Kevin offered. George stopped mid-bite, still not taking his eyes off his intruder. He sighed and put his fork down into the mash.

"What do you want, Yim?" he finally retorted. Kevin furrowed his eyebrows, dejected by George's workplace formality. George hadn't called him by his last name in over a year. He knew this would be complicated. He was told that George would probably subject him to personal insults. But mission briefings, for their government meticulousness, didn't prepare him for an emotional sting.

"I'm here to check you out of here," Kevin revealed.

"Fuck you. I like it here. Get out."

"They thought you'd probably say... *something* along those lines," Kevin said. "Unfortunately, this comes straight from the top."

"Tell Boddaring to fuck off, too."

"As much as I'd love to," Kevin chuckled, "the order didn't come from him. It came from President Buynak."

Silence fell between the two again as the gravity of the information sank into George's gnarled mind. George opened his mouth to speak, but his reasoning betrayed him. His eyes began to search the room for something - anything - to give him the inspiration to speak.

"W... Why?" he finally croaked out.

"Wendell's still alive," Kevin replied. George reacted as if he'd just been hit with a Taser. He nearly fell off the bed. His plate came crashing down to the ground. He needed his medication. He began searching for a pill, any pill. He checked under the mattress, where he kept a hidden stash. Nothing. He jumped out of bed and checked the bedside table drawer. Empty.

"How do you know?" he spat back at Kevin. "More shitty

information? Guesses?"

Kevin raised his hands in self-defense. "Woah, Woah! He sent us a message." George's search for self-treatment turned considerably more frantic. He pushed Kevin aside and began mashing the red call button.

"And specifically mentioned you."

"Dr. Sansor? Dr. Sansor... *George!*" George stopped in frustration and turned to Kevin.

"*What?!?! What did it say?!?!*"

"Well his message was mostly in-decipherable. All coded. But he did say that he's somewhere called 'The Beyond.' And that we need to hurry to get there."

About the Author

Jeff Perilman is a dedicated husband, father, and law enforcement officer. Since he was a child, he has been writing short stories, poetry, and music. He is the proud founder and owner of Jeffcore, LLC. He enjoys heavy metal, comic books, Nic Cage, and tattoos. He is an avid connoisseur of buffalo wings, popcorn, and pretzels. Jeff graduated with a Bachelor's degree from the Wright State University in Dayton, Ohio, where he resides with his wife, children, and dogs.

You can connect with me on:
- http://www.jeffcore.com
- http://www.twitter.com/jeffcorellc
- http://www.facebook.com/jeffcorellc